ALSO BY LYNNE GRIFFIN

Fiction
Sea Escape
Life Without Summer

Nonfiction
Negotiation Generation
The Promise of Proactive Parenting: Sea Change

GIRL

SENT

AWAY

LYNNE GRIFFIN

Permissions requests may be addressed to
SixOneSeven Books
21 Wormwood Street
Ste. 325
Boston, MA 02210
www.sixonesevenbooks.com

Grateful acknowledgment is made to the following for permission to quote from copyrighted
material:

Chandos Music for permission to reprint an excerpt from "Diamonds and Rust," music and
lyrics by Joan Baez, (c) 1975; and to Houghton Mifflin Harcourt for permission to reprint
an excerpt from "Myth," from Native Guard, by Natasha Trethewey, (c) 2006.

New York / Lynne Griffin — First Edition
ISBN 978-0-9831505-7-2

Printed in the United States of America

(sixoneseven)BOOKS

To Caitlin and Stephen—for the music

Mount Hope Wilderness Camp, New York
Workbook Entry #12

Some day in May

Memory hasn't always been my enemy. For eight years, there's been a wall of water between me and what happened to my mother and sister in the little village of Phuket, Thailand on December 26, 2004. The worst day of my life started out all clear blue sky and palm trees. My mind holds a pretty picture of Mom and Poppy standing motionless on the sugar white sand of Patong Beach. That much I remember. As hard as I try not to untangle the rest of it, still my thoughts loop and circle back to before the punishing water, and then to after, when my father dumped me into the arms of a stranger, an Asian man with a camera I can still feel digging into my skin. It's the middle—the minutes that connect the perfect life I had to the one I'm stuck with now—that's what the wave erased.

I don't know how much longer I can keep them there, walled off in that faraway place. Mixed up images steal my sleep and crowd my days. I hate everyone and everything, and I don't even love my music anymore. Part of me thinks I might be saved if I dare to remember. If only I could bring myself to talk about them. To tell my dad what's happening to me. But when I think of him harassing me for drinking too much or hanging out with freaks, or sending me here—every time a counselor tells me I'm a liar and a loser—I think none of them deserves to know what's going on inside me. How my brain is shorting out. How split off from myself I'm becoming.

The last time police brought me home, my father asked me straight out if I needed help. He actually accused me of starting to remember. I told him, no. I lied right to his face. And he believed me.

Now I'm telling the truth and nobody does.

I thought things were bad back then, the night I blacked out standing on those train tracks. But that was before my father had me kidnapped.

PART ONE
THE RIFT

LYNNE GRIFFIN

ONE

One Month Earlier

When silent fights were all that filled the rift between Toby Sedgwick and his daughter, he stood in front of her bedroom door trying to muster the courage to provoke her. Any emotion would be better than none, he reasoned. *You can do this. You have nothing to lose—no, you have everything to lose.* Toby opened the door.

Ava sat on the couch by the window, staring into a cup of black coffee, her knees tucked under her in an impossible move only a teenager can finagle.

"I made an appointment with a counselor," Toby said. "For today at noon."

Ava lifted her head, brushing stray hair the color of autumn from her face. His daughter had fiery looks, a handful of bold freckles on light skin and green-blue eyes that questioned everything. Yet she looked at Toby now without passion, as if only just noticing him standing there.

"I'll drive you to school if you hurry," he said. "I'm meeting with Mr. Graham first thing about your grades. Then I'll go to work for a bit and come back for you."

Toby expected to see a flash of anger on Ava's face, the way her brow would tense, the disgust she could level at him with the slight narrowing of her eyes. Right on cue, there it was. And then just as quickly gone.

"You can't make me go. I don't want you talking to teachers about me either. School's my business, not yours." Ava's protestations were juvenile. Like everything about her lately, they lacked her usual conviction.

At least now she was up, storming toward her adjoining bathroom, making more noise than seemed possible given the soft soles of her Keds. Toby followed her, in an odd way heartened by her reaction.

"You are my business," he said. "And school called me, which means they're worried about you too."

Up close, Toby could tell Ava hadn't showered. Caught up in a ponytail, her hair was noticeably greasy, not recently combed. Alcohol breath hung in the air between them. He was tempted to accuse her of being hungover again, but what good would that do? She would deny it. It would only add to the likelihood that he'd set off their particular kind of shouting match. Ava would tell him to get out of her room. To leave her alone. He would remind her that she was only sixteen, and that under his roof, the rules were the rules. Back and forth it would go, each of them reciting his or her worn out lines. He needed to get her to that appointment so he let it go.

In a shocking turn of events, Ava said none of these things. Still she expressed herself. When she threw her half-filled mug into the sink, the sound of glass shattering went right through her. Both hands flew to her temples. After running a shaky hand across her forehead, she brushed past Toby. With her backpack slung over her shoulder, she turned to him. "Well, are you coming?"

Was he coming? Toby had all but admitted he was out of his league dealing with her, about to bring a professional stranger into the mix, and Ava barely made a show of resisting him.

"It's Tuesday. Don't forget your guitar," he said.

Ava stopped for a moment above the open case. Her cherished instrument was a dark-sounding acoustic with rosewood back and sides, a slim tapered neck. When his daughter played—and standing there waiting for the next thing to happen, Toby couldn't remember the last time he'd heard her—it was a guarantee that anyone listening would get lost in the beauty of the guitar's full-bodied sound and Ava's expertise with dynamics and tone.

"I don't have a lesson today. Miss Kelly's gonna be out. Let's just go."

So father and daughter climbed back into their quiet corners, and Toby drove toward Wellesley High.

Ava got out of the car at the main entrance. Without a word or a look, she moved toward the double doors, disappearing into the sea of other teenagers.

The admin office was bustling too. It was strange to see so many kids Ava's age with so much energy moving about this early in the morning. Except for school days, Ava didn't get going till after noon, one o'clock. Toby looked at his watch, then grabbed the Journal. The other times he'd had occasion to be in this office— to learn about PSATs or summer music programs—he'd waited twenty plus minutes.

"Mr. Sedgwick," the secretary said. "Right this way."

It wasn't until he crossed the threshold to the conference room that Toby realized this was no ordinary check-in to talk about crummy test scores and overdue projects. All but one seat was occupied at the round table. Tim Graham motioned for him to take a seat next to Ava's music teacher. Not one person, including Miss Kelly, made eye contact.

"We're glad you could come in," Tim said, crossing his hands over a stack of paper-clipped pages. Tim was a sharp guy who dressed well and spoke with confidence. He'd worked his way up from middle school guidance counselor to high school vice-principal. Everyone knew he had his eye on superintendent.

"You're making me nervous," Toby said. "I thought this was about Ava's grades."

"It is. It is," Tim said. "As you know, they've dropped precipitously of late. In every class including music. I've known Ava since sixth grade and I've got to say there's been a real change in her. She isn't coming to school available to learn. Ava's uncharacteristically quiet, and she's spending a lot of time on the fringes. Frankly, Dad, she looks unwell."

Toby shifted in his seat, strangely enough, feeling blindsided. Things sounded so much worse put together, all laid out on the table. Sitting there, he did his best to imitate a father who knew what he was doing, when in truth he had no idea. If Lorraine were here, she'd know what to say, what to do about their daughter. All Toby had to go on was an ever-increasing series of confrontations and a heavy dose of dread.

"We'd like to hear from you," Tim said. "Is there anything you can think of that might account for the change in Ava? Up until the last several weeks, she's been a model student. Ava's always been so solid, such an all-around great kid."

Ava's still a great kid, Toby wanted to say. His girl had never been difficult, not when she was two or twelve. Not even after Lorraine and Poppy died. Cautious, yes. Sensitive, certainly, but never trouble—or troubled. His girl was even-tempered, kind. The way she used to keep an eye on her sister, holding Poppy's hand wherever the two of them went. It was an image Toby would never forget. Yet one he couldn't afford to linger on at the moment.

Up until recently, Toby would've said he and Ava got along okay. She didn't open up to him like she did when she was little, but how many fathers and teenage daughters really talked? Everything was per usual until a random day back before the holidays when Ava just seemed different. Like a stereotypical adolescent who suddenly found her father to be a constant source of irritation.

There was that argument about her less than stellar report card, and the times he'd smelled alcohol on her breath. At first when he'd confronted her, she'd made up seemingly harmless excuses. *I just wanted to try it. No one had been driving.* Ava had been convincing, and she promised to get her act together. In the beginning, Toby had let it go, chalking things up to what was normal for a girl her age.

"I'm taking her to a counselor. This afternoon," Toby said.

"Oh, excellent. Ava's willing to go then?"

Toby couldn't come out and say his daughter had actually agreed. He'd sound like an idiot if he told Tim and the teachers that he was counting on her lack of opposition as consent. "You seemed surprised," Toby said.

"I've talked to her about getting help," the music teacher said. "Sorry to say, Ava hasn't been terribly receptive."

North of sixty, Miss Kelly was on the verge of retirement. Toby imagined the woman was the butt of the snarkier kids' jokes for her sweaters bedecked with musical notes and clef symbols, but Ava talked about her talented teacher like she was a rock star. Or at least she had when Ava talked to Toby about such things.

As the woman spoke, he remembered Ava's guitar sitting lonely on his daughter's bedroom floor. "You're in school. Does she have a lesson today?" Toby asked.

"Yes, right after dismissal. Why?"

Toby's mind was on overdrive. Maybe Ava hadn't put up a fight about counseling because she'd already been considering it, thanks to Miss Kelly. But why then, had she lied about not needing her guitar?

"No reason," Toby said. "Is there anything else? I'm getting the distinct impression there's something you're not telling me."

"It might be a good idea to get to know Ava's friends," Tim said. "Tell her straight out about your concerns—and ours." He slid the stack he'd been resting his hands on toward Toby. "Look, you're a man of some means, so I'd be remiss if I didn't make you aware of the resources available to you. If counseling goes well, terrific. But if you suspect Ava might benefit from something... more intensive, you'll know what else is out there."

Toby accepted the stack of brochures. Something about the tagline on the top one—promising to teach children to stand up and reclaim their lives—put him off, but he found the pictures of smiling teenagers sitting around a campfire and hiking, the backdrop of the Adirondacks framing each shot, reassuring.

"I'll let you know how the appointment goes," Toby said. "And thanks. I appreciate all of you looking out for Ava."

Heading to his car, Toby couldn't shake the feeling that there was more Tim wasn't saying. Of all the teachers at the meeting, only Miss Kelly spoke up. What were the rest of them doing there if not to talk of Ava's academic death spiral? Was Toby expected to figure the subtext out on his own?

He replayed the conversation word for word, searching for darker undertones. *Ava looks unwell. She's spending time on the fringes. You might want to get to know her friends.* There was no arguing his daughter was going through a rough patch, but was Tim suggesting Ava took drugs? No, Toby told himself, he would've come right out with that. Now that Toby had kicked things into gear with this afternoon's appointment, he would keep his high hopes pinned on the counselor visit.

Then hope scaled the back fence of the football field. Toby didn't believe it was Ava running from school property until a shock of red hair flying behind her betrayed her attempt to flee him.

What the hell was she doing?

Toby flew into panic mode, pulling his car out of the visitors' lot. Almost too late, he spied a boy sneaking a cigarette behind a truck. After beeping at the kid, he floored it, desperate to get to the street that ran parallel to the high school, to find Ava before he lost her.

Had Toby pushed her too far, or not far enough soon enough?

By the time he got to Seaver Street, Ava was nowhere to be seen. Down one road, up the next, Toby tried to track her. He circled the grassy green of Wellesley Town Hall, then drove by the Free Library. No Ava. Toby had jumped into the deep with no idea where he was going.

He rang her cell but, no surprise, she didn't pick up. He made a mental list of the kids he should call. But they'd all be in school. Except Tim Graham as much as said Ava had new friends. Ones Toby didn't know. Sketchy ones—if he was reading Tim right.

After searching all the places he could come up with, Toby went to the police. A female cop sat behind a desk wolfing down a sub. Shreds of lettuce hung from the corner of her mouth as she spoke. "Take a number."

Incredulously, Toby looked around for some kind of dispenser. The cop cracked a smile. "It means wait your turn," she said.

"But there's no one else here and it's urgent. I need to speak to someone about my daughter."

"She dead or bleeding?"

"God no, Ava took off from school and I need help to find her. She's sixteen, wearing jeans and a sweatshirt." Jesus, he was describing half of Wellesley High. "Ava's got red hair. Here, I have a picture." He pulled out his phone and called up a months-old picture of his daughter. Looking at Ava, so impossibly young, worry hammered him like a fist to his chest.

"I can save you the wait," she said. "You can fill out a report if you want to, but we don't do runaways. Now, if you can prove she's been kidnapped, well, then we can help."

Was she kidding? Toby had just told a cop Ava took off, did she really expect him to change his story in order to get her to put down her goddamned sub? Dismissing her, Toby ran from the station to get back behind the wheel.

Fear flattened time as he drove around and around, through Wellesley into Needham, toward Newton. Without credible guesses for where his daughter might be, Toby drove blind.

Hours into his search, he went home in hopes Ava had snuck back in while he'd been out looking for her. No such luck. Back out he went. Driving down side roads, up favorite streets. By cafés and gift shops, behind bookstores and bagel joints. Anywhere he could think that she might go.

By the second nightfall, after he'd missed the appointment with the counselor and canceled dinner with his foundation's wealthiest donor, Toby was wrecked, distraught over thoughts of Ava braving the cold, by now hungry and afraid. He couldn't stop his mind from imagining her being someplace dangerous, doing something stupid.

Fighting to keep his eyes on the road, Toby hunted the glove compartment for a stray roll of Tums. When he had two discs crushed to chalk in his mouth, he tried Ava's cell for the umpteenth time. One ring and like all the other times, the call went to voicemail. "You know what to do," Ava said, her lyrical voice betraying the trouble she was in.

Toby told himself it had to work out. Ava would be okay. Try telling that to the peptic acid snaking its way up the back of his throat.

Willing his daughter to pick up, he dialed her again. At this point Toby would've been happy to listen to his daughter complain about him breathing, or existing. With no clue where else to look, with no family to call, there was nothing to do but go home. Never had being a single father felt so solitary.

When he opened the door to their rambling home, all lights still off, he called out anyway. "Ava? You here?"

Room to room he went, turning on lamps, praying he'd find

his daughter sprawled on the couch or upstairs, safe and sound in her bed.

As Toby reached the bottom of the stairs that led to her room, blue light filled the foyer. Round and round it circled his head, dizzying him, frightening him. Toby watched a police cruiser pull into his driveway. Time stopped as he watched the cop step on to the pavement, and then reach inside the back seat to haul his daughter out.

Toby ran to the door to meet them. Ava moved up the stone path, head down, staring at the ground, her focus either on walking a straight line or avoiding her father. Here we go again. His daughter delivered home by police; this time, her lovely face covered in scratches, twigs and leaves clinging to her clothes. When the police officer dropped his hand from her upper arm, Ava glanced over at him, but not at her father. No one moved until Ava broke from the trio. Skirting Toby, she took slow and careful steps upstairs to her room.

The cop crossed both arms over his barrel chest and rocked back on his heels enough to get Toby's attention. "Your daughter was standing on a railroad track, facing down a train. Wigged her friends out so bad, one of the kids called us."

Toby reached for the door in an effort to remain standing.

"Does she have any history of psychiatric issues? Take drugs as far as you know?"

"No. No." As Toby said the word over and over, he prayed what he chanted was true.

"It's highly unusual for a group of underage kids who've been drinking and smoking pot to think it's a good idea to call us. You get me? Whatever your kid was doing out there, Mister, you better take it seriously."

Admonition over, the cop turned on Toby. He headed back out to serve and protect. That was it? That was considered helpful?

The acid resurfaced, roiling in the back of his throat as Toby took the stairs to Ava's room. Sticking his head in, all he could see were piles of clothes obscuring the carpet. Her bed was a jumble of comforters and pillows. He was about to poke them to see if his slight daughter lay under the heap, when he saw her.

"Where were you?" he asked. "I've been looking everywhere.

You scared me half to death."

Ava leaned over the back of her couch, her head out the window. It didn't look to Toby as if she were coming in or going out, more like the position he'd assumed when he was her age and used to sneak cigarettes out his bedroom window.

When she turned toward the door, he saw her striking hair was a mass of sweaty tendrils. Even in the dim light, her face shone white, her cat's eyes dilated and vacant.

"You need to talk to me," Toby said. "What's going on? This isn't you, Ava. This has to be about Thailand."

"How many times do I have to tell you I don't remember. And I don't want to talk to you. About anything. Now get out," she shrieked, slapping one hand over her opposite arm.

Goose bumps covered her arms and legs, her tank top and short shorts inadequate for meeting the cool night air. Her slowed reflexes sabotaged her deceit. Even with her hand covering the petals outlined in black, the imprint on her upper arm was unmistakable. A tattoo of one delicate blue poppy. A new, yet permanent reminder of her sister's namesake flower.

Toby backed away, closing the bedroom door, wishing he could lock Ava in there for the next five years, or at least until he could come up with a better idea.

Plummeting grades and skipping school could be excused, explained away as adolescent rites of passage. But to Toby's way of thinking, this girl, fragile and angry, was barely recognizable to him. It didn't make sense to him that now, all these years later, out of the blue, Ava would be grieving her mother and sister. But that had to be it.

Years ago he'd consulted a series of doctors and trauma experts, all of whom told him that while Ava acknowledged her mother and Poppy were gone and that she missed them, she had no memory of the actual events of their ill-fated vacation. According to those in the know, she'd adjusted to their circumstances remarkably well. Blocking things out was a trick of the mind, the doctors had said. Ava's way of protecting herself.

Toby wished his brain could play such games. It was insufferable to think about Lorraine and Poppy. Replaying their final moments as a family was pure torture. So when father and daughter returned home from Phuket, he took his cues from Ava. Toby lulled himself into believing the strange logic that closure could be found by keeping the tragedy in the past. Ava had shut it out for good reason. So he made a silent agreement with her not to talk about it—or them.

Standing there now, Toby believed distant eyes, clammy palms, and shaky hands could only be symptoms of one thing. It was bad enough Ava drank, but now it looked like she'd gotten into much worse.

No matter what was responsible for the change in his daughter, Toby knew he had to do something. Take drastic action before she really hurt herself.

Downstairs he went to unearth the stack of brochures given to him by Tim Graham. Toby sat at his desk sifting through them while his desktop came to life. Then he Googled programs for teens. The search turned up pages and pages of simultaneously alarming yet strangely comforting information about troubled kids. Boot camps, boarding schools, residential treatment facilities. Site after site offered Toby and parents like him, quizzes and inventories aimed at estimating just how out-of-control their kids had become.

Fill out this assessment, get a score, and one of our counselors will contact you immediately, they promised.

Does your teen disregard rules? Come home late? Forget to call?
Is your teen having problems in school? Poor grades? Skipping class?
Does your teen hide things about his/her life from you?
Does your teen hang around with teens you've never met?
Do you feel like every conversation becomes an argument?
Do you suspect your teen uses/abuses drugs and/or alcohol?
Has your teen had run-ins with police?
Are you worried your child is suicidal?

Toby answered yes to every question. For a brief moment, he wondered how many boxes other parents of sixteen-year-olds might check about their kids. How many might his own parents have checked back when he was a teenager?

Then, there it was on the screen. The photo he'd seen back at school, from the exact same program brochure he held in his lap.

Mount Hope Wilderness Camp: A crisis intervention and treatment program for adolescents with substance abuse and emotional issues.

The solution to Ava's problems was within driving distance of their home and came recommended by a team of teachers who cared about his daughter. Toby's next move was obvious.

In took less than two hours to fill out the online forms and speak with the intake coordinator at Mount Hope. Hardly any time at all for Ava Sedgwick to be enrolled in the place that would change her life. Toby minimized the screen, feeling certain that someday she would thank him for what he'd just done.

TWO

≈

The man with almond-shaped eyes wears thick-rimmed glasses and holds a camera to his face. Click, he points it at me, focusing and refocusing the long lens, turning, turning, turning. I'm running, but getting nowhere. He shouts at me, but I can't understand. I stop suddenly, puzzled when his voice comes out sounding like a woman's. Someone familiar. As soon as I stand still, he disappears. Yards and yards of blue poppies take his place. They keep coming and coming, a field of them rolling toward me. Flowing over me. I can't breathe for all the flowers crammed in my mouth, stuffed in my ears, covering my eyes.

"Ava wake up. I've picked out a school."

Heavy with sleep and slightly hungover, Ava curled to one side of her canopy bed dripping with ruffles, her eyes shut against the world. Pieces of the nightmare flew away from her as her father shook one shoulder. His voice was too loud and too close, his hand too firm on her arm.

It couldn't be time for their morning routine: him telling her to get going and Ava rolling on to her other side clutching the comforter to her chin. What was he doing in her room so early? What did he mean picked out a school? Once her eyes came unglued, Ava could tell by her father's outline, courtesy of the hall light, that it was closer to midnight than morning. In an instant, two strangers, huge men, blocked the glow as they made their way into the room.

Ava pulled her knees against her chest, clutching a pillow in front of her.

"They're taking you to a place," her father said, his voice shaky, his words not making sense. "It's a wilderness program for kids who need time to figure things out. They can do a lot more for you than I can."

His wrinkled shirt untucked, he wore the same clothes he'd had on yesterday. His hair stuck up in a million directions. His eyes were squinty and wet. For a second he didn't look anything like her dad. No tailored clothes fresh from the dry cleaner's, no comb tracks through what was left of his hair. Where were his bribes to make Ava breakfast if she hurried? Where were the threats to make her walk to school if she refused to get up? Right now!

Shaking her head, trying to breathe, Ava told herself this couldn't be happening. What exactly was happening? It had to be just another one of her freak-outs, a bad dream she hadn't met yet. But the headboard digging into her spine felt real. The bruises in the making as the bald guy took her arm and yanked her to the edge of her bed—all real.

"Say good-bye," the taller one said, moving Ava's dad out of the way so he could stand in front of her bed too. Four legs the size of tree trunks kept Ava from making a run for it. "Time to leave, Mr. Sedgwick."

As her father bent down to switch on the bedside lamp, the scarf she left draped over it fluttered to the floor. The room filled with blinding light. Ava squeezed her eyes tight against what was happening. But she could hear him.

"I can't watch you all the time, honey. I'm afraid you're going to hurt yourself. They promised to help us."

Ava's eyes flew back open. "No, please. Is this because of what happened that night with the train? I didn't do it on purpose. This is hurting me." Ava shouted at her father, and then at the men. "Let go of me!" She tried to think up something to say to make her father change his mind about sending her away. Ava's whole body came off the bed as she flailed and struggled against the man pinning her there. He didn't break a sweat or loosen his grip. He pinched her harder. It didn't take Ava long to realize she was no match for a guy three times her size.

"Why are you doing this?"

When her father didn't answer, Ava screamed three words that came from the deepest place inside her. "I want Mom." Her voice, louder and clearer than it had been in weeks, moved her father toward her. Their eyes met.

"She would never do this to me." Ava spewed the desperate words out. Instead of feeling bad enough to call things off, her father backed away.

"Leave now, Mr. Sedgwick. You're making this worse."

Ava thrust her arm out, her whole being pleading with him to take her hand. "Daddy, no! Please. I'm sorry. I'll be good. I'll do whatever you say." Too late. He listened to them, not her. After her father disappeared into the hallway, Ava heard his bedroom door shut tight against her.

"Bet your ass you'll do whatever we say." The tall one who gave all the orders picked a sweater and a pair of jeans from the pile of clothes on the rug and threw them at Ava. "Put these on."

The bald guy flashed a pair of handcuffs. "We can do this the easy way or the hard way. It's up to you." His voice was deep, so low only Ava could hear the threat.

She put the jeans on over her pajama bottoms, the sweater over her cami. No way was she changing in front of these goons. One of them shoved her from behind when she stopped to wipe the tears racing down her face. "Daddy, please!" Ava cried out, but only once. The handcuffs were back, dangling in front of her face.

Through her sobs, Ava asked, "Can I take some of my things? My guitar?"

The guy scanned the room. He wore a disgusted look as he took in the clothes tossed over the couch, the laptop on her desk, the flat-screen TV anchored to the wall. "Brat," he muttered. Then when his eyes rested on the guitar lying in its open case he said, "Musician," like everything about Ava suddenly made sense. "Won't be time for that where you're going."

The whole way down the stairs, Ava searched her brain for

something, anything she could say or do that would stop them from pushing her toward the driveway, putting her in that car. It happened so fast. The guy in charge went around the other side to get in back with her. Ava rattled the door. She'd known it would be locked, but she had to try.

Bald Guy in the driver's seat looked at her in the rearview. "What, you think because we're big, we're stupid?" When he laughed, phlegm jiggled in his throat. She smelled stale cigarette smoke; the matted sheepskin seat covers reeked of it.

Ava took the metal clip of her seat belt and started banging the window. A giant hand reached over, grabbed the buckle, and locked her in like a child. Tall Guy's arm grazed her chest. She fought the urge to throw up, figuring if she did, she'd be left to sit in her own vomit for the time it took to get wherever they were taking her. All she wanted to do was go back to her room, to lie down on the cool tile of her bathroom floor.

Ava screamed and screamed, though there was no way anyone could hear her. The street was dead and not one light filtered out through a single window. Except for her father's. Toby Sedgwick was backlit by the lone bedroom light. His shadow watched his daughter go.

"Where are you taking me? I didn't do anything," she said.

"That's not what he thinks." The man sitting next to her used his hand to make an up-and-down motion like he was pulling the whistle on a train. "Look, sit back and shut it. All we gotta do is get you there. Few hours from now we'll be out of your hair."

Hours?

No matter how hard it was to talk to her father, she should've told him what happened two nights ago on those tracks.

It wasn't the first time memories came looking for her, but it was the scariest. After Ava ran away from school, all she could think to do was to get as far from Wellesley as possible. She took the train into Boston thinking that by the time she got there she'd know where to go, what bus she could take to get out of town. Or maybe she could hop the next one no matter where it was headed. The closer she got to South Station the more Ava knew she couldn't leave her father. Not like this. One minute there and the next out of sight. It would kill him.

But her body was worse off than her racing mind. The muscles of her arms and legs were rigid, every bit of her skin tingled, her head pounded. Ava was a jazzed-up mess. If she didn't find some kind of release soon, she worried she'd end up screaming right there on Tremont Street in downtown Boston. The jangled way she felt made her finally understand the girls who cut. That's when Ava saw the sign: *Tattoos. No waiting.*

No need to look through the book of choices. She knew what she wanted before she opened the door. The blue poppy turned out beautiful. And it hurt. A pain so real and exacting, it erased everything else she felt. It gave Ava the jolt she needed, a newfound confidence to head home.

By the time she got back to Wellesley Hills, she'd changed her mind yet again. Not ready to face her father, Ava slept on a bench inside the station. During the day, she wandered around town, dodging him, making plans to meet up with some kids. Her plan then was to down a drink and sneak back home. It was too cold to spend another night on a bench. Ava figured a single hard lemonade would give her the courage to face her father and the power to dull her nightmares, making her less afraid to close her eyes. Two more drinks offered Ava the promise of uninterrupted sleep.

Her group of friends sat huddled together on the ground, passing around a bottle of Jack. With arms outstretched, Ava walked the rail like a balance beam. Without warning, the sky opened up sending rain down on her. She tipped her head back, drinking it in as the ground began to quiver beneath her feet. Part of her knew there was a train rounding the bend, but Ava never saw it coming. She didn't hear the train's thunderous approach. An air rush didn't chill her. As the vibrations tingled up her legs, Ava started to disappear. The prickly sensation made it to right below her knees, and then like that, she blacked out.

This freak-out came on quicker than most, and it didn't last long enough for images to linger. Or maybe Ava didn't remember anything because some kid she'd just met snapped her out of it when he pushed her out of the way of the train, landing on top of her, thorny brush scraping their cheeks in the fall. Waves of rust, her hair mingled with his blood, weren't enough to hide his look. The kid thought she was crazy.

Ava feared he might be right.

Her father thought she'd completely lost it too, otherwise he wouldn't be doing this. Sending her away. Why didn't she stop drinking when he asked her to? How hard would it have been to promise no more running away, no more sneaking out of the house at night? As much as Ava didn't want to deal with whatever was breaking apart inside her, she should've told him something was wrong. Or gone to counseling when he begged her to. It couldn't have been any worse than this.

"Where are you taking me?" Ava asked the men again, modulating her voice, middle C for calm.

Neither one of them spoke as they drove north of Wellesley. Let the school be in Maine, Ava thought, near our summer place above the Reach. She hadn't been there in eight years, but she could live alone at Herrick House, or with her mom's best friend Mrs. Purcell, at her house in Center Harbor. Ava would be able to handle being up there again, going to school there. She could. Visions of what she thought she could manage met reality when they got as far as the Newton town line and Tall Guy pulled out a blindfold.

"Are you kidding me? Why can't I know where I'm going?" Ava shifted in her seat, uncrossing her legs, crossing them again in the opposite direction.

"New kids are a flight risk. Put it on. Don't make me pull out the cuffs. And quit humming. It's annoying."

Ava's mind worked double-time trying to figure out where they were taking her; she wasn't aware she'd been humming. They'd refused to let her take her guitar, but they couldn't stop her from using music the way she did.

For the rest of the trip, with the blindfold tied behind her head, Ava fantasized but didn't speak up. She plotted but didn't fight back. Her father was dumping her at some school—against her will—and Ava sat in that car, her back numb against the seat, convincing herself that the best thing she could do now was not make trouble. Her instincts told her things would turn out better that way. Alone in the dark, the blindfold tight against her skin, the truth was she was petrified.

Hours later, Bald Guy whipped the blindfold off. Stepping

out of the car into late night, Ava had no idea where they were. Thousands of different types of pine trees stretched their arms out to touch each other, blocking any evidence of a road. A coyote's high-pitched yelps drowned out the hoots of a distant owl. Judging from the mountains surrounding the place and the time it took to get from her bedroom to hell, Ava guessed the place was in New Hampshire or Vermont.

A guy with a marine haircut, shirt buttons near to bursting, met them at the door to a log cabin.

"Hey, Justice," Tall Guy said.

In the presence of this man, Tall Guy acted all nice. His voice was tempered, and he kept a good distance from Ava.

With every muscle in her body clenched, Ava took the smallest steps she could toward the cabin, even though what she needed to do was run to a bathroom. Looking around without being obvious, Ava put all her energy into squeezing her butt and thighs. It was no use. She couldn't hold it any longer.

With hands crossed low in front of her, warm liquid began soaking her jeans and tears took off down her cheeks. Ava bit her lip and prayed the guy was talking about something else when he called her a baby. Then he to pointed at her crotch. Tall Guy and the driver leaned over to look. All three of them burst out laughing when they saw the dampness creeping toward one knee. Ava froze, standing still in that spot, but her body wouldn't stop shaking.

"Lucky for you I'm your intake counselor," the guy named Justice said, as the men left, mocking her all the way back to their car. "I know a few here who'd punish you for that. Get a move on." He grabbed Ava's arm, shoving her forward, forcing her deeper into the log-cabin shack.

Justice deposited Ava in an empty seat in the row of chairs against the wall. A girl with a nasty black eye and a boy with his head down were parked on either side of her.

Justice reached up to take a pair of hospital gloves from a box on the shelf above Ava's head. The plastic fingers made snapping sounds, again and again, as he adjusted the fit. "Take out all piercings and give me your rings, necklaces, anything you weren't born with. Time to hit the showers and change those clothes. McEttrick, listen up. I'm only giving this spiel once." He cuffed the boy in the head.

Black-Eyed Girl said nothing, but her shoulders shook; even her cries were silent. The boy with bangs like fringe moaned, repeating the words, *no shower*. The third time Fringe mumbled something under his breath, the counselor got up in his face and started yelling.

"Look, Seed, you know the deal. Shut it till you're in group. Understand? That's the place to grumble and gripe about how bad you have it."

The boy didn't stop. He kept ripping skin from around his scabby fingernails, repeating, "No shower."

Justice hit him harder, this time on the other side of his head. Fringe stopped talking, closed his eyes tight, and placed one hand over his ear.

"I don't care how many times you've come through here. Right now, you're back to the beginning. You're a Seed. A nobody." Justice kept pulling things off the shelf. "All the kids here start off at Level One. Do what you're told, and you'll move through the ranks, earn more privileges." He dropped a backpack at Ava's feet and into her lap, a pile of clothes, khakis, a T-shirt, and matching sweatshirt. After sizing up her feet, he put a pair of hiking boots in front of her on the floor. Then he repeated the same deal for Fringe and Black-Eyed Girl.

Two bolts, wrought-iron and heavy, separated them from freedom. A few hours into captivity and already the counselor had Ava thinking of the other Seeds—his word for detainees—as kids without real names.

"Outside of group, you're only allowed to talk to another student if your level numbers add up to four. No talking to counselors without permission. Follow the rules!" The counselor screamed in Ava's face, his bulbous nose less than an inch from her tiny one. "Everything here is about discipline." His breath reeked of tomatoes and garlic. At first it disgusted her, then it started Ava counting. Was it ten or twelve hours since she'd last had something to eat?

If Ava weren't so afraid of Justice, she would've challenged every one of his ridiculous rules. No water between meals. Bathroom breaks twice a day. Forty-five minutes of writing in workbooks in the morning and again at night. One, two, three, he tossed black and white composition notebooks on top of their piles.

"Put everything in your pack and let's get this show on the road. Outdoor showers are down the hill. Your first hike starts in an hour. What are you waiting for?" he screamed at Black-Eyed Girl, sending a shudder like dominoes through the three of them sitting there. "All of you. Move it," he shouted.

Ava visualized tripping Justice before he could crowd Black-Eyed Girl as she tried to move past him toward the locked door. She screamed, bully!—idiot!—bastard! in her head every time he yelled at the boy with the bangs for moving too slowly or staggering under the weight of his pack.

Not knowing where they were going, the group of three, carrying identical backpacks filled with atomic orange shirts and hiking boots, trekked down a path. They followed Justice, their way lit by searchlights every few feet. Not one of them made a run for it. If Black-Eyed Girl and Fringe came there like Ava did, blindfolded, maybe even handcuffed, what was the point?

"You can't see it now," Justice said, "but your parents did you losers a favor."

Dodging stones and tree roots on the trail made Ava dizzy. Her feet went numb. The drenched jeans were cold against her skin. They walked by a counselor younger than Justice but older than Ava. The woman wore a cap with a Mount Hope logo and clothes of her own choosing, cargo pants and a camouflage jacket. As Ava watched her stoke the logs in the fire pit, she tried to convince herself the sweat on her forehead came from being out of shape and walking too close to the flame. The queasy feeling in her stomach from not having eaten since yesterday. But the word *parents* kept ringing in her head. Ava couldn't remember a time when she'd wanted her mother more than she did in that moment.

Stop thinking about her. Don't have one of your freak-outs here. Not in front of them, she told herself.

The lady counselor with big teeth stared right back at her as the little parade circled the pit following Justice. Ava pictured an imaginary string pulling her nose up, making it impossible for her to cover her chops. Seemed like no one here had a reason to smile.

"By the time I'm through with you," Justice said, "you might be ready to go home. You might actually turn out to be something."

Ava followed two sparks as they flew upward and away from the fire, vanishing into the dark sky, their glow replaced by a glittering mass of stars. It was no good looking up, thinking about home and the only parent she had left. Stars didn't shine like this in Wellesley, where she lived with her father. Toby, the traitor.

THREE

Dad,

I hate it here. And I'll hate you forever, unless you come right now to take me home. Did you even check this place out? To see what they do to kids? As if being dragged out of bed in the middle of the night by strangers wasn't scary enough, once I got here they strip-searched me in front of this evil guy named Justice. Every time he looks at me now, my skin crawls. And I have to spend a million hours a day with him because he runs the Learning Center, if you can call it that. Hour after hour we sit in hard plastic chairs without moving, listening to him tell us what losers we are and how we need to own up to what we've done to hurt the people who love us. Love? If you loved me you never would've dumped me in a place that calls dog food a meal, serving the same thing twice a day—if I'm lucky. They make us sleep with the lights on when we're in the bunkhouse. All we ever do is hike. Without water! Justice says I better figure out how to make fire with a piece of wood and a stick before our first overnight or I'll have to sleep on the ground without my sleeping bag. Do you really want me to freeze to death?

What did I do that was so awful? I told you I don't drink. Or do drugs. So I stay out late. Why do you care? You're never home anyway. Unless you want to get rid of me so you can work more. And spend more time with Jill. Why won't you admit she's the reason you sent me here? I *don't care what she told you about her stupid daughter. Becky still does drugs.*

How many times do I have to say I'm sorry about the train thing? I wasn't trying to kill myself. And even if I was, this is the last place on earth to send a person thinking of offing themselves.

Toby couldn't read the rest of his daughter's tirade. He dialed the extension of his VP of Finance to leave a message. "Jill—when you're out of your ten o'clock, please stop by my office."

Turning his gaze out the bank of windows, taking in the Boston skyline, Toby replayed the program director's warning. *The first letter will be a rant against you for forcing your daughter to accept that she's out of control. Don't believe any accusations of abuse. These manipulations are all too common among our students.*

Though he'd been told to expect a letter like this one, that didn't make it any easier to read. Sixty days, Toby told himself. He'd only enrolled Ava for the two-month program.

The waistline of his slacks was tight. With one hand he tugged at his belt and with the other he swept the last piece of cinnamon roll into the wastebasket, revealing the glossy brochure he kept on his desk, the tangible reminder that he'd done the right thing.

Toby fiddled with his wedding band; it wouldn't budge. One look at the gleaming gold and he was flooded with thoughts of Lorraine. A mother was supposed to be there to ask the difficult questions so a father wouldn't have to resort to buying the tough love Mount Hope was selling. Pulling out the contract he'd signed giving the escort service permission to transport Ava, and the school the power to treat her, he felt awful about how it went down. Ava had looked completely blindsided, because she had been. Toby had been told it would be safer not to tell her ahead of time so she wouldn't run before they got there.

In one of their early phone conversations, the program director led him to believe that counselors would be the ones to come and take Ava to the school, a therapeutic community with an Ivy League tuition price tag. When the escorts got there that night, Toby questioned them downstairs—wondering out loud if maybe he had changed his mind. They said all kids put up resistance in the beginning. This was the way it had to be. They knew what they were doing and they promised Ava would be fine.

Still, he'd nearly stopped breathing when his daughter cried out for her mother. Another piece of him died when she'd stretched her splayed hand out to Toby.

But what else could he do? He'd done his best, raising Ava alone, tiptoeing around anything that might call up memories of her mother and sister. True, Toby tended to spoil Ava. At some point, he was sure someone from Mount Hope would tell him that he was part of the problem. It wasn't like he hadn't heard it before. More than once, Lorraine had accused him of indulging both Ava and Poppy.

Toby looked around his office on the forty-seventh floor of the luxury office complex he owned. The Arne Jacobsen furniture and Dan Christensen artwork—all things unchanged from another time—were evidence he was good at making investments. He took pride in his job to decide which humanitarian organizations could most benefit from his family foundation's money. Toby had worked tirelessly and effectively to grow the endowment, to pay his good fortune forward to those less fortunate. What he had no trouble admitting was how inept he felt as a father. How little he knew about teenagers.

"Hope I'm not interrupting."

Toby hadn't heard Jill knock. He hadn't noticed her standing between his office and the reception area, but there she was, poking her head in, looking as concerned about him as ever.

"No, of course not. I called you. Come in." Toby got up from his desk and moved toward the sitting area of his office, gesturing for Jill to join him.

Everything about her appearance was unremarkable. Jill was neither too tall nor too thin. Her mid-length brown hair was neither stylish nor mousy. Her clothes were well-tailored though nondescript. When Toby interviewed her for the VP chief counsel job, she hadn't done much to make an impression until she started talking about her experiences in law school, her work with other foundations. Jill appealed to Toby's intellect. Now, after years working with her, he couldn't imagine running the Sedgwick Foundation without her.

"You rang?" she asked.

"I did. Close the door. It's personal."

"You have questions about Mount Hope, am I right? I wondered how long it would take you to reach out to me. I didn't want to push." Jill sat down, relaxing her posture, taking on more of an after-hours pose. Toby could almost picture her with a glass of Merlot in hand. While Jill was a terrific gal and he did enjoy her company at work-related dinners and the like, peel away her education and work experience, replace her tailored clothes with jeans and a flannel shirt, and she reminded Toby a little too much of Lorraine's best friend, Biddie Purcell. Which meant no matter what Ava thought, Toby would never date her.

"I didn't remember that your daughter went to Mount Hope until Ava reminded me. In her letter," Toby said.

"Oh God, you already got the first letter. And you survived?"

"Barely. Talk about twisting the knife."

"Becky went to Mount Hope two and a half years ago. Stayed for six months. But I remember the experience like it was yesterday. That girl was so lost after my divorce."

"I apologize for not really registering the details at the time. I get it now, how worried you must've been. You probably took me for a heartless boss back then."

"Not at all. I don't think anyone can really know what it's like until they go through it. That's why places like Mount Hope exist. It's for the parents as much as the kids. It really helps knowing you're not the only one struggling."

"At first I thought Ava was working through typical teenage stuff and then suddenly things were so far south I wondered how in the hell I could've missed that she was in trouble."

"My situation was different. Becky was difficult from day one. Colicky baby, a kid who never slept. All through grade school she had trouble making friends. Then high school was a monumental disaster. Drinking. Drugs. My ex and I fought constantly about how to parent her. Both of us absolutely clueless. We didn't need Mount Hope to tell us we were part of the problem."

Toby took a deep breath.

"No, no," Jill said. "I'm not saying you are in Ava's case. I'm saying they helped us. They showed us the error of our ways. I can't say it was easy, but Becky is better for it."

"So she's all right now?"

"It took time to reconcile the damage we'd inflicted on each other. But we did—we're still working things through. Becky started Massasoit Community College this semester. She's living on her own in an apartment in Brockton, with her boyfriend."

Something in Toby tensed infinitesimally. Jill was telling him more than he wanted to know.

"If you don't mind, I'd like you to take the dinner meeting with Bob Verde," he said getting up, brushing out the creases in his slacks, digging inside his pocket for keys. "I'm going bend the rules a little. Head up to see Ava, take her out for coffee or something. I think it'll help us both to feel better about the way we left things. If I leave now, before rush hour, I'll be in upstate New York by nightfall. I'll be back in the office tomorrow by noon."

"You really didn't survive the first letter, did you?"

As Toby and Jill looked at each other, he got the distinct impression she wanted to hug him.

"I guess not." Toby backed up, loosening his tie, jingling his keys.

"Look, there are no contact rules for a reason," Jill said. "You owe it to Ava to let her get used to the place. To learn the rules. Don't interfere. She needs time to build a solid relationship with her counselor. Trust me. I know how hard it is to let go, but let go you must."

"I need to explain to her why I sent her there. Maybe all she needed was a wakeup call and now she's ready to talk to me, to tell me what's going on with her."

"At Mount Hope Ava has the right people to talk to. Counselors who know how to get her through whatever it is she needs to figure out. By the end of the program, you'll see, she'll be a different kid. On a better path. Leaving the crooked one she's on behind."

Jill had given Mount Hope a glowing endorsement, and still Toby couldn't let go of his urge to see his daughter. To get in his car and speed north.

All he wanted was one ten minute visit with Ava. Hell, a two minute phone call would do. He needed to make sure she'd forgiven him for their middle of the night fiasco, for everything. But if Ava already was in a better place, he'd be screwing that up too. God, it was impossible to trust his instincts given the mess he'd made of parenting thus far.

As impossible as this was, Jill was right. The situation called for Toby to put his daughter's well-being above his own desires. So he would. Toby shoved his keys back into his pocket. He'd do anything for Ava.

FOUR

Thirty seconds after Ava woke up, the best part of her day was over. Squeaky bedsprings above reminded her that the overweight girl who smelled like vinegar and cheese was still there. A vague memory of a dream came to Ava in which the bunk came crashing down on her in the middle of the night, metal coils trapping her, feathers and sheets clogging her mouth, making it impossible to breathe. In the seconds before Ava realized it was another freak-out, she remembered feeling grateful to the girl for putting her out of her misery.

Like every other morning she'd been at Mount Hope, reality smackdown came full on when Ava removed the pillow from over her eyes to find the lights blazing, realizing she wasn't at home. Across from her in the barracks was a cot that contained the sleeping body of the supervising girl, the only person in the bunkhouse Ava was allowed to talk to.

She didn't know a thing about Mallory, the girl who watched her every move when she was awake, who told Ava her own name meant bad luck. After hearing that, Ava didn't have the heart to give her a nickname.

Even though they were allowed to talk, Mallory hadn't told Ava her story. Ava hadn't told Mallory hers either. Mostly because she didn't have a complete version to tell.

Mallory flipped over in her bunk so unexpectedly Ava bit her lip. "Staring at another kid, category one punishment—lose ten points," Mallory whispered, drawing a circle around her face. "Keep to yourself if you want to move up a level and get more privileges."

With that, her ally's first subversive advice of the day, morning was broken and gone was the closest thing to safe Ava had felt in minutes.

Mallory jumped out of her bunk and started changing into her uniform of khaki shorts and designated colored tee. Ava got up and grabbed her own clothes, looking the other way as Mallory dressed right out in the open, but not before she saw the ugly scar that ran the length of her roommate's stomach.

"Get up. Make your bed," Mallory said, poking the shoulders of the overweight kid. Cheez pretty much kept to herself, as much as a girl could keep to herself in a room the size of Ava's bathroom at home. Mallory lifted the ratty shade, slapping it against the casing by accident. The girl bolted upright in her bunk, nearly hitting her head on the ceiling. "Sorry," Mallory said, having shuddered herself at the sound. Guess Ava wasn't the only one with a reason to be jumpy.

Their boots got locked up at night so no one could run. After getting them back, the three girls made their way single file behind a long string of other kids walking toward the shed, a building where gear was stored. Carrying her day pack, Ava was thankful it wasn't too cold out and that it had stopped raining. At least it wouldn't be wet on their first overnight. The sun was low in the sky. If Ava were home, she'd have at least two more swats on the snooze before she'd have to get ready for school. Pine and blueberries wafted through the air, and with each crunch of their hiking boots Ava thought about her mother and sister.

Up in Maine, a Sedgwick family breakfast included a giant stack of pancakes dripping with syrup. Poppy used to dump so many wild berries into the batter that the silver dollars their mother made turned out a funny shade of teal. Ava pushed those memories out of her way as she moved down that path. She'd already learned that eyes filled with tears made it impossible to hike. Ava's stomach growled so loudly that Mallory shot her a look. Forget about pancakes, Ava would've settled for a pinecone oozing sap.

Creepy Justice waited till the whole group had gathered around. "Listen up." Two piles of bigger backpacks lay in a heap. "You're each going to carry a pack that makes the one you've been carrying for the morning hike feel like a lunch box. Twenty pounds for the girls. Thirty for boys."

"I know you're up to the challenge," a woman said. The counselor Ava had seen at the fire pit on her first night at Mount Hope had her hands on her hips, a whistle dangling from her neck, her thick calves and broad shoulders inches below Justice's.

He turned to the woman, pointing his index finger at her like a gun. "Everybody here met Honor? She's our new counselor. You'll be her first group. Welcome," he said to her, cocking his head, smiling like the pair of them were at some happy freaking summer camp.

"Justice and I will be organizing this overnight together," Honor said, stuffing that ridiculous whistle inside her jacket, zipping it up with one hand. "Tonight after we set up camp, we'll decide which of you will be assigned to me for your one-on-ones."

Ava flashed a smile the woman's way. If she stood a chance of convincing anyone she was here by mistake, it would be better to get the newbie counselor. Ava didn't belong with delinquents. She hadn't done anything to deserve being sent away, shipped off to the wilderness camp for the hopeless.

Justice and Honor took turns talking the group through what to take from the day packs to add to the rucksacks. An extra pair of shorts, a shirt, a pair of long pants, a thermal blanket, cans of beans, instant soup, a sleeping bag. A fluttery feeling danced in Ava's chest. "I don't have a water bottle," she said, forgetting once again to ask for permission to speak.

"Level Threes carry the water," Justice said. "Seeds don't know a damn thing about rationing. Be quiet and put your sweatshirt on." He poked her arm till it hurt. "Skin like yours will fry up faster than catfish in a skillet."

Ava pulled the sleeve of her T-shirt down as far as it would go, trying to cover the tattoo she'd once wanted so badly. Now that Justice had touched the outline of those petals, she wished it would up and disappear.

"The ten of you to my right are with Justice," Honor said. "The rest of you follow me. We're going together but I want you to stay in your groups. Keep your counselor in sight at all times."

Ava swung her pack up and on, adjusting the waist belt in front. She'd lost five, maybe six pounds since she'd landed there. Vowing never again to count calories, Ava watched poor Cheez struggle with her belt. She wondered how much more the girl had weighed when she first got to Mount Hope. Rumor had it Cheez had already been there three months. Hiking single file, Ava walked in front of Honor and behind Mallory. Their pace was steady, and Mallory acted like she knew where they were headed. Fringe pulled up the rear in Justice's group, putting Ava in a better position to be invisible. Maybe this wouldn't be so bad.

Within a few hours of winding gravel roads and balsam-lined trails, the walk became a climb. Bushwhacking the trail, blowdown had covered the path, and it was sloppy with mud. Sweat trickled down Ava's waist into her shorts. Blackflies bit the backs of her knees, and her bulky pack made it impossible for her to reach down to swat them. When her calves started cramping and a brick-size knot lodged in her lower back, Ava heard Fringe start to complain.

He hadn't said anything the first two times he'd fallen. It was Justice who let the group know he was the weakest link.

"Get up! What are you, a faggot? Can't climb a little hill?" He shouted loud enough for the whole line to hear.

"I need to stop," Fringe said. "I have to change and put on my sweatshirt."

Even though he was behind Ava, she could hear his teeth chattering. An acrid smell, from some kind of swamp-like vegetation, started making her sick to her stomach. For the first time, Ava appreciated the lack of a breakfast. The canopy of trees trapped moisture in the forest, blocking out the sun, rotting things that had been there longer than she had.

"Jesus, you shit your pants," Justice said, covering his mouth and nose, trapping the netting he wore over his face to keep the flies out. "I told you before we left to put on a goddamn sweatshirt. There's a clearing up ahead, you're gonna have to wait."

Ava wasn't the only one to use the clash between the two to

pause and catch her breath. Honor turned back to see if Justice needed help. He had Fringe by the elbow, forcing the kid to stand up.

Mallory shoved Ava's arm and spoke through clenched teeth. "Stopping without permission—another category one."

The line was moving again, and inside of a few minutes, they reached a flat space. For the first time the group was allowed to rest. The sun was warm on Ava's back, and she was thankful for her wide-brimmed hat and its ability to block the glare. Still, the pair of sunglasses she'd left sitting on her bureau in Wellesley would've been nice.

It was the kind of view that made Ava want to write. She'd make up lyrics about the extensive trails winding their way around the hill, a collection of veins running down an arm. The shadowy valley, a secret treasure, was inspiring. Present company was anything but.

Fringe had his head down, one hand placed like a visor on his forehead. It looked like he was shielding his eyes from the sun; then he swiped under both of them with his fingers. He started to shiver, his arms clutched tight to his chest. He kept mouthing, *I'm sorry, I'm sorry,* to no one in particular. Ava looked away, scared she'd get caught staring, or worse go to him and get in trouble for being nice. She was embarrassed for him when she noticed his khaki pants were tie-dyed shades of brown.

Cheez panted, fanning the collar of her tee while loosening the strap on her pack. Ava was about to do the same, unbuckling her rucksack, when Mallory butted in.

"If you take off your pack at breaks, it'll be harder to get it back on. And never, ever take your boots off until nighttime."

What would Ava do without Mallory's dribs and drabs of useful information? She was about to thank her when Mallory thrust a water bottle out to her. "Drink to here," she said, pointing to a line on the plastic.

Savoring sips, Ava wondered when she'd get her next drink. The break didn't last nearly as long as she needed it to. A circle the size of a quarter had begun tingling inside her left boot. A blister. Ava visualized the skin peeling away from her foot, filling with a nasty colored fluid. An hour into taking the trail down into the valley, she was trying to concentrate on the terrain, but the thing nagged her like her father.

Moving forward, hour after hour, Ava was distracted by rage at her father and the hot pain spreading its wings inside her boot. It wasn't until Honor yelled back and pointed forward that she saw the narrow stream.

"Untie your packs and hold them as high as you can above your heads. We're wading across."

Ava stood on her toes, squinting, trying to take the scene in. The noise the water made flowing over rocks and stones got louder and louder. Or maybe that was her heart beating, shooting blood up her neck. Bang, bang, bang, into her head. Mallory looked back at Ava and nodded. "It's not that deep," she whispered.

Ava couldn't catch her breath. She felt her throat close over as if she'd been stupid enough to swallow a stick. Then the dizziness came, leaving her no time to make the decision to sit. As soon as Ava realized she couldn't stop this one, she surrendered.

Daddy tries to place me inside a small plane. I grip the exit, petrified he is sending me away. "I'm coming too," he says. "It's okay. It's okay." But it is not okay. Poppy and Mom are not with us. He won't tell me where they are. I grab his arm as he buckles me into the seat across from his. Bloody cuts and scrapes cover every inch of his skin. I wonder if I made those marks. Did I hurt my father with my grip?

"Don't look out the window, Ava. Promise me, you won't look down."

I pretend to obey, closing my eyes down to slits. Still I look. Buildings are broken, roads flattened, everything is gray or brown. There are so many people, all of them digging through heaps of trash, piles of wood, stacks of stone.

I imagine a flash of pink. My mother lighting up the darkness. She is wearing one of the pretty Thai costumes my father bought her in the shop beside the beach. Is she watching me lift off to fly toward home? Why isn't she reaching for me, crying for me, shouting for me to stay?

Ava came to when Justice slapped her on her right cheek; the sting of another smack lingered on her left. The bump on the back of her head throbbed.

"Get up now or you'll lose your pack. C'mon, faker. Stop your little act."

Awake but dazed, Ava could see the curved bank of the stream come into focus. Coarse grass sticking out of the flow waved at her, telling her not to be afraid, tempting her to come in. Without any effort, Ava stood. Somehow fear wasn't keeping her back, it was propelling her forward.

Then she felt Mallory. The girl had taken one arm, and Fringe, the other. Side by side, combining their scraps of strength, they helped her up, raised their packs high, and waded the water.

FIVE

≋

Ava stayed awake nights thinking about the kids who came before her, the ones who tried to run. She especially hated the determined few who'd made it out. Their bravery was the reason the rest of them had to walk heel-toe whenever they went bunkhouse to mess hall, gear shed to Learning Center, fire pit to bunkhouse, a counselor or supervising kid always at their backs.

God forbid Justice let Ava take the straight path to Honor's cabin by herself on therapy mornings.

Mallory had volunteered to walk Ava to her one-on-one, holding tight to a belt loop on the back of her khakis as Ava led the way. The other times they'd done this, they talked for the ten minutes it took to get to Honor's. This morning, Ava didn't pay attention to Mallory until she tugged at her waist, pointing out a branch ready to smack her in the face.

"Got any tricks for keeping track of all these rules?" Ava asked, holding back the branch, making way for Mallory.

"You just do it," the girl said, cocking her head, telling Ava with her eyes to keep going.

"I'm pretty sure I'm moving up a level today, which means I'll be giving my dad an earful by dinner. Level Twos get phone calls, right?"

Mallory let go of the branch, thwacking it back on a neighboring tree.

"How should I know? Hurry up. If I'm late getting back we'll both end up in Worksheets."

Mallory ran hot and cold. One minute she was telling Ava the things she needed to know to stay out of trouble, the next she got ticked at Ava for asking a simple question. She wasn't the only kid at Mount Hope who acted like that either. Bad moods could spread through the place like the flu through a high school, making it impossible to know who to trust.

Honor met students in her shoebox of a cabin perched hillside. The screened-in porch where kids talked about as little as possible faced away from the main buildings that made up the camp. For an hour twice a week Ava could almost pretend she was on vacation. Early morning fog, draped in places, was a sheet tumbling off a bed. The hills were dressed in purple and yellow wildflowers. There had to have been songs written about that mountain.

Mallory let go of Ava's belt loop so she could climb the two steps to the cabin door and knock on wood. "Permission to cross threshold," Ava called out. Five points for following counseling etiquette.

Twin rockers creaked and sighed. Honor and Fringe materialized out of the dim porch light. Behind the screen, Fringe looked like a regular kid. His shoulders hunched, he didn't claim his height. He ran his hand through his hair, but it refused to go where he sent it, landing once more in strings on his zitty forehead.

"Arthur, can I trust you to cooperate with Mallory, getting back to the Learning Center? I'd rather not wait for Benno. Ava and I have a lot to discuss." Honor shoved her hands in her pockets and rocked on her heels. She raised a brow, looking for Mallory's consent.

Benno was the boy version of Mallory, and because of their higher levels, each had extra responsibilities, like keeping the rest of the kids in line. Instead of objecting to being belt-looped by a girl, Fringe lifted his orange tee and aimed his butt toward Mallory.

"No problem," they both said at the same time.

With three out of four of them oblivious to the intimacy of

the gesture, Mallory took hold of Fringe's belt loop and they made their way down the path. She was the master; he was the dog.

Honor bent down to tie a loose bootlace. Ava watched Mallory steal a glance back at the cabin. As the pair came to the top of the embankment, Mallory let go of Fringe's belt loop, and through the hazy screen, Ava saw her take his hand.

"Have a seat," Honor said.

Ava knew Mallory felt bad for Fringe, but what was that?

"I hope you'll be more focused today," Honor said, opening a manila folder. "This is your fifth session in almost three weeks, and you've got to start owning up."

Owning up was Mount Hope-speak for offering a full confession in 3-D. Kids told wild stories every night at The Circle—about taking drugs, drinking, and doing the deed.

Ava had been introduced to the school's lying fest on her first overnight. After setting up camp, one by one the members of her group sat on the dirt, legs crossed, making one of two semicircles around the fire. There was a man she hadn't seen before, poking at the wood with a long stick.

"Welcome to The Circle," Fire Guy said, still focused on the log and flame.

Justice went around confiscating boots, putting them with the backpacks he'd already taken from the group. Honor sat down creating a divide between Ava's cohort and a larger collection of about twenty kids. On the riffraff side of the campfire, most heads were down, two girls kept sighing, and all the boys had their arms crossed over their chests. The kids on the other side sat up straight like windup toys, their attention focused on Fire Guy. Ava didn't need to be a counselor to know which kids were new to Mount Hope and which ones had already been programmed.

"I'm Pax," the man said as he laid down his fire stick and picked up another with feathers and ribbons tied to its ends. He motioned for two kids to scoot down, taking a seat next to Honor. "This is an orientation meeting aimed at letting you know how we run The Circle."

"We want you to be comfortable sharing what brought you here," Honor said. "Why you think your parents turned to us for help."

Pax interrupted her. His nose flared as tiny lines crinkled around his eyes. "We use the Native American talking stick during group." He raised the thing like he was the star of kindergarten show-and-tell. "When it's in your hands, you hold the sacred power of words. All others are to remain silent out of respect. The eagle feather tied to this end will give you courage to speak truthfully. The rabbit fur on this end is a reminder that your words must come from the heart. The shell, iridescent and transformative, is a sign that people and situations can change. I guarantee you, you will be changed by what happens to you here."

"You'll be changed," Fringe mumbled as he wiped dirt from his hands on his pants. "You'll be changed all right," he said again under his breath.

Honor reached out to take the talking stick from Pax like she'd run The Circle before, like she was operating from experience. But how could she be? According to Justice, she was new there too.

"Let's start with you," Honor said, passing the stick to Mallory.

That's when Ava found out that her roommate had a baby. She didn't believe most of the crazy things kids shared at The Circle, but Ava had seen the evidence that Mallory's crackhead boyfriend cut the kid right out of her. As her bunkmate told the story, her tears were real; her need to work the program so she could get her boy back seemed legit.

Other kids straight-out lied. Ava could tell which ones told the counselors exactly what they wanted to hear. The better the performance, the more praise kids got. More praise, more points, more privileges.

As she rocked in her therapy chair in Honor's cabin, Ava got up the nerve to ask her counselor about it. "You don't think all the stories those kids told last night at The Circle are true, do you?"

"Some Seeds take responsibility for what landed them here. You don't seem to want to."

Part of Ava wanted to tell Honor about every shard of memory that haunted her during the day and the ones that jabbed her while she slept. Mosaic pieces of glass that didn't exactly fit together. Honor was the only person Ava had met at Mount Hope who didn't make her want to hurl when she spoke. But how was

Ava supposed to talk to a stranger about something she couldn't even tell her own father?

Careful, Ava told herself. Mallory had warned her to watch what she said around Honor. If taken for crazy, she might have to stay longer, or wind up someplace worse. She could feel Honor's eyes on her. The pressure to own up was getting intense. So Ava caved and gave up the obvious—the thing she knew everyone wanted her to talk about.

"It kinda freaks me out sometimes, you know, thinking about my mother and sister." Ava hated the quivering inside her chest at the mention of them. The hollow feeling in her gut that had the power to erase her. She kept her focus straight ahead on the mountain, the flowers. No part of Ava wanted to watch Honor's reaction to her bringing them up.

After what felt like a long time, she looked over at her. The counselor wasn't saying anything, just kept rifling through some folder. All Ava could hear was paper catching wind.

"What about them?" Honor closed the folder and wrapped her arms around her chest, barricading Ava from the papers with her name on them.

"They died. In Thailand." Ava's words came out harsher than she'd meant for them to. She pointed at her file. "It's all there."

"Forget this. Why don't you tell me what happened?" Honor's tone was encouraging, but her face remained stern.

"It's all kind of cloudy."

"How old were you?" Honor asked, opening the folder, writing down the things Ava said.

"Eight. My sister was seven. My dad had business in Phuket. We went with him on Christmas vacation."

"That would've been, what, 2004?"

"Yeah. December. 2004."

"You're making this up on the spot," Honor said, closing the folder again.

"What?"

"I read the papers, Ava. I watched the news. That part of Southeast Asia was decimated in a tsunami, and you want me to believe you were there on vacation?"

"We were. We were there when it happened."

"So now who's making up stories? Come on, I'm new to Mount Hope, but that doesn't mean you can pull this one over on me."

"Why would I make something like that up?"

"I don't know. You just accused the other kids at The Circle of doing it. Look, I'm well aware you guys will do anything to get sympathy around here."

Ava got up and started pacing the porch, trying to put it all together. With each stomp of her boots, she wondered how it was that Honor didn't know about Mom and Poppy.

"I'm not lying."

Honor put her hand out to stop Ava's rocker from dancing.

"Okay, I'll give you the benefit of the doubt," Honor said. "Convince me. Tell me what happened. Give me details."

Ava stopped moving, as if quieting her feet would slow the thoughts racing through her brain. "My dad said at first it was perfect. We went to the beach like every other day. Then he said the wave came. We ran, I guess."

Honor leaned forward. "I asked what you remember."

Ava wanted to scream, *nothing, okay? I don't remember anything.* Her head felt like it was about to explode. Was this some kind of a joke? There had to be something in that stupid folder. Up till now she'd thought Honor was different, but suddenly it was like she was trying to trick her.

"Give me a minute, will you?" Ava asked. "I feel like you're grilling me."

"It's my job. I'm a counselor." Honor paused, like she needed to convince Ava that being a counselor was what she was doing there.

"My father and I don't talk, okay? It's not easy to bring it up. Or talk about what happened. If I try, he looks so pathetic, I end up changing the subject."

"Yes, I've noticed you're good at that. Five sessions and eleven workbook entries and you're still refusing to own up to what landed you here."

"Wait, you read our workbooks?" Ava tried to remember what she'd written since the beginning. Then it hit her. "Justice reads mine too?"

"We do what it takes to get inside your head. Speaking of workbooks—"

When she looked over at Honor, she could tell her counselor wasn't having the same trouble recalling Ava's confessions. "You have it all wrong," she said.

"What? You didn't do those things?"

"I didn't do anything to deserve being sent here."

The file was back open; Honor held up her notes. "Cutting school. Sneaking out of the house at night to go drinking. Standing in the path of a train." She counted out Ava's infractions on her fingers.

"Don't forget," Honor said. "I was there when you pretended to pass out to get out of hiking. And I know about the spell you faked in the kitchen. I'd call that a whole lot of something."

"What do you mean that I faked?"

"It's the oldest trick in the Mount Hope book. Pretending to need medical attention to get special favor. I won't share which Seed wrote about it in his or her workbook, but the point is, you're not cooperating with treatment."

Ava controlled her breathing and turned from Honor. Staring at those mountains through the screen, the thin mesh could just as easily have been bars. She was beginning to understand why kids agreed to the counselors' lies, letting go of their real stories.

To get out of this prison, she needed to move up levels.

"Okay, I drink. My father doesn't care about me. He works too much. And he won't admit he has a girlfriend." Ava turned to face Honor. "I hate Jill. And sometimes, I hate my father too, okay?"

Honor steadied the rocker with one hand and motioned for her to sit down.

Ava took her seat, looking straight ahead. She didn't tell Honor about the flashbacks of the last time she saw her mother, the nice bits that kept coming to her, all bright sky and sunshine. In those memories, her mother's alive, walking along that stretch of paradise. Poppy's there too, jumping around, being Poppy. Like her father's one-liner goes—at first it was perfect.

"I've been keeping track," Ava said, willing the tears to stay where they belonged, trying to push thoughts of her mother and sister back where she kept them. "I think I have enough points to get my red shirt. When can I call my dad?"

As mad as she was at him for sending her here, what Ava needed now was to talk to her father. To ask him straight out to explain things.

"Permission to cross threshold," a boy's voice called through the screen.

Startled, Ava slammed her elbows into the back of the rocker.

"Denied," Honor said. "Benno, step back. Ava and I aren't finished here."

SIX

≈≈≈

Toby hit Send/Receive for the third time in five minutes. After he'd played phone tag all of yesterday with the director of Mount Hope, finally chasing the man down, Pax had promised that today was the day Toby could expect an e-mail update outlining how Ava was doing. Toby hit the tab again. Still nothing.

If a report didn't come through by lunchtime, he'd call again. Policy or no policy, this time Toby would put his foot down.

He pulled at his collar, wishing he could undo his top button, wondering if the cleaners had shrunk this cotton dress shirt too. As he sat staring at the screen, an alert message sounded, with the wrong chime. This is ridiculous, he thought. It wasn't an e-mail from the director. Instead a meeting reminder. Kiet would be here in fifteen minutes. Toby's Thai project manager would surely be on time. The man was nothing if not a model of good manners.

Facing down the computer wouldn't make the message about Ava come any faster. He hauled himself out of his office chair and moved toward the glass windows, his view of the State House and Boston Common mesmerizing even on a rainy day.

The first time Toby had brought Lorraine here, she'd acted like a girl, flitting from one side of the bank of windows in his office to the other, asking him to point out Boston landmarks.

Lorraine had never been impressed with Toby's money, and at first, that's what he'd liked about her. She didn't care about the restaurants he took her to, or the clothes he offered to buy, the gifts of jewelry. Lorraine's enthusiasm was always tied to the beauty around her. No matter where she was—his office, the summer house in Maine—she'd take in details he'd never even noticed. Later, having captured it in her poetry, a certain play of light on leaves or the echo the wind made, she'd read to him by candlelight, from her leather-bound journal. Only then, in a cloud of her lavender perfume, would Toby realize that because of Lorraine, he was seeing things for the first time.

As if it were yesterday, Toby remembered a bright spring day when his family stood right here by this window; had to be ten years ago.

It was April vacation, and his wife had convinced him to beg off work for a few hours to take a family walk on the part of the Freedom Trail that snaked its way through Beacon Hill. Lorraine, Ava, and Poppy were prolonging their visit by stopping back at his office.

"It wasn't a walk in the woods, but it was nice," Lorraine said, aiming little Poppy in the direction of the leather sofa across from Toby's desk. Of her own accord, Ava took her seat like the ideal second-grader that she was, as if just in from recess, while her little sister bounced up and down on her cushion. Toby walked up to his wife and from behind, wrapped his arms around her waist. The couple stood facing the wall of glass, taking in the panoramic view, his cheek next to hers. Still annoyed with him, Lorraine escaped his arms, and with a deft touch, slipped her journal from her canvas bag. Mumbling under her breath, she plopped down in the center of the sofa, one daughter on either side. Wisps of hair obscured her eyes as her pen began to leap across the page.

"Trees cut down. Form from memory. Silver stacks grow your lonely city."

Poppy kept bouncing next to her mother. "Read it again, Mommy."

"Shhhh," Ava said, tapping her sister's shoulder. "Let her get the words down first."

Before Lorraine had fully captured her inspiration, Poppy

was up, pushing with all her might one of Toby's conference table chairs over to the windows, stopping only once to shake out her tired arms. "Show me where we trailed, Daddy." She took a deep breath before scrambling up, her sneakers leaving an impression on the upholstery. Ten pudgy fingers pressed against the glass; she looked right and then left.

"We didn't trail," Ava said. "It's called a trail."

Ava had taken to correcting her sister, though Poppy tended to ignore the older girl's pleas for accuracy. Toby watched Ava curl her long limbs under her in an attempt to get a better look into her mother's poetry journal. She was nearly settled in when Lorraine tapped Ava's knees, reminding her without words: no feet on the furniture.

"Poppy, please get down," Lorraine said. "And take your hands off the glass. You'll leave prints."

"It's okay. I can clean it later," Toby said, moving closer to Poppy, getting ready to point out the route they'd walked. "Ava, check the top drawer of my desk. There might be a little something sweet in there for you and your sister."

"No wonder they don't listen to me when you're around," Lorraine said, closing her journal, slipping it back into her bag. She relaxed back against the sofa, wagging an accusatory finger at Toby. It was getting harder to know when his wife was seriously perturbed or merely being playful with him.

"Sorry," he said. "The least I can do is let them have a little fun in Daddy's office. I'm the one who fouled up our Maine plans."

"Do you really think it's a good idea to remind me?" Lorraine tucked her hair behind one ear, turning away from Toby, rejecting his contrite expression. "I've been thinking I might take the girls up to Herrick House for a couple nights anyway, toward the end of the week," she said. "With your attention on the board meeting, you won't even notice we're missing."

"Look, Daddy," Ava said, pointing to her sister, who was standing up straight and tall, towering over her father from the perch overlooking Boston. "Poppy's all grown up."

"I'm bigger than Ava," Poppy said.

"Maybe someday, honey," Toby said, giving his little pixie a squeeze. He wondered how it was that Ava, a child so young, could recognize the perfect time to distract her bickering parents, for the time being staving off their recurring spat. "When you're all grown up," Toby said to Poppy, "you might be as tall as your sister."

The intercom sounded. Toby bypassed accepting his secretary's announcement by phone in favor of meeting Kiet at the door.

"*Sawatdee-kah,*" Toby said with a bow.

Kiet put his briefcase on the floor by his side and returned the traditional Thai greeting, then put his hand out to reciprocate the hello with an American handshake.

"Please sit." Toby gestured for Kiet to enter the office and take a seat at the round table he used for private conferences, the site of their biannual meetings.

Kiet bowed before taking his seat. His business attire was impeccable: Tailored suit, perfectly knotted tie. Kiet's cuff links flashed as he folded his hands, placing them on the table across from Toby.

"Good to see you again, Mr. Sedgwick."

Toby engaged in the customary pleasantries, inquiring about Kiet's flight, and of course asking after his wife and son, when all he really wanted to do was open the folders he had in front of him. To go over the projects Kiet was responsible for overseeing in Thailand, to move the meeting along.

"Your daughter, how is she?" Kiet asked.

Toby swallowed hard, using the pause to ponder what to say.

"She's away at camp. A kind of outdoor adventure school. In fact, if you won't consider me rude, I might suggest we take a break at some point. I'd like to check my e-mail in case there's a message about her."

"*Mai pen rai*—no problem. I appreciate your fatherly concern."

An accomplished, well-connected man in his native country, Kiet spent the next two hours going over one project after another, along with the positive impact each was having on the continued rebuilding of Phuket and Khao Lak. As Toby's trusted liaison in the region, Kiet recommended the extension of three projects—one pediatric hospital program and two infrastructure initiatives—funded entirely by grants from the Sedgwick Foundation.

Toby tuned in and out, doing his best to be polite, listening to Kiet while trying to curb his impulse to return to his desk every time a ping alerted him to a new message in his in-box. On the one and only break he did take, to see if the update from Mount Hope had indeed arrived, he wished he hadn't. It wasn't there, and its absence only served to make Toby more anxious. He noticed the time stamp on the lower right side of his computer screen, trying to gauge when he'd be able call the director to demand a phone conversation with his daughter. Another hour with Kiet ought to do it as far as business was concerned. Toby could get a call in while his associate went back to his hotel to freshen up for the bi-annual dinner on the foundation.

Despite the coffee roll Toby had picked at during his project manager's ongoing reporting, his stomach growled. He was getting weary of the social mechanics of the meeting, tired of trying to stay engaged when all he could think about was Ava.

Finally, Kiet closed the last project folder, placing it back into his briefcase. The time had come. Yet nothing else came out of the man's satchel. Kiet's soft speech became almost inaudible.

"I'm afraid, as was the case with our last several meetings, there is nothing new to report about Mrs. Sedgwick and your youngest daughter."

Toby closed his eyes briefly, as if Kiet's words were a blow, even though this was what he'd come to expect. Whenever Kiet had leads on a possible sighting, he would phone Toby. There hadn't been an overseas call regarding his family in years.

When Toby opened his eyes, he found Kiet's hands folded on top of the table. The man wouldn't even place a working folder between them to give Toby false hope.

Opening the final file in his own stack, Toby pulled out two photos, one of Lorraine, the other of Poppy.

"I had new ones done," Toby said. "It's what they would look like now. I want you to have them."

Kiet made no effort to reach across the table, to take the photos from his boss. "They are beautiful. But I don't—"

"Please. For me. Take them."

"I work for you, yes. But you are also friend, Mr. Sedgwick. In my country, the focus of life is to enjoy. We say it is *suay*—unlucky—to hold on to the past. I will take the photos only if you insist."

There weren't words to explain to Kiet what it felt like—not to know. So Toby neither persisted nor did he relinquish his request. He laid the age-progression pictures of his wife and daughter in the center of the table. And he waited.

SEVEN

Ava's heels hurt from stomping all the way back from counseling. Benno could barely keep up. She didn't know what she hated more, that the hottest guy at Mount Hope had someone else's permission to put his hand on her pants, escorting her back to the Learning Center, or that she wasn't moving up a level. According to Honor, Ava had work to do. There'd be no phone call home.

"Someone ratted me out," she said, more to herself than to Benno.

They came into the clearing where counselors were running activities. Clusters of kids sat around picnic tables for craft class, identical robots pretending to like making dream catchers and cornhusk dolls.

"I can't believe all my points. Wiped out." Ava snapped her fingers. "I'm back at the beginning."

"Did Honor tell you what for, or do you already know? When I first got here, they laid all kinds of crap on me, things I didn't do. Justice especially loves to watch a kid deny the stuff he made up. Looks right at you, smirking. Sick bastard."

Benno was a wild kind of cute. Glossy black hair without relying on sunshine. Dark eyes with barely any lid, all mystery and danger. Which was probably why he landed at Mount Hope in the first place.

"Yeah, she told me." Ava replayed the scene Honor had referred to. The last blackout happened when she and Fringe were on kitchen duty. In twenty minutes, they were supposed to peel an entire boatload of carrots, with Mallory sitting on a stool watching them.

Fringe started talking about not having a mother. Everything he said came out sharp or flat, and suddenly Ava's ears were filling with cotton, all airy and soft. She moved toward Mallory, thinking she had time to push the girl off the stool so she could sit down and put her head between her knees. Ava never made it passed the edge of the counter.

The mother is dressed in a plaid skirt, her blouse tucked in at the waist. Her hair is pulled to one side with a barrette. Standing on a hill by the shore, she pours milk from a bottle into a glass. She starts to speak, but her voice belongs to a girl. "I'll take good care of Jane. I'm a big girl and I can watch so she doesn't tumble into the water." Then the voice changes; it belongs to a woman, but it is hush and shush. She holds a book. She fans the pages. "Let me row, row, row your boat." Her voice lulls me. "See, the lyrics are really poetry. Would you like to swing, swing, swing on a star?"

Twenty-four hours after Ava collapsed in a heap, those images were landing her in trouble. The mother and sister in that flashback were so veiled in a mist, she couldn't even tell if they were hers. Walking now with Benno, Ava wasn't worried about how those pictures fit into her life or even if they did. Mostly what she was stuck on was that Mallory and Fringe saw her hit the kitchen floor and one of them wrote in a workbook that she had been faking.

"What kind of person assumes a kid is pretending unconscious instead of making sure she's not for real," Ava asked Benno. "Is there even a doctor on this mountain?"

"Too bad. I took you for a smarter chick."

"What do you mean?"

"The number one stupid thing people do? Pretend to pass out. *I'm starving. I can't hike another step,*" Benno whined, exaggerating kids' complaints. "Ever see McEttrick pull it? Makes it look real as hell. He even does this thing when he comes to, where he looks around and starts talking to people who aren't there. Christ, if you're gonna try to get out of here on a medical, you're gonna have to do better than that."

"What's a medical?"

"Eat enough of those purple berries to puke your guts out. Or waste your water till you're so dehydrated you go comatose. You got to go big. It's got to be real."

She'd seen those berries on the trail to the Ledges. Tempting little treats Honor warned them not to pick. On every single hike, Ava counted the steps to her next sip of water. She couldn't imagine ever letting the dirt have her share.

"Don't bother trying, Ava. You don't have what it takes." Benno pushed her head the way a brother does. But there was nothing brotherly about the way he let his hand linger in her hair.

Ava shook his hand free, hating him for thinking he could touch her without asking. Mostly she despised him for assuming she was weak. Benno didn't have a clue what Ava was capable of doing to survive.

"You're pretty," he said, softly. The word sounded funny, dainty coming from Benno. Ava could imagine him telling a girl she was fierce or hot, but not pretty.

Ignoring the flattery, she nodded like a good Seed to Pax as they rounded the admin building. Herr Direktor was sitting on the front stoop with his clipboard.

A few yards from the Learning Center, Benno pretended to trip. Right in her ear he whispered, "If you want more freedom around here, form alliances with a couple of kids. If you want to graduate the program, give it up on everyone else."

That's what Ava thought she had with Mallory—an alliance. After seeing her holding hands with Fringe, that's what Ava figured Mallory had with him too. God the girl was moody, but Ava hadn't found a single kid here who wasn't. She didn't peg Mallory for a snitch. She'd been helping Ava so far. Which left the boy with the bangs.

Fringe had been through here enough times to know counselors read their workbooks. He had to be the one who said Ava was a faker.

The door to the Learning Center was open. Benno let go of her belt loop once they were standing in front of Justice. He was leaning back in his desk chair, both arms raised and crossed behind him. Huge pit stains framed his big fat head. Not one Seed looked up from writing in their workbooks.

"Ten points for a co-op walk. Perm to ask?" Benno asked.

The clipped phrases that made up Mount Hope lingo were becoming second nature to Ava. She'd cooperated on the way back, so she got points. Benno asked permission to speak, so he got some too.

"Go ahead," Justice said, staring her up and down.

"Ava asked to make amends, sir. She wondered if she could volunteer time in Worksheets or have extra practice with the bow drill."

Three weeks ago Ava would have shouted, *no I didn't!* Why would she ask to spend the rest of the afternoon in a room hotter than this one, listing her faults, copying them over and over until she ran out of paper? Worksheets was a punishment, and Ava hadn't done anything wrong. But she was catching on. "Making amends" moved things along. Benno figured she'd be one of his allies if he taught her to make fire, since Ava still couldn't do it without help.

"Even the feisty ones end up coming around. You own up with Honor?" Justice asked her.

"Yes, sir," Ava said, and so she wouldn't get in trouble for exaggerating her progress, she added, "I'm working on coming clean, sir."

"Benno, keep escorting. I got two Seeds who need to go to counseling. When Mallory gets back, I'll have her show City Girl how to get a spark from a stick. Wouldn't want her freezing her butt off on our next overnight. She complained enough for three of you on the last trip."

When Benno turned to go, Justice ran his fingers over Ava's hand. It took every cell in her body not to react. Not to shake his paw off. Not to push his chair, sending him into the wall, tipping him onto the floor. Ava had to believe her dad would go ballistic if he saw this creep working his hand up her arm, brushing his hand across her breast.

But Ava needed to get to Level Two. Red shirts got phone calls.

Her mind raced trying to figure out how to fib her way to get what she needed, to be cunning. Why shouldn't Ava make stuff up? Every kid at Mount Hope was pegged a liar. How many came in that way, she couldn't say. But she was sure that's how every single one of them would go out.

Backing up, Ava bumped a chair and sat down. She didn't get one page of lies written in her workbook before Mallory walked into the Learning Center. Ava was making up some unoriginal story about the first time she drank when she heard Justice tell Mallory to take her to the pit.

Mallory belt-looped her there, not saying a word.

Ava never had any trouble with the first steps in making fire. Whittling the board and drill was easy. So was stringing the bow. While she went through the motions of the stuff she could do, Mallory sat cross-legged on the dirt, waiting for Ava to get to the part she still couldn't master.

"You've got to lock your wrist against the upright leg. It'll keep the drill steady. That's it." Mallory was a good teacher, real encouraging.

"It's killing my arm," Ava said, unable to get enough friction. Each time her muscles were tested, she wanted to let go. Part of her didn't want to be strong. "I can't do it."

"Yes, you can. Last night you told me you're a musician. Pick a song with the right rhythm. Sing it in your head. Or do what I do. Think about an overnight without your sleeping bag and the thing will light up before your eyes."

With hers half-closed, Ava hummed a song she wrote a long, long time ago. She let the words run through her head.

"Look," Mallory said.

A hint of smoke wafted up out of the fire board. Ava lifted it to find a small black dot visible on the coal catcher.

"Fan it. Lightly. There's no hurry now."

Smoke kept coming, like memories, hazy and impossible to see or hold on to. Without Mallory telling her to, Ava knew to transfer the coal to a small pile of leaves. Picking them up, cupping them in her hands, she blew gently. Mallory clapped when the spark of flame burst free. The last person to clap for Ava after she sang one of her songs might have been her mother.

"Fringe wrote in his workbook that I faked a blackout in the kitchen," Ava said, trying to shake her mom from her mind. Tending her fire, seeing the process through from leaves to wood, she kept her eyes on what she was doing. "I made it to the next level with points to spare. I was on my way, and now I have to start all over."

"Who told you he did that?" Mallory grabbed a handful of leaves, ripped them to shreds and tossed them into the fire.

"Well, you didn't do it so it had to be Fringe. He was the only other one there."

"His name is Arthur, and you can't blame him. He's sick."

"Benno says he's a faker. Passing out. Pretending to hear voices."

"That's what everyone says you're doing. Faking. We both know you're not. You've seen him. Kids like him shouldn't be here. He needs—"

"I saw you holding hands with him in the woods. What was that about?"

"Did Honor see?" Mallory's hushed voice filled with panic, but her body didn't give her away.

Ava shook her head as she transferred her fire to the pit.

"Listen," Mallory said. "You can handle starting over. You're smart. If you want to, you can figure out how to work the program. He can't. It's his third time being dumped here by his father."

"Why would you form an alliance with him? Risk your own level?"

Mallory stopped throwing leaves into the pit. She looked both ways, then positioned Ava's fire board and drill on the ground.

"What? Tell me," Ava said, moving closer to Mallory, keeping her voice down. "You can trust me."

Mallory started playing charades, getting down on one knee, showing Ava the same motion she'd just nailed to make the fire that was roaring in front of them. Even though Ava didn't see a single kid or staffer, Mallory kept rotating the drill, pointing to the ground. Her make believe teaching moves didn't fit what she was saying.

"Tonight at The Circle, Pax is going to announce who's moving up." She pointed to the drill again, as if she were showing it to Ava for the first time. "I'm the new junior counselor assigned to Honor," she whispered. "Benno's gonna be with Justice."

Ava picked up a couple of pinecones, chucking one and then the other into the fire. She hated that it suddenly smelled like Maine.

"I'm getting out the Mount Hope way," Mallory said, grinding the stick into the plank of wood. "But I'm gonna figure out how to take Arthur with me."

"Are you crazy?"

"He's not just weird," Mallory said. "He needs a psych hospital."

Seconds passed, the fire crackled. It was the only sound between them until Ava spoke. "Take me too."

Mallory alarmed her when she didn't say anything. It made Ava sick to think her father sent her here, sicker still to think he might not have told anyone what happened to her mother and sister. Ava needed a backup plan in case he never came for her. It looked like that would have to include Fringe and Mallory.

"I can help you." Ava lied, not having a clue what she'd say if Mallory pushed her to say how.

"You want an alliance? Then you can't badger me. I'll tell you the stuff you need to know, when you need to know it. Haven't I so far?"

Ava nodded, pretending she was appreciating Mallory's fire-starting technique.

"Don't you dare tell anyone," Mallory said. "You rat me out and we'll see who they believe. The girl sent back to Level One, or the Mount Hope star who'll do anything to get her kid back."

"I swear," Ava said, under her breath.

The temperature must've dropped ten degrees since they'd started. Ava put her cold hands out over the flame, bumping into Mallory's on purpose. This, her pathetic way to make their deal official.

EIGHT

≋

It was impossible to pull the splinters out of her swollen fingertips without tweezers. New kids equaled no sharps, not even supervised by a counselor. Curled into her bunk, with Cheez snoring a symphony above her and Mallory turned to the wall, Ava worked at the biggest one, lodged in the index finger of her right hand. As she kept on digging and plucking, all Ava could think of was that time Poppy took red grapes, hollowing out enough of the insides so they'd stick one on each finger. If hers didn't hurt so much now, Ava might've smiled remembering her sister flashing jazz hands until every grape went flying.

It was Ava's own fault, how messed up her fingers were. Last week, the punishment for failure to complete a workbook assignment was two hours in the prayer position. Hands clasped above her head, standing saint-still with nothing to lean on, it was a consequence she was willing to accept for refusing to write in that stupid thing. But yesterday, Honor changed things up; instead, she banished Ava from group to the woodpile because she wouldn't write about her biggest fear so that everyone at Mount Hope could read it.

Two hours stacking logs with no gloves, and thirty-six hours later Ava was still picking at slivers.

Blowing strands of hair from her eyes, she gave up on her hands. Undoing her ponytail was easy, pulling it back again was anything but. By the fourth wince, Ava had had it. She gave in to silent sobbing.

That's when she saw Mallory move, sliding soundlessly from her cot. On her way over to Ava's side of the room, she mouthed a comforting shhhh. Like a mime, she motioned for Ava to make room, and sitting down behind her, she began to braid her hair. Ava could tell she wasn't very practiced at it, her hair was so short. Mallory started, then restarted, trying to smooth out the bumps as she went. Ava didn't care. Her touch was kind. Like a sister's.

"I believe you," she whispered in her ear. "About Thailand."

She turned abruptly, making Mallory lose the grip she had on her hair.

Ava mouthed the words, "Who told you?"

Mallory tipped her head and, using only her face, she called Ava naïve. That's when Ava realized Benno had been listening to her session with Honor long before he knocked on the screen door. Which meant by now everyone at Mount Hope knew what she'd talked about in her one-on-one.

"I had a sister too," Mallory whispered. "Emmy had a kind of heart condition. She died during the surgery they did to try and fix it."

"Oh my God. How old was she?"

"Twelve. It happened four years ago. My parents still have a freaking shrine to her in our living room. Pictures, candles, the whole nine. Every sentence begins with Emmy this, Emmy that. I loved her, but when I'm at home I can't breathe."

"My dad's the opposite. It's impossible to talk about Poppy or Mom without him looking like he's going to crack in two at the sound of their names. So we don't."

"That's the same with my mom where my baby's concerned. I don't think she's ever once said his name. Michael Vincent, my beautiful boy."

Ava wished she could see a picture of Michael, but she knew that even if Mallory had been beyond clever, she wouldn't have been able to smuggle one in.

"It's like they're punishing me and him for living," Mallory said.

"Who's taking care of him while you're here?"

"He's in foster care. My parents wanted me to give him up for adoption, to one of their friends who can't have kids. When I wouldn't, they shipped me off."

Could Mallory's story get any worse?

"I still can't understand why my dad sent me here," Ava said. "I don't think he had any idea what it's really like."

"Some parents know and don't care. Others have no clue because Pax tells them a load of crap. Who doesn't want to believe there's an easy way to fix us?"

Ava hadn't felt broken until Mallory talked about them needing to be repaired.

"Look," she said. "Your dad sounds like a saint compared to mine. The last thing I heard my father say was that no baby should have a lousy mother like me, or a father who's capable of doing this." Mallory patted her stomach.

Ava was relieved when Mallory didn't lift up her shirt to show her the scar. It was as if she knew Ava had already seen it.

A month ago, Ava might've agreed with Mallory that her father wasn't so bad. He wasn't around much but he was never mean. She couldn't remember a time when he'd hurt her on purpose.

Until he sent her to Mount Hope.

Mallory went back to braiding Ava's hair, pulling it tight without hurting her. "Don't tell me you didn't do stuff to get this place on your dad's radar," she said.

"Yeah, I screwed up. But not on purpose. It's hard to explain."

"You can tell me," Mallory said.

"I'm remembering stuff. About the day they died. It's a jumble. Doesn't make much sense. But it's messing with me." Finally saying these things out loud made Ava feel small. "I think a lot about my mother. I'm kinda mad at her for leaving me. I'm such a freak. It's not like the tsunami was her fault."

"Maybe you're not really angry with her. Just at the horrendous situation. I mean, shit Ava, it had to be unreal."

As much as she wanted an alliance with Mallory, to stop feeling so alone, Ava couldn't keep talking about that place, on that day. Not right before closing her eyes.

"Some of what comes back to me is good. Nice things about my sister Poppy. She was the funniest kid ever."

Cheez flipped over in her bunk, banging away on her bedsprings, letting out a pissed-off sigh. Mallory and Ava froze. She mouthed sorry, pointed an index finger toward her cot, and in three steps, Ava's ally was back in her bed. Slumber party over.

It took forever to quiet her thoughts. To stop thinking of Mallory and her baby and that scar that practically cut her roommate in two. Ava didn't dare summon her mother. Instead she focused on Poppy. Until her mind wandered over to her dad. At first Ava had to agree with Mallory that he wasn't so bad. Then the last thing she wondered before the slow sink into sleep was how he could've sent her away.

There's a tap on my shoulder. "Ava, wake up." I twist and turn, tangled in bed sheets, trying to follow the sound. I open my eyes to find my father standing over me. He looks different, thinner, with more hair on the top of his head. It's him, only younger. I want to ask him what he's doing here at Mount Hope. Has he come to take me home? Nothing comes out. Then I realize my hands are covering my mouth. One on top of the other, spread wide, like they're glued to my lips. My stomach rumbles, something liquid sloshes around inside, making me queasy. "I told you not to talk about them," he says. My father shoves me hard. My whole body shakes in waves bigger and more violent than any chills from fever. The tremors are uncontrollable, but they loosen my hands from my mouth. As soon as I take them down, a flood escapes me. I watch as the force of the water blows my father back against the cinder-block wall.

"Get up. You're gonna make us late for group."

Ava woke to find Mallory and Cheez standing above her, blocking the light.

She touched her hair. The braid was tight, which meant confiding in Mallory last night wasn't part of the dream.

"Sorry. It'll only take me a minute."

Ava pulled on her khakis, stiff from not having been washed

for days, and grabbed her orange tee from under her pillow, stealing a glance to the other side of the bunkhouse. Only halfway out of her early morning fog, Ava needed to check to be sure her father wasn't lying there under the window in a pool of her venom.

They made it to group with minutes to spare. Wednesday mornings before breakfast, a handful of kids sat in a circle on Honor's porch floor and took turns reading out loud from workbooks. Before they got started, Honor pulled Mallory aside to tell her something private. Everyone else moved the chairs.

"Ava, I understand you've had a change of heart on completing assignments. Do you want to go first?" Honor asked.

Like she had a choice, Ava nodded, accepting the workbook Honor handed her, flipping through until she found the writing prompt in bold letters on the top of the page: Write about a time when you were out of control.

When Ava finished telling the group how she stole a six-pack of strawberry daiquiris from a liquor store, got smashed, and drove into Boston in her dad's car, randomly picking out a tattoo, then driving back home, Ava closed her workbook and looked up to see Honor smiling at her like she'd just learned to ride a bike without training wheels. Mallory and Fringe had their heads down. The rest of the group looked bored. Ava's stories were getting better, but they couldn't compete with the tall tales and fake fables the other kids made up. If she didn't know they were in therapy, she'd think they were in creative writing class. Ava's honors English teacher at Wellesley High would be handing out A's like they were number two pencils.

"Does anyone have anything they want to ask Ava? Any comments to share?"

Nobody said anything. Not one kid asked for permission to speak.

Honor tapped Ava on the knee. "I think you've successfully managed to turn things around. In one week, you've moved up a level."

She couldn't believe her ears. Doing everything Mallory had told her to, she'd made it to Level Two. Good-bye, orange shirt. Hello, phone call!

In the week since they'd formed their alliance by the fire

pit—except for the lapse that landed Ava in the woodpile—she'd put her energy into working the program instead of messing around trying to keep track of things. And she'd watched Mallory. Looking for signals, waiting for the conversation where the girl would tell Ava how she was going to get them out.

"Can I say something about what Ava shared?" Mallory turned away from her roommate. She sat up straight like a counselor did just before calling a kid out.

"Of course. I'm interested in how you experience Ava," Honor said.

Leaning in, both elbows on her knees, Honor folded her hands like she was praying, resting her chin on the tips of her fingers. The other kids perked up. Nothing got the group's attention better than a whiff of confrontation.

"Ava told me she had a sister named Poppy. Which means the stuff she wrote in her workbook about randomly picking her tattoo is a lie."

In slow motion, Ava felt her jaw drop. What was Mallory doing? And why was she doing it to her? If Ava lost a level because of her, she wouldn't be held responsible for wrapping her hands around Mallory's neck.

"Maybe it hurts too much to talk about her sister," Fringe said, his eyes all glassy, tears ready to break free any second. Ava was starting to see why Mallory felt bad for him. What Ava couldn't understand was why she was intentionally getting her in trouble.

Honor's voice became distant, as if the words were coming to Ava through a large shell. "Stay after group, Ava. We need to talk."

The back of her neck tingled with sweat. "I'm sorry I lied. Will I still be allowed to talk to my dad?" Ava hoped Honor couldn't hear the B-flat that sailed out with her words, riding on the falseness in her voice.

Honor put her hand on Fringe's arm, patting it once to reassure. That's when Ava noticed him staring past her, zoning out. The kid was a wreck.

"Arthur, are you all right?" Honor asked. "Did Ava's lying upset you?"

Fringe swallowed hard, as if whatever else he wanted to say was trapped in his throat. "Everything upsets me," he said. "I'm not tough like the rest of you." Tears ran a race down his cheeks. Wiping and wiping, he was no match for them.

"Being in this world hurts too much," he said. "They tell me it would be better if—"

"You're only sixteen," Ava said. "Things won't always be so bad."

"Ava!"

"Sorry, I just think he's too hard on himself—"

The bell rang, and collectively the group shuddered. No matter how many times a day those things clanged, instant panic showed up on all of the kids' faces.

"Arthur, you and I have a one-on-one later today," Honor said. "Are you comfortable continuing this conversation with me then?"

"Okay." He took a deep breath and nodded.

"Ava, help me put back the chairs. Everyone else, follow Mallory to the mess hall."

When Honor turned to open the screen door for the group, Ava gave Mallory a menacing look, one full of questions she wouldn't be able to answer until tonight when they got back to bunks.

As Fringe walked by, Ava wanted to tell him everything would be fine. Instead she gave him a pitiful smile that he didn't return, and then he was gone with the rest of the group, walking single file down the path through the woods following Mallory.

Ava took the broom from the corner and started sweeping the porch. Honor shook the welcome mat outside the door. They moved in silence, putting the rocking chairs, which had been parked off to the side to allow the group to spread out, back in their therapy places. When everything was where it belonged, Honor pointed to a chair.

Ava sat.

"I don't like what Mallory did," Honor said. "I don't abide throwing you under the bus. But there's nothing that bothers me more than lying. Ava—you're impulsive. You don't think things through before you do them. Or say them."

"I'm sorry about the workbook. I won't do it again. I'd like to own up about losing it at the end of group. I experience that kid as needy, and sometimes scary. He's so down on himself."

"Arthur's got a lot of problems, but you should spend a little more time worrying about your own. Leave him to me. I came to Mount Hope to help kids like him."

Ava hesitated, trying to control her so-called impulsiveness.

"You can make this work. I'm living proof."

It took a second for it to sink in. "You were a Seed?"

"Like lots of kids here, my family was dysfunctional. And like me, Arthur will be fine. Focus on your own issues."

She couldn't believe Honor had been here, imprisoned, and then came back of her own free will. And why was she telling her now? How come nobody gossiped about Honor having been a shirt? Ava tried to freeze her face, not blinking, not smiling. Honor had her all self-conscious about having no willpower. She wanted to pin Honor down, ask her if she'd lost her phone call, but it was like Honor read her mind.

"You made a mistake with the workbook. I take it you've learned your lesson. Don't do it again. This time I won't subtract points for your behavior in group. And I expect you to keep this conversation between us."

Ava slapped her thighs and called out, "Thank you."

"I'm warning you—learn to control your impulsive behavior."

"I will. I promise."

"You'll be able to call home later today. Benno will come find you and bring you to Pax's cabin."

Honor got up and moved toward the door but not before Ava heard her stomach growling. Maybe even the counselors got hungry here. "There's more. Good news."

Ava braced herself, holding tight to the arms of her chair. Good news at Mount Hope wasn't like good news anywhere else. Honor motioned for Ava to follow her out the door, down the path to the mess hall.

"Your father's been assigned to the next parent session. He starts with a new group this weekend. I'm looking forward to talking to him about you."

Ava's stomach flipped upside down, but it wasn't because she was hungry. She should've been happier that her dad was coming, that she could ask him her questions face-to-face. Make him finally tell Honor about Mom and Poppy.

The problem was, Ava's tattoo story wasn't the only thing she'd lied about. If her father got to read her workbook, he'd know that too.

Between now and the weekend, she had to find a way to destroy it.

NINE

Toby swallowed the last bite of half-sour pickle and tossed the crumpled deli wrapper into the wastebasket. He'd thought a working lunch, reading from the stack of requests for funding, would make the time until the call pass more quickly.

2:39.

2:40.

The long hand on the wall clock took its sweet time rounding the bend, heading toward three. Waiting twenty more minutes to hear Ava's voice was going to put him over the edge. He'd never gone this long without talking to her. Reassuring phone calls from the program director once a week and two e-mail reports weren't enough. He hadn't spoken to Ava in a month.

For the first few weeks she was at Mount Hope, Toby tried to get around the system. He'd unsuccessfully challenged the no-contact rule, insisting that it would be better for their relationship if he could explain to his daughter why he'd sent her there, what he'd hoped she'd get out of it. It didn't matter how many times the director listed the benefits of letting her experience the consequences of her behavior. Toby only backed down when the director convincingly wrote about how well Ava was doing, learning to rely on her own strength, facing her issues head-on.

There was nothing Toby wanted more than to know what those issues were exactly. He rummaged inside his desk drawer, reaching for the handful of letters she'd written him. It was the softened tone of the latest one that had convinced him maybe the director was right, perhaps the staff at Mount Hope knew what they were doing after all.

Dear Dad,

I'm writing to apologize for scaring you with all my craziness lately. When I disappeared that night, I should've known that, plus my freaking out all the time, didn't just hurt me. I hurt you too. Trust me, I know now I should've come to you. Asked for help. I know you sent me here because you want the best for me, especially to keep me safe. I'm working hard with my counselor to own up and take responsibility for my actions. I'm working the program as hard as I can so I can come home. On schedule. Changed for the better.

This week, one of my assignments was to write about a place I was really happy, where I felt safe. Remember the summer house in Maine? I have the clearest picture of it in my mind. The pond out back with the little red canoe Poppy loved. Views of the Reach from every window. All those secret rooms upstairs, great for hide-and-seek. Mom's poetry books lined up on the shelves in the sunroom. I remember one time she yelled at me for coloring inside her favorite collection. I really wish I hadn't done that. I never meant to make her mad at me.

Anyway, maybe when I get out of here, we could get away from Wellesley for a while. Not to go there. I know you won't want to go where there are too many memories of them. But another place. Where we'd have time to talk, you and me. We could do whatever we want, go wherever we want. My counselor says it's a good idea to put some distance between me and my old ways, especially in the beginning. You can take time off, right? You are the boss.

Honor says—she's the counselor I keep mentioning—I have a way with words. I'll let you be the judge.

At the sound of the knock on his office door, Toby swept the letters off his desk into the drawer and closed it.

"I stopped in to wish you luck," Jill said. "I'm happy to lend an ear when you're through."

"Thanks, I'll see how things go."

"Gosh, Toby, you look exhausted. Can I take you to dinner? Or if you'd rather, I could whip up something healthy at your house."

"I've got to finish these," he said, patting the stack of proposals.

"Sure thing. But really, there's no need for you to stay late." Jill walked over to his desk. After separating the pile in two, she handed him a few and took the rest. "I've already gone through them. I know you like to review everything, but I've flagged the only real contenders. You've got to take better care of yourself."

There again, Jill was right. With Ava gone, he'd been working even longer days, only to toss and turn when he did hit the sack. He'd resolved to work out before heading to the office each day too. That had lasted all of two mornings.

Now his full stomach was putting pressure on his diaphragm, making it hard for him to breathe. He shouldn't have eaten that huge sandwich before talking to Ava. Too late now. The pastrami was already leaching into his arteries.

The intercom buzzed, and Toby gave his secretary the go-ahead to put the call through.

"Good luck," Jill said. Before she left, she caressed Toby's left hand, letting hers linger over his ring finger.

Toby dismissed Jill with a wave of his hand and turned his attention to the call.

"Hello Mr. Sedgwick. I have your daughter here," the director said. "What a terrific girl! Ava's made a lot of progress this week. She could well move up another level if she keeps this up."

"Wonderful, put her on," Toby said. There was a pause, but no hum of noise in the background as the phone exchanged hands.

"Hi, Dad."

Her voice was timid; it held not a single note of the enthusiasm he'd longed to hear. What a fool he'd been to think Ava would call to fill him in on what it was like at camp, all marshmallows and "Kumbaya."

Elbow on his desk, he rested one hand on his forehead, covering his eyes. "How are you, honey? Everyone says you're doing great."

"I'm working. Owning up."

"I miss you so much."

"It's hard—to miss anyone here. We're so busy. It's pretty—the mountains, I mean. I learned to make fire in time for our next overnight."

"Good for you. When's that?"

"Saturday."

"Did anyone tell you I got into the next parent session? It's this weekend. Took some finagling on my end. The director said they like kids to be further into the program. But I figured since you're doing so well, I'd just as soon move things along."

"Honor told me—" Ava's tone was flat.

Toby would've given anything to see her face. To know if she was still mad at him for sending her there. If he saw her, he believed he would know.

"Maybe you should wait a few weeks," Ava said, haltingly, filling the final space with what sounded like canned phrases pulled right out of the Mount Hope Wilderness Camp brochure. "The program works. Honor's living proof."

"There's no reason you can't come home early, you know," Toby said. "We could go to that counselor I found in Boston. Or how about Maine? I would go there if you wanted to."

Ava spoke so quietly, he could barely hear her. "That would be nice," she said.

Toby heard the sound of a slap, louder than anything Ava had said during the entire phone call.

"Ouch!"

"What was that? You okay?"

"Bees. Just a bee. I got stung. Pax's cabin needs new screens," Ava said, all panicky, her sentences a string of jumpy beats.

"Go to the nurse, okay? You're allergic."

"No, Dad," Ava said with a sharp intake of breath. "That was Poppy."

"Oh, God, honey, that's right. I'm sorry." Toby clenched his teeth and shook his head, as the sound of his missing daughter's name sent shock waves through the phone line. "I knew that. I'm out of sorts with you gone, that's all. Mixed up. You know?"

"I've got to go. There's a ropes course I have to take."

"Are you sure you're okay?"

"Here's Pax."

"I'll see you this weekend, okay?" Toby asked. But just like that, his daughter was gone. Eerily like before. No time for good-byes. No "I love you"s floating on air.

"Mr. Sedgwick, as you can hear for yourself, your daughter's doing well. Once again, I'd like to encourage you to postpone the parent component until Ava reaches a higher level. In fact, I propose you extend her stay here by at least a month. Perhaps two. She's uncovering some very deep emotional pain in her sessions. These things take time."

"I've talked to a lot of doctors over the years, and every single one told me kids are resilient. Ava was so little, most of what happened would remain a blur. Better not to keep dredging things up, they said. But if she's remembering what happened to her mother and her sister, well, there are things I need to explain."

"I'm going to agree with the other professionals you've spoken to. Ava was young, and memory at that age is unreliable. This is simply a case of a young woman needing to process being motherless. Using drugs and alcohol was her way of escaping feelings of loss."

On some level, Toby wanted the director to be right. To tell him this was all normal, a stage Ava would successfully pass through. Toby needed to believe what everyone kept telling him so he wouldn't have to go back there. Never again to revisit that beach.

The director made a good point. Ava had been dropping her mother into more conversations in the last few months than she had in the last eight years. Poppy, too. And then there was the tattoo.

"I assure you," Pax said, "Ava is like the hundreds of other girls who come through our program every year. We believe in what we do here at Mount Hope. You can trust me."

The director almost had him. He'd nearly convinced Toby to leave things to him. Until that one sentence—a mere handful of words—woke Toby up. She was just another kid to him. To Toby, Ava was the world. He might be a lousy father, one who didn't know what the hell he was doing, but he could learn. He would learn.

"Where is the parent session taking place?" Toby asked. "I'm coming. This weekend."

TEN

≋

Walking back from Pax's cabin after talking to her father, with Siamese twin Benno still attached to her hip, Ava entered the clearing. There Fringe was, standing off to one side. Alone. Everybody else was already paired up for the double-trouble rope challenge.

Could this day get any worse? First there was the nightmare where Ava blew her dad back against the concrete wall, and then Mallory nearly cost her the phone call by freezing her out in group. Ava tried not to think about Pax standing next to her in his cabin, his head beside hers, listening to her talk to her dad, one of his fingers tracing the length of her hair. Without saying a word, he told her with his eyes that he could cut it off at a moment's notice.

Ava knew he would. She'd seen Mallory's hair and nothing else could explain it.

Her father had sounded so close. Ava wanted to ask him why her memories were so messed up, why the things she remembered were so odd and unclear. But Pax wouldn't take his threatening eyes off her. His hot breath fanned her cheek. All Ava wanted to do was beg her dad to hop in the car and come quick. Before she knew what she was doing, Ava told him, yes, she would go to Maine with him. Then Pax stomped on her foot and slapped her hand. His glare made it clear: lie, baby, lie. Mount Hope is the place you want to be.

Now, here she was, having to rely on Justice's least favorite kid to pass low ropes—the boy with the bull's-eye on his back.

"I'm lifting the level-to-level talking rule," Justice said. "For this challenge only, you can speak to anyone you're paired with. Don't take advantage of my good nature. I find you talking about anything but how to cross that cable and it'll cost you." Justice looked right at Ava when he threatened them. He paced back and forth like a drill sergeant, flicking one rope and then the other every time he passed by. She wondered how many kids looked at those twisted braids hanging down from those trees and thought about putting them to better use.

Fringe motioned for Ava to come over to where he stood. He looked relieved to be on somebody's team. If she had to put a number on how many times he'd been picked last for gym, she would've guessed a million.

"Benno, get on up. Let's show them how it's done." Justice climbed the rungs built into the tree and stepped onto the cable. The line went from one tree to the other, strung tight. Leaning against his tree, holding a rope, Justice waited until Benno took the exact same position on the other side.

"Your goal is to make it to the middle, exchange ropes, and then work your way to the other person's side. It can't be done unless you work together."

Justice tried to make it seem easy, but compared to Benno, he looked ancient trying to find his balance. Halfway to the middle, he teetered on the wire. His body swayed forward, then back. Ava would've bet every single kid there wished he would fall on his face. She was tempted to jiggle the line.

Benno made it to the middle before Justice. He hung out there, acting cool, waiting. The rope switch in the center was effortless, and in a few seconds, they were on opposite sides. Justice jumped down off the cable, a cloud of pine needles flying in all directions. Benno leaned against the tree waiting to see if a repeat demo would be required.

"It's only four feet off the ground, but don't be a lazy Seed. Work with your partner to stay on the line or I'll make you do it again."

Everyone crammed into the middle of the group. No one wanted to go after Justice and Benno. That's when Ava noticed Mallory wasn't there. She hated ropes even more than Ava did. How did she finagle getting out of it? Ava would've volunteered to do whatever dumb job Mallory got assigned. Clean the bunk room bathroom. Peel a boatload of potatoes. Anything to get out of doing this.

So of course Fringe and Ava had to go first.

"Take small sideways steps. Sideways steps. Until you get used to the give of the cable," Fringe said, as he made his way on to the line. "If we move at the same speed, it won't shake. It won't shake as much."

Ava was uncoordinated climbing the rungs to take her place opposite him. As he spoke, she realized he'd done this before. A Level One pro, Fringe had had the chance to do it over and over.

The cable was impossibly thin, and her hands, still swollen and filled with splinters, were burning within seconds of gripping the rope. Leaning against that tree, Ava willed herself to concentrate, but finding her balance was harder than she'd thought it would be. Tensing her upper arms, she wondered how exactly she would make it to the middle, never mind all the way to the other side. What Ava couldn't have known until her feet were off the ground, her boots wobbling on the line, was that muscles held memory. As Ava stood between those two trees, images came like the waves once did.

The umbrella of feathered leaves shields me from the bright sun. My body is wet, cold, so very tired. My father pulls my arms from around his neck and forces me into those of a stranger. The lens of the man's camera digs into my flesh. "Reaw-khao!" my dad shouts. "Hurry."

"Ava," Fringe shouted, his voice far away. "Don't! Don't look back."

Her arms ached. Her heart boomed. She couldn't take a deep

breath, as if being smothered by a towel. *Stop it. Stop,* she chanted in her head. *Don't remember here.* Not now with Justice watching.

"Focus on me," Fringe said. "Not where you've been. Pay attention to where you're going. Come on, do it with me. Step together. Step together."

Only a few feet in front of her, Fringe wore a halo of fog. Ava forced herself to look at him, praying the freak-out would pass. God knows what would happen to her for "faking" it in the middle of ropes.

"Three more steps. Steady," Fringe said, his voice getting clearer and more confident each time he spoke. "Keep going. Good. We're doing it."

Ava wanted to rush toward his bright orange shirt, but her hands were glued to the rope.

"We're almost there. When we get to the middle, don't hold on to me or we'll fall."

Fringe was in charge, and she could tell he knew what he was doing.

"I won't take you down," she said.

Halfway there, standing in midair, Ava suddenly felt like she could do it. After they exchanged ropes, it was clear they were each going to make it to the other side without falling.

Fringe jumped down, falling on his knees. Scrambling up, he came over to Ava's side, offering his hand like some kind of knight. She'd made it because of him and she was grateful, but that didn't mean any part of her wanted an alliance. Especially not after what Mallory did to her. Ava climbed down on her own and went to the end of the line.

Kids took turns completing the challenge while she stood there going back over the memory of her dad abandoning her to a stranger.

For the rest of the afternoon, through dinner, right up until The Circle, Ava kept replaying what she'd remembered during the ropes challenge. The more she tried to recall what came before it, the hazier things got.

When Ava had her dad on the phone, why didn't she scream, "Get me out of here, I'm a prisoner!" Even if Pax had hit her upside the head and punched her in the stomach, it would've been worth it. Her dad would be here now. He could mix her up with her sister all he wanted, as long as by the time The Circle was over, Ava was asleep in the passenger seat of his car heading as far away from this place as he was willing to take her.

Ava stopped worrying about herself when she got to the fire pit and there was no sign of Fringe. He hadn't been at dinner either. Where could he have gone between ropes and The Circle?

All the counselors were there. Two groups of kids too. Mallory was directly across from Ava with her head down; she wouldn't look over at her. Couldn't face her. Well, she wouldn't be able to avoid Ava once they got back to the bunkhouse.

No thanks to Mallory, Ava finally got her red shirt, and so did two other kids from their group. It didn't feel as great as she thought it would. After having heard her dad's voice, Ava could admit she missed him. And she was worried too. What if he came to the parent weekend and Pax convinced him not to take her home?

When everyone got up to head back to the bunks, Ava overheard Benno whisper to the kid next to him that Fringe was in OP. She wanted to ask what that was, but Honor glared at him. She flashed the fingers of one hand twice, which meant Benno had lost ten points. Which meant OP had to be bad.

It didn't matter what level Ava was, or the color of the shirt on her back, someone was always there to remind her that she still couldn't talk when she wanted to. Lining up to go back to the bunkhouse, and the whole way up the path, being careful not to trip over tree roots and rogue stones, Ava practiced what she'd say to Mallory. As much as she wanted to blast her roommate for what she did in group that morning, she wanted to know about Fringe.

Outside the bunkhouse, one by one, each kid took off her boots. Ava handed hers to Justice, and he gave her back her workbook.

"Too bad I ain't got me a strawberry daiquiri," he said under his breath, fingering his chest in a gross way. Ava threw up in her mouth when she took the workbook from him. The slimy feel of the cover had reminded her that Justice could read it whenever he wanted.

It didn't matter where Ava was—the bathroom, the bunk

room—the sound of that metal bolt sliding over the door echoed through the whole building. A numb feeling started in her head and raced through her body, landing at the bottoms of her bootless feet. Ava hummed a song she'd written, so softly no one could hear her. It didn't help.

Cheez, Mallory, and Ava were alone in their bunk room with more freedom than they'd had all day, and no one said a word.

Before scooching under her blanket, Ava yanked a corner free to scrub the cover of the workbook. She wanted any trace of Justice off it, every single fingerprint gone.

Cheez took forever to climb into her bunk. Once she hoisted her body up there, she kept shifting side to side. She straightened out her covers. Fluffed her pancake of a pillow. Ava was running out of patience waiting for her to fall asleep. Watch, this would be the night she'd decide to write in her workbook. But within five minutes, the squeaking stopped and she was pretty sure Cheez was asleep. Ava looked over at Mallory. The girl turned her face toward her in slow motion. They locked eyes. One finger to her lips, Mallory signaled for Ava to come to her side.

Inching out of her bunk, Ava looked up to make sure Cheez was deep-breathing. Like a slow-motion version of hopscotch, avoiding the creaky spots on their floor, she made her way toward Mallory's cot.

Mallory sat cross-legged at the head of her bed. Ava did the same at the foot, still holding her workbook. The only thing missing from this cozy camp scene was everything.

"I didn't know he was going to say anything about killing himself," Mallory whispered.

"What are you talking about?"

"Arthur said something to Honor about how maybe it would be better if he weren't around. You know, not wanting to live."

"That's not what he meant. His life sucks. He's a mess like the rest of us."

As soon as she'd said like the rest of us, Ava wanted to take it back. No one was more miserable than Fringe. And big surprise, telling the truth didn't get him any help, it just got him into some kind of trouble.

"That's not what Honor thought after their one-on-one,"

Mallory said, scratching the back of her neck. "She took it up with Pax, and tried to get him transferred out. Next thing, before The Circle starts, Benno's carting him off to OP."

"What the hell is OP?" Ava fanned the pages of her workbook.

On the page with the assignment she'd read that morning at girls' group, the words strawberry and daiquiri were underlined, but not by Ava.

"Observation Placement," Mallory said. "You know, like solitary confinement in jail. The quiet room in a mental hospital." She made a circle next to her ear like Fringe was nuts.

"I'm not so sure he's crazy." Ava thought back to him on low ropes, capable, confident even. She was starting to think the kid was just plain strange. Or maybe like everyone else around here, he was sly. "Honor says we should focus on our own problems. She'll look out for him—"

"How many times do I have to tell you, he's sick. Now they've put him in a goddamn box. Would you want Justice or any other creep counselor watching you more than they already do? Benno told me they take your clothes. And you're not allowed to eat. What are you now, Honor's best friend?"

"She was nice to me. Didn't take away points after you sabotaged me." Ava slammed her workbook shut. Mallory put her finger to her lips again and looked over at Cheez, who'd stopped snoring in her top bunk. Neither girl moved or spoke for what seemed like forever. Relax, Ava told herself. Cheez is asleep. Ava could tell. She'd been listening to her breathe for thirty-two nights.

"Look, I'm not perfect," Mallory said, finally. "I might be ahead of you level-wise, but I don't know everything. Yesterday before group, Honor accused me of playing favorites, so I needed to show her I'm not into alliances. I wasn't trying to screw you. I figured you'd only lose a few points for the tattoo thing, not enough to make a difference. I never meant for Arthur to get freaked out by it and land in OP."

Mallory told a good story, but Ava didn't believe her. "Yeah, well, when are you going to tell me your plan for getting us out—"

"Shhhh."

Mallory picked up Ava's workbook and put her hand out for the pencil, a stub of a thing with no eraser, the kind people use to keep score at mini-golf. Ava could barely write with it, never mind figure out how to hurt herself with it. But some kid who came before must've tried death by full-size pencil, so now the rest of them had to write with cramped fingers.

"No way," Ava said, grabbing her workbook. "You're not writing anything in here. Justice reads mine, probably every damn day."

If Fringe knew the counselors read their workbooks, then Mallory had to know it too.

"I'll rip out a page."

"Are you kidding? That'll put me back to the beginning. I thought I could trust you."

"You can. I have an idea."

Cheez rolled over, the bedsprings screeching. "Will you two shut it?" she hissed. "The only thing I look forward to around here is sleep. Keep it up and I'll tell Justice you're planning shit. You'll be locked up in OP before breakfast."

Squeak, sigh, squeak. Cheez heaved her body onto her other side, her face to the wall. Ava scrambled back to her bunk, hitting every whiny floorboard on the way. Mallory waved her hands to get her attention and then pointed to her mattress. She smoothed out the wrinkles on her blanket and started to spell on cotton.

Forget it, Ava mouthed, fighting with her blanket, covering her eyes with her pillow.

Trying to express yourself in a wilderness therapy camp shouldn't have been so impossible. Or dangerous. Fringe got locked up for saying he was depressed. Cheez was threatening them with OP. And since counting on her dad was a wild card, that left Ava with only erratic Mallory to trust. Her bad luck.

ELEVEN

Toby's GPS had him driving in circles. Shouting back at "the voice" wasn't moving him any closer to Mount Hope. When he couldn't listen to her say the word *recalculating* one more time, he pulled over to the shoulder and reached in back to dig through his bag for the directions.

"Damn it." Right there in black and white, it warned him exactly when during the trip the GPS would go awry, and where he'd lose cell coverage. He could've kicked himself when yards beyond where he'd turned around the last time, certain he could find the place on his own, he saw the sign. Twenty minutes after he started following the directions, Mount Hope came into view.

Toby scanned the parking lot. He didn't really expect to see Ava standing on the grounds waving to him. Still, he was disappointed when she wasn't leaning over the railing of the grand porch, or waiting for him by the lake on one of the benches made from twigs. Ava wouldn't be running to him, throwing her arms around his neck, hugging him tight. But he replayed that scenario in his mind anyway. Soon, he told himself. It had been a little over a month since she'd left home, and in no time he would see his girl.

The parking lot contained other bedraggled travelers. Parents summoned on a Saturday morning to learn where they'd gone wrong. Only a handful of men made their way toward the lobby, alone, like him, not part of a couple. Mostly women rolled designer suitcases or carried leather satchels to the entrance. No matter how large or small the bag, every person's shoulders were hunched, an air of resignation accompanying their steps.

As Toby was about to open his door, another car ripped into the spot next to him. Why, with all the empty spaces in the lot, did someone always follow the pack, parking right by someone else? Toby took in the view of the lake. Unlike him, it was serene; not one ripple disturbed its demeanor. Don't get annoyed this early on, he told himself. Otherwise it'll be one hell of a long weekend.

The woman in the car next to him mouthed the word *sorry* when she saw Toby. When her car was parked and quiet, he got out of his, heaving his bag onto his shoulder.

"I didn't realize someone was still in there," she said, over the top of her car. "I'm Nan. Nan McEttrick."

Nan and Toby closed their car doors—slam, slam. Hit remote locks on their key rings—cheep, cheep. And met at their respective trunks.

"I'm kind of frazzled," she said. "My cell isn't working, and I got lost. I just want to get this show on the road."

As the woman rambled, Toby couldn't help but notice the silver threads woven through her black hair, at odds with her youthful face. She must've been a teenager herself when she had her child. Nan was pretty, but that wasn't what captivated Toby. She had eyes like Lorraine's, bright, round, and blue. He couldn't stop himself from staring.

"Toby Sedgwick." He reached out to shake her hand. "Trust me, you're not the only one who's nervous. All I want to do is see Ava. Daughter or son?"

"Neither," Nan said. "Arthur's my nephew. I'm in the process of getting custody. It's been a yearlong battle so far, with three admissions to Mount Hope against my wishes. This is the first parent session they've let me attend. Long story. By the end of the weekend I'm sure we'll know more about each other than we care to."

Maybe this woman was prepared to air her family's private business, but Toby had no intention of spilling his guts about his, talking about Ava with a group of strangers.

Nan pointed her finger at the main building. "I'll tell you this. I will get him out of this place. Arthur won't ever have to come back here again."

Toby's plan had been to show up and listen, and already this woman was reeling him in.

"Mind me asking why he was admitted to the program three times?"

"Arthur's mother took off. His evil stepmother wants him out of her house, but my brother keeps changing his mind about signing the final papers to let Arthur come to me. Guilt is a powerful thing."

As they entered the lobby, teenagers in green shirts with pasted-on smiles pointed the way to a table filled with dwindling rows of pocket folders and pre-filled name tags.

Toby ignored a boy offering to take his bag, moving toward the table that boasted the coffee urn and a tray filled with pastries. One small paper cup of coffee wasn't going to be nearly enough. Though he supposed that no matter how much of it he drank he'd never be in the mood for the awkwardness of icebreakers, the confusion of breakout sessions, and oh, God, team-building exercises. He was out of there if things deteriorated into the lifeboat activity or the dreaded group hug.

Over the years, Toby had hosted plenty of leadership seminars at the Sedgwick Foundation, but when organizers touted the benefits of him getting in touch with his feelings, he would always feign competing priorities, like a meeting he simply couldn't miss.

In an effort to wall himself off from some of the more suspicious nomads, Toby hung by the coffee table until Nan collected her things, after she too had disregarded the boy scouting for luggage.

"Tell me to take a hike if you'd rather go this alone," he said.

Nan stole a glance at his plate loaded with Danish. Toby tossed a napkin over his pitiful breakfast.

"Right back at you," she said, as they walked into the conference room. "It's likely to play out the other way around, though. I'm going to try to keep my mouth shut, but I can't make any promises."

Together without discussing it, Toby and Nan gravitated to two seats toward the back of the hall, near the door. The room was warm and the seats too close together. He apologized to Nan when they sat and his hip brushed against hers.

"Mind me asking why you're so down on the place?" Toby asked, shoving his bag and folder under his seat. "Looks pretty nice to me."

Right out of a travel brochure, the lodge was rustic with log walls, thick carpeting, and Native American tapestries hanging from the ceiling. Except for the lone moose head mounted on one wall and the frightened-looking deer on the other, if Ava had digs like these, and her days were filled with hikes through the breathtaking backcountry, things couldn't be that bad.

"I don't think it's a good idea to cut kids off from family. I haven't been able to talk to Arthur since he got here."

Three weeks ago Toby would've agreed with Nan about the lack of contact rules. That first letter from Ava nearly did him in. Lately though, her notes home were insightful; they had a calmness about them. The phone call would've been great too if he hadn't been the one to screw it up.

"May I have your attention?" A gaunt man at the front of the room spoke into a microphone. "If you're still carrying luggage, even a simple overnight bag, please hand things off to our students. Let's show your children how to follow directions," he said, tacking on a false laugh.

"That's Paxton Worth," Nan whispered. "The director. Something about him rubs me the wrong way. Don't you think the counselors' names are odd? Who are these people?"

Toby hadn't given much thought to the contrived names of the staff, but now that Nan mentioned it, he wondered, were they real?

A teenager appeared at the end of their row. Toby stood up, planning to carry their bags to the cart that was parked outside the door. It took a few seconds to dislodge himself, to work out the ache in his back.

"Your names?" The girl held a Sharpie and a few blank name tags like the ones from the table in the hall. Her hair was uneven, and not in a stylish way. It looked as if she'd whacked it off on a whim.

"I'm Nan McEttrick. I'll take the name tag, but I'll keep my bag."

When Toby told the girl his name, she looked from one to the other but didn't write anything down.

"We don't have all day, Mallory," Pax said, giving the girl a wholly parental glare as he stepped in front of her. He put has hand out for Nan's bag. "As the program progresses, we're going to need space to move around." The director explained louder than was necessary, clearly for everyone's benefit.

Nan pulled her bag close to her chest.

Toby recognized the director's voice from their handful of phone calls. His tone had the quality of a television news anchor. He didn't look anything like what Toby had expected. Yellow-gray complexion, no chin, ears flying off both sides of his head. His face was made for radio.

"I'll keep it out of the way," Nan said. "It stays with me."

Toby disarmed the uncomfortable moment by moving out of the row, toward the girl the director called Mallory. Pax said *perfect* under his breath as he moved on to assert his authority over two women a few rows back. Toby didn't miss the hint of a smile Pax put on the minute he turned away from Nan.

Together Toby and Mallory carried the disobedient parents' belongings to the cart in the hallway.

"Do you know my daughter Ava?" he asked, as he pushed some of the lighter totes off to the side to make room for the larger duffels, all the while keeping his eyes on the girl.

At first Mallory didn't say anything. She was intent on rearranging bags. Her head was down, so Toby couldn't see any recognition on her face. The back of her scalp was red raw like she'd gone at with her fingernails. When she reached up to hang the garment bags on the gold pole running across the top of the luggage cart, her T-shirt came free from her khakis, revealing a jagged cord that snaked its way up her abdomen out of sight. Toby looked away, instantly uncomfortable. Poor kid, he thought, what happened to her?

Mallory looked up and down the hall, and when it was clear they were alone, she made eye contact.

"Yeah, I know her," she said, pulling the Sharpie out of her pocket along with the sticky-backed name tags. "How do you spell Sedgwick?"

Toby spelled his name as he watched the girl write.

Mallory added a number to the upper right hand corner of the tag, peeled off the back, and slapped it on his bag.

"Do you know when I get to see her?" he asked.

She was silent, doing her job, moving around to the other side of the luggage cart. Mallory leaned on a suitcase and began writing again. This time she folded the tag in half. Looking both ways, she handed the slip to Toby. "You'll need this," she said, tapping his bag.

Toby shoved the claim ticket inside the pocket of his jacket, keeping his eyes on the girl, waiting for an answer. She looked like she was about to say something when Pax's booming voice interrupted her.

"Mr. Sedgwick, we'd like to begin. I'd hate for you to miss anything." His tone was cheerful and the expression on his face polite, welcoming even. "Mallory, finish with the bags, then head back up the mountain. You'll be with Justice for the rest of the day."

Toby felt transported back to high school when for the rest of the morning, four hours straight, Pax drew interconnected circles with arrows in all directions on a freestanding whiteboard at the front of the hall. A few eager beavers in the front row answered all of his questions. Toby was glad he and Nan had chosen seats toward the back, so he didn't have to pay much attention. And so the director couldn't hear Nan.

He didn't know if he could sit one more minute wedged into the hard plastic chair hip to hip with Nan. His neck was stiff and his back screamed for some Advil. When the guy next to him apologized for his stomach growling and the woman ahead of him started passing around Tic Tacs, Toby wondered what time they'd planned to break for lunch. His own blood sugar had taken a nosedive twenty minutes after he ate his Danish, and a headache had seized his forehead soon thereafter.

He was cataloging his complaints when he saw Nan's hand go up. Then she was out of her seat.

"Excuse me, I have a question. When are we going to see the children?"

Pax stopped talking, his hand poised before the whiteboard. Parents in the rows in front of Toby first turned to see who was speaking, then quickly looked back to take in the director's reaction.

"I think I speak for a lot of parents when I say our time could be better spent connecting with our kids," Nan said.

"Ms. McEttrick, our program has served many families for many years. Would you concede that perhaps I know what I'm doing?"

"Mr. Worth, if that's your real name, why don't you ask the rest of the parents if they feel the same as me? Who else here wants to see their kids?"

Several hands shot up—all the men in the room and a handful of women. Then tentatively, one hand after another, until there were only a few holdouts. Clearly most in the room were on Nan's side. Even Toby raised his high.

"I appreciate your feedback," Pax said, moving down the center aisle, getting closer to his allies in the crowd, the smile back on his face. "There's a certain progression to the day's activities. I was about to break for lunch, but I'd be willing to forgo that in order to complete the exercises we need to do, getting you ready to reengage with your teenagers. Does that suit the group?"

Toby was dying to eat something, but he was willing to starve if it meant getting closer to seeing Ava. He checked his watch; it was approaching one. Toby was wondering how the director would squeeze everything in so they could see their children before they went on their overnight when a man bellowed from the back of the room.

"How long's that going to take? Why can't we eat while we do the damn exercises?"

"Yeah," said a woman behind Toby. "Let's get this over with. I'm about to pass out."

"I want to see my son," another woman shouted.

As soon as a few parents began to rebel, murmurs and questions rippled through the group. With one nod from Pax, several men came forward from the back of the room. Not a single one of them spoke. Within seconds it became clear they were intent on moving the chairs into a circle. People were up. Some stood, confused by the commotion. While others reoriented themselves and started to help reconfigure the furniture. Following the men's lead, this new upheaval was communicated with actions, not words. The director didn't entertain a single question.

When a perfect circle had been formed and everyone sat, the room went quiet again. Toby couldn't get a handle on what had just happened.

Then Pax pointed a finger at Nan. "May I start with you? Please stand."

The director stood in the center of the circle. Parents were sitting chair to chair, in a looser arrangement than before. Still Toby felt trapped. This is ridiculous, he thought. He was done, about to leave, when he realized he didn't know where to go. He had no idea how to find Ava. Then Nan stood, her shoulders square, not an ounce of panic on that pretty face. Toby couldn't tear himself away from the strength she radiated.

Pax stared her down but spoke to the rest of the group. "Don't you find it interesting that with only a few sentences, Ms. McEttrick was able to influence the group to achieve her own interests? Some teenagers mirror adult behavior exactly like hers. Others reject it at a heavy price to their self-esteem. It should come as no surprise to each of you that either way, your self-absorbed, self-indulgent, self-destructive behavior is affecting your child."

"This is ridiculous," Nan said, reaching back to grab her bag. "I want to see my nephew. Now!"

"Does anyone else experience Ms. McEttrick as controlling?" Pax asked. "It's no wonder poor Arthur sees himself as incompetent. He's incapable of completing even the simplest of tasks. At sixteen, he cries and carries on like a much younger child."

Nan was all brass—until she heard her nephew's name. Her eyes went glassy, and in that moment, Toby saw fear. Nan's vulnerability was tied to loving the boy. So he stood, placing a firm hand on Nan's back in an effort to support her. "I don't see how this is helpful," Toby said. "You're upsetting her."

"I imagine you don't, Mr. Sedgwick. Yet unpleasant emotions, though difficult to confront, simply must be acknowledged.

To be honest, I experience you as passive, someone not terribly self-aware. I'd guess you avoid conflict at any cost. Am I right?"

Toby found himself nodding.

"Perhaps that's why Ava's behavior is escalating—stealing, lying, drinking, taking drugs. Being promiscuous. She's done one risky thing after another in order to get your attention. Your daughter tells us she is desperate for a parent—not a friend."

Nan and Toby stood in the center of the circle while all the other parents looked on. Some didn't move an inch. Others leaned back, sinking deeper into their chairs. No one wanted to be the next parent in the hot seat. It was true Toby had been worried about Ava's safety and he knew she needed help, but he never thought she was as out of control as Pax was making her sound. And even if she were, what purpose did it serve to call Toby out in front of a bunch of complete strangers?

"At Mount Hope, we effectively replace learned negative behaviors with healthy ones." Pax placed one hand on Nan's shoulder, the other on Toby's, pushing them down into their seats. "For your sake and the sake of your children, we can show you how to open yourselves up to new ways of being in relationship with your teenagers. Your sons and daughters want to reclaim their lives. Let me help you help them. How does that sound?"

The punch-drunk group collectively agreed, nodding their heads. Pax waved his hands as if he were conducting a symphony. On cue, the double doors opened. Cold drinks, fresh baked goods, and sandwiches on trays materialized, wheeled in on silver carts from the hallway.

For a second Toby wondered if he wasn't being paranoid. Had the whole thing been planned to work out exactly this way, first embarrassing and upsetting Nan, then humiliating him, all with the goal of keeping the group in line?

Toby couldn't deny that the director had made accurate points about his less than perfect parenting. And who would refuse to sit through something if it meant helping their kid? So Toby did what he often did when feelings overwhelmed him. He reached for a plate and piled it high.

TWELVE

Fringe wasn't Fringe when he came back on Saturday.

At first, Ava didn't see him when she walked into the mess hall. After she got her tray and turned toward their lunch table, there he was. It was as if he'd appeared out of nowhere. Even from a distance Ava could see his eyes were dry, the teary film gone. His shoulders were pushed back. Fringe looked taller, broader, and he was wearing a red shirt.

"Hey." Ava took a seat across from him. They both started chowing down on rice and beans. She wondered why he wasn't saying anything even after he swallowed. He kept staring past her.

"We can talk, you know." Ava pointed to her shirt and then to his. "You moved up."

Fringe touched his sleeve. "I didn't have to wait for The Circle. They said I did a good job deescalating. Whatever that means." He started patting his chest like it didn't belong to him, like he was some kind of dog.

"Mallory's such a liar," Ava said. "She said OP's like prison. You look good."

"They say I'm better. Better. They say I know what to do now, Ava. What to do."

Mallory dropped her tray onto the table with a clang. Ava

jumped out of her seat as Fringe's juice sloshed over the cup's rim, spreading all over his tray. She shot Mallory a look.

In slow motion, Fringe started drawing marks and symbols with one finger in the pool of his juice. He stared at the mess, like he was afraid to look at Mallory. "They say I should forgive you for getting me in trouble."

Justice came up behind Fringe and punched him in the shoulder. "Don't waste food. Clean it up."

"OP is the devil's hole. But you can't shut me up with a new shirt." Fringe started ripping his napkin into smaller and smaller pieces. Blowing the scraps across the table, he puffed. "Orange. Red. Yellow. Green."

"One more word and you'll be back there so fast your head will spin. Pick those up." Justice hit him so hard on the back of the head it made a horrible whack, but Fringe wouldn't stop.

Why didn't it matter to him, that Justice kept punishing him, when he was finally something higher than a zero?

Justice must have realized Fringe didn't care, or couldn't. He leaned down and put his fat lips next to Fringe's ear, whispering loud enough for everyone to hear him.

"Give me one more goddamn reason and you won't go down the mountain to see Auntie."

Like someone had lifted a shade, Fringe's eyes opened wider. "Perm to sit alone?" he asked, sitting up straight again.

"Pick that up and get your butt over there." Justice pointed to a table in the corner where Seeds could go if they were on their last nerve.

When both of them were finally gone, Ava leaned across the table to Mallory.

"Everything about this place—including you—is messing with me. One minute he's fine, just weird. The next minute he scares the shit out of me."

Mallory looked across the room at Justice, then over at Fringe sitting by himself. For a second it seemed like she was trying to figure out who Ava was talking about.

"Know anything about his aunt?" Ava asked.

"Saw her down at the parent session," she said, shoveling a spoonful of rice in her mouth, eating the food like it was actually good. Ava almost told her not to worry—no one was going to steal it from her.

"You were there?"

"I signed people in. Collected bags."

"Did you see my dad? He's kinda losing his hair, a little over—"

"He's there."

Ava didn't get to ask Mallory anything else because there was Justice right behind her, booming out new directions.

"Last rope challenge before your overnight. Let's go."

Snarfing as many bites as possible on the way to return her tray, Ava got in line behind Mallory in case she had another chance to ask about her father. Justice put his hand on Mallory's back and made a circular motion over and over, dipping lower with each rotation.

Even though his hand was on Mallory, Ava felt it. The prickly feeling on her skin made her hate herself for being glad Justice caressed Mallory's back and not hers.

On the way to the clearing, she tried to work out how long her dad had been on the mountain, and how long it would be before she saw him. Last week, they left for their overnight right after dinner. If the challenge took an hour, there was still time to see him before the hike.

When they got to the ropes, Fringe came to stand next to Ava. Without being told, Benno hopped onto the metal footrests on a utility pole planted in front of a wooden wall.

"He's going to let down the knotted ropes you'll use to climb the wall," Justice said.

Mallory kept her eyes on Benno. Once he made it to the top and dropped them, the ropes swirled and bounced, until both of them straightened themselves out near the ground. Ava had passed low ropes thanks to Fringe, but she still didn't like the idea of this challenge. Mallory was more coordinated then the whole group put together, and she hated ropes. Ava half expected Mallory to volunteer her to go first. Then she raised her hand.

"Perm to demonstrate?"

Mallory put the harness on like she'd done it before. Ava knew she hadn't. Talking late one night in the bunk room, she'd told Ava that she was afraid of heights, and that she was getting good at finding ways to avoid rope challenges. No one would've guessed it by looking at her. How she anchored her feet on each rung, using the rope and her arms to hoist herself up the wall.

It didn't take Mallory three minutes to make it to the top. Holding onto the rope with one hand and the uppermost edge of the wall with the other, she hesitated, then gave Benno the cue to belay her to the ground.

"You were unbelievable. I thought you couldn't do it," Ava said when Mallory landed, both her feet firmly planted in dirt.

"I'm gonna do whatever it takes to get out of here. You should too," she said under her breath.

Justice came over and unclipped her harness, his hands lingering on the clasp near her crotch. "Turns out you're real good at this junior counselor thing. Don't screw it up," he told Mallory.

She didn't look away. Ava did. But not before she saw Mallory flinch as he pulled the harness off her, tossing it to another kid. "Move this along. I want everyone to do it at least once. Then we'll hightail it over to the shed to collect our gear. We're heading out early."

Ava felt her shoulders drop; her whole body slumped like someone elbowed her in the gut. The overnight. Leaving before dinner?

"Sedgwick. Over here." Justice backed up away from the climbing wall, moving out of earshot from the group. Crooking his finger, he told Ava to follow. "You probably want to know about seeing Daddy. It's not going to happen. Tomorrow after we get back from the overnight, you'll go down to the lodge and have a session with him and Honor."

"Perm to ask?" Ava could barely get the words out.

"What?"

"Do you know if he's upset about not being able to see me till then? I mean, if he gets mad he might want to take me out early or something."

Justice got a sicko look on his face. "Don't you worry, Red. Pax has the group in the palm of his hand." He flicked the end of her braid, the tip of it hitting Ava on the cheek. His hand came up, and he pulled her close to his face by her chin. "By the time you see

Daddy tomorrow, you'll be signed up for at least another month. If Pax is in good form, might even be two."

THIRTEEN

Justice slept on the opposite side of the fire pit, the trash bag of boots tied to his wrist. On this overnight, Ava had been able to make fire, so she got to keep her sleeping bag. Trying not to be obvious, she waited till he claimed his position, and then unrolled her bag as close to the pit and as far from him as she could. That was four hours ago.

The snap, crackle, pop the flames made was quieter now, almost nonexistent. Even though the fire still cast a glow and Ava was wrapped in down, she was colder than the last time she'd slept on dirt. Her teeth chattered and she'd lost all feeling in her toes.

Turning on her side toward Mallory, Ava scrunched her eyes, trying to focus on her friend's face. She was wide awake, her eyes darting back and forth. Mallory's fingers curled over the top of her sleeping bag, gripping it near her mouth. As lightly as Ava could, so she wouldn't scare her, she reached one hand out of her bag and tapped Mallory's shoulder.

"Move closer. It'll be warmer," Ava said in the softer-than-whisper way her music teacher called *sotto voce.*

Mallory nodded, and both girls inched over, meeting in the middle when their shoulders touched.

"Are you okay? You look petrified," Ava said.

"The dark's the worst. Makes you appreciate leaving the lights on in the bunk room."

"You're different since you came back from the parent session. More nervous."

Mallory wiped one eye with the back of her hand. It was the first time Ava had seen her cry since she'd been at Mount Hope. Fearless Mallory had climbed the dreaded wall in ropes class, and now she acted like they'd just spent the night telling ghost stories around the campfire.

"I did something stupid," Mallory said.

"Tell me about it—I figured out it was you who told Honor I faked a blackout in the kitchen."

"Not that. Way worse."

"Arthur doesn't blame you for sending him to OP. He said so at lunch."

Mallory didn't say anything, but Ava could see her staring across the pit to where Justice lay.

"What happened? Did he do something to you?"

"Shhh. He's evil. Don't go anywhere alone with him, Ava." Mallory moved back to her spot on the dirt. "Whatever it takes, stay out of OP."

Ava wanted to ask what he'd done to her, and to find out more about Observation Placement, but the crinkle of plastic—Justice rolling onto a garbage bag filled with their boots—stopped her heart beating. She went stone-still.

Watching steely night become morning, Ava cried over the biggest regret of her life: not telling her dad about the day her mind started cracking into pieces. Everything was fine until right before Christmas. Ava woke one morning and realized it was Poppy's birthday. That's when bits and pieces of things started coming back to her. Slowly at first. A palm tree here, some white sand there. Poppy swimming. Her mother.

If only Ava hadn't fought it. All she'd had to do was ask her dad to fill in the gaps and breaks, to shine light on the dark places of her memory. If she had, would he still have sent her here?

Finally it was morning and a cloud the shape of a G clef materialized as Ava lay in her sleeping bag looking up. When they were little, she and Poppy would argue over which crayon was better for drawing Mom's eyes. To Ava, they were robin's egg. Her sister swore they were the color of midnight. Mom settled it. Poppy, as always, was the winner.

First out of his sleeping bag, Benno stoked the embers and added branches to the pit. Mallory's job was to sort the boots and return them to their rightful owners. Justice pulled their workbooks from his backpack, one by one flinging them at their feet as they tied their laces.

Damn. She was meeting with Honor and her dad for a session this morning, and Ava still hadn't found a way to get rid of her pack of lies, to lose her workbook.

"Don't anybody mess with me this morning," Justice said, yanking the hood of Fringe's sweatshirt so tight he gagged. "Screw up today and you'll be sorry. Got it, Seed? Real sorry."

With the other counselors down at the parent session and the whole large group to himself, Justice acted tougher on this overnight. Yelling at everyone—not just Fringe—and giving them less to eat at dinner. He even collected their boots before dusk.

"Get into your groups and write for ten minutes. Benno will have breakfast ready by the time you're done."

Ava watched Benno unload food supplies from another backpack. He was counting out cans when Fringe tried to help him by putting a skillet on the grate over the flame. Benno flicked his finger in Fringe's ear, then pushed him away from his chore. It was like the more Justice treated Benno like a real counselor, the more he acted like one.

Mallory gave him a mean look as she took Fringe by the arm, leading him toward an area overlooking the vista with a collection of rocks to lean on. Cheez and Ava followed them, neither of them belt-looped. They posed no risk, because in that direction, there wasn't anywhere to run. With all three of them in front of her, Ava glanced back to be sure Justice wasn't watching. She stepped on one of her bootlaces, pulling it free, making sure to leave a long tail.

"Okay, so, this morning's assignment is to write about a person you want to say you're sorry to. And why."

Mallory looked at Ava and mouthed the words, *I'm going to write about you.*

"Stop telling me what to do!" Fringe shouted like he was trying to get Benno's attention back at the pit. "Stop. Yelling. At me."

"Arthur! Look at me," Mallory said, lowering her voice, trying not to draw attention to their group. Cheez scootched away. Ignoring them all, Ava opened her workbook. It didn't matter what she wrote this time. No one would ever see it.

I remember your eyes
Were bluer than robin's eggs
My poetry was lousy you said

"When was the last time you saw your aunt?" Mallory asked Fringe.

Ava could see she had a real knack for dealing with him. He began rocking, gently at first, like it soothed him to let his back come in contact with a rock.

"Aunt Nan. She can fly."

Okay, it was official, the kid was crazy. Mallory leaned forward and opened his workbook, flipping past page after page of intricate drawings, tapping a blank space toward the back.

"Write about her. Come on."

"Cessna. Skylane. Nan can fly." Fringe kept repeating Nan can fly while he drew in his workbook. For ten minutes, Ava kept writing classic Joan Baez lyrics in hers.

"Chow time." Justice's booming voice was a gunshot at the starting line.

It was now or never.

As everyone stood, so did Ava. Placing her boot on the loose lace, she intentionally stumbled. When her knee hit the ground, she released it. The workbook arced out over the ravine. The pages fluttered, reminding her of the baby bird she and Poppy saw one morning in Maine. Crouched under a pine tree, they were sneaking a look inside Mom's poetry journal when they saw the little thing. Like that helpless sparrow flapping its wings, Ava's workbook tried to stay airborne. She watched it fall, landing underneath a balsam like a Christmas present.

"What the hell did you do that for?" Mallory asked, slapping her thighs.

"It was an accident," Ava said, rubbing her knee, pretending it hurt.

"It's gone." Fringe peered over the edge. "Ava's in trouble."

Cheez put both hands out in front of her as she backed away. Not at all conflicted about which direction she was willing to go, she chose not to get involved.

"You idiot. Your dad already saw the workbook." Mallory pulled Fringe back from the ledge. "Now you're never getting out."

Justice stormed over to see what was keeping them. "I said I wasn't up for any bull this morning. What are you Seeds fighting about?"

All four of them stood there without saying anything.

"Mallory, you're back two levels for not being in control of your group. The rest of you, own up, or you'll have the pleasure of my company tonight. I'm itching to send the lot of you to OP. We could have a goddamn party."

Mallory, the tattletale, started in. "Ava's—"

"He threw my workbook down there," Ava said, interrupting her, pointing at Fringe, her hand shaking. "I was minding my own business working on my assignment and he went ballistic."

Fringe tipped his head and looked at his hands, turning them palm up as if without his knowledge they'd done what Ava had said.

Justice gripped him by the throat, nearly lifting him off the ground. "What'd I tell you, huh? I knew before Nanny-cakes got here that you wouldn't make it down the mountain to see her."

"I'd like to make amends, sir," Mallory said. "I can go get it."

"It's too far." Ava spoke without asking permission.

There Mallory went again, looking out for number one. She knew right then that they'd never had an alliance. All the times the girl had been nice to Ava, she was just reeling her in, setting her up.

"Quiet!" Justice pointed at Ava, his fat finger so close to her eyes, he could really hurt her with it if he wanted to. "Or you won't be going down to see Daddy either." He turned to Mallory. "Go ahead, get a rope from Benno. Make it quick. Then we're outta here. This overnight is officially over."

Ava hadn't meant to make a mess of things. Fringe was heading back to what he called the devil's hole, and this time it was her fault. Worse, he wasn't going to see his aunt. Now Mallory was going to retrieve the workbook Ava was too weak to throw far enough, the one her dad had already read. When Mallory got back up to the Ledges, after collecting the evidence of who everyone thought Ava was, she knew Mallory would lie and lie, telling Justice what Ava had done. She'd end up in OP right next to Fringe, wearing God knows what color shirt or—if she could believe anything Mallory said—nothing at all.

Justice looked down at Ava's boots. "Better tie that, Seed. You wouldn't want to trip now, would you?"

Between willing herself not to puke and trying to figure a way to get out of landing in OP, all Ava could do was stand by watching Mallory secure the rope to her waist with the help of Benno's expert hands.

Mallory rappelled toward the cluster of firs to get the workbook. Benno and Justice held the rope. Fringe sat down, cross-legged in the dirt, still looking at his hands.

Justice called out to Cheez. "If you wanna go straight to junior counselor, get the rest of those clowns packed up and put the pit out."

Cheez didn't wait for more direction. With the promise of a new job, off she went. For a second, Ava envied her moving up so easily to the level she herself had been striving for. Fringe stood, confused by all the commotion. Mallory's feet had barely hit the valley floor when she started to remove the knotted rope from around her waist.

"Leave it on," Justice shouted down at her. "You can reach the damn workbook without coming untied." He tugged at the line, but Mallory had been too quick for him. Without resistance, Justice lost his footing and fell backward. "Bitch. Get back up here. Now!"

Fringe covered his ears and sat down. Keeping his eyes on Mallory, he started to sway.

A few yards from the cluster of saplings, Mallory made no move to get the workbook. Cupping her hands around her mouth, she made a do-it-yourself megaphone.

"Ava, tell your dad," she shouted. "Let everyone know what it's really like here."

At first Ava thought Mallory had bent down to tie her own laces. Then a horrible crack echoed off the narrow valley walls, then another. It didn't make sense—what Ava saw her roommate do. Over. And. Over. It took three whacks for Mallory to fall to the dirt after smashing herself in the head with a rock.

"You're not telling anyone anything!" The sound of Justice shouting at Ava was muffled, his hands suddenly clapped hard over her ears. He held her head so tight, she pictured it popping off her body. In her mind Ava knew this was the most terrible thing that had happened since she'd arrived at Mount Hope, yet strangely, she felt calm. More disconnected from herself than ever before, Ava kept her eyes on the blood pooling around Mallory's body.

"Look at him!" Justice forced Ava to look to the place where Fringe sat rocking and moaning, "No, no."

"He's been here three times," Justice said. "You might be able to get Daddy to take you out today, but the next time you come home late or don't clean your room, he'll ship you right back. It's what parents do with losers like you." Justice turned her face back to his, his sour breath hanging between them. "He'll say he loves you. That all he wants to do is help you. But back here you will come. And when he sends you away again, I will be right here waiting for you. I will make your life a living hell." He pushed her down on the ground next to Fringe, then he smacked Benno across the face. "Don't just stand there. Run and get Medical up here. Don't you dare tell a single Seed on the way."

Benno dropped the rope at their feet, and before Justice could say or do anything else, he took off down the mountain.

FOURTEEN

Toby could hardly see straight as he made his way down the grand stairs to the lobby for day two of parents' weekend. After they'd all been shown to their respective rooms well after midnight, he'd slept in fits and starts, his mind preoccupied, reviewing the barrage of indictments Pax had leveled against him in front of everyone, trying to sort out which rang true.

He'd never claimed to be father of the year, but Toby had a hard time accepting that all of Ava's problems were squarely and solely his fault. Sins of omission he could swallow, but his daughter's claims that he intentionally, maliciously pushed her away, driving her to self-destruct? He didn't believe that.

Nan stood at the bottom of the stairs nervously tapping her wristwatch. She looked like she was ready to storm the dreaded conference room, while Toby had to force himself to put one foot in front of the other.

He arched his back, stretched his shoulders, and placed a hand on his chest as he walked over to Nan, his heartburn acting up again. "You got any Zantac in that big bag of yours?" he asked her.

"Sorry," Nan said, noticing him. "That's not the only thing I wish I'd packed." She pointed a finger to her head and with her thumb pulled an imaginary trigger. "This place is killing me. How guilty do you feel this morning?"

"I just want to see Ava. If she's doing as well as they say, maybe I could buy all this." Even as he said it, he didn't believe it. Toby couldn't get past the fact that along with some wild confessions, Ava had written some blatant lies in her workbook. How much could they really be helping her if she was still lying?

"You didn't do it, did you?" Nan asked, placing her hand on Toby's forearm, sending a tingle up and down his left arm.

"Sign her up for another month, you mean? God, no."

"Shall we get right to it?" Pax asked, flinging open the double doors. A cluster of parents trailed him. Most of the group chose the same chairs they'd sat in the day before. Pax made his way to the raised platform at the front of the room. "Your children are due back shortly from their overnight. Sessions with counselors start at ten. There's one more exercise we need to do before they get here."

Pax chose three women from among his admirers to go to the head of the class. Each one took a seat on the opposite side of a long table, staring out at the rest of the group. Toby wondered if these women, and a handful of other parents, were planted in the session to lend credibility to the director. One woman in particular was always thanking Pax, talking loudly enough for everyone to hear. She must have said a dozen times that he'd single-handedly saved her son's life. Toby didn't see how that could be true if the kid and his mother were still here.

"When I call your name, I'd like you to come up and plead your case in front of these judges. In this mock trial exercise, you'll need to prove to them, and to the rest of us, that you deserve to have your son or daughter back," Pax said.

Here we go again, Toby thought. He looked at poor Nan. The group hadn't been sitting there a full minute and she was already sighing. He couldn't blame her. She'd told him how awful it was fighting her own brother for custody of Arthur. It seemed heartless to make a game of what this woman was actually going through.

"Mr. Sedgwick. We'll start with you."

Toby stood, stretching one leg at a time, working out the

aches his body had memorized from spending so many hours the day before in those hard plastic chairs.

"I'd like to file a motion to postpone," he said, smoothing out the wrinkles in his slacks.

No one laughed.

"You find this funny?" Pax asked. "Are you aware that Ava arrived here not a moment too soon? Had you postponed your decision to send her to Mount Hope, your daughter could have killed herself. Need I remind you of the train incident?"

"No, of course not. I guess I just don't see the benefit of pleading my case to them." Toby pointed to the women presiding over him. "Call me a skeptic, but they're here too. They know as much about teenagers as I do."

The woman who sang in Pax's choir gave Toby a disgusted look. The other two sat there, arms crossed, playing their roles as adjudicators.

"To tell you the truth, I can't focus on another one of these exercises. I'd rather spend my time with my daughter. I need to see her, talk with her about what she wrote. I need to know she's all right." Toby rubbed his chest again. A sick, unsettled feeling came over him when he talked about Ava. Ten o'clock couldn't come fast enough.

Pax moved to the center of the raised platform, standing behind the judges. "You're glib, Mr. Sedgwick. You should be more responsible. Learn about what you don't know. I've explained repeatedly, all teenagers embellish their workbook entries in the beginning. That's one of the reasons we ask overeager parents to wait until the students reach a higher level. It takes time for them to sort out the reality of their situations."

Toby felt weak in the knees thinking about Ava's lies—and the things he'd been keeping from her.

"Here's the cold, hard truth," Pax said. "Ava can't be authentic with you, because you're not being real with her. When she was home, did she avoid you? Then seek you out only to argue with you? Yell at you? Lie to you?"

All Toby could do was nod.

"I assure you, when you see Ava this morning, you won't recognize her. She'll be a different girl. Calm. Polite. Centered. You see, Mr. Sedgwick, you are at the root of your daughter's problems. You're emotionally detached. If you and Ava are going to learn to communicate effectively, you're going to need to stop taking things so literally. Stop being obtuse. In your session today, force yourself to look at the emotions behind the words. Stop stuffing your feelings, as you so clearly do—with food."

Pax maintained eye contact as he threw the final zinger.

"Look at you," he said. "Out of breath from getting out of your chair. Your belt on its last notch. It's long past time you look at what you're eating *and* what's eating you."

There it was.

Toby had wondered when the director would point out that he'd let himself go. Pax had thrown a light on every other character flaw Toby had. He couldn't think of a single thing to say in response.

Tugging his shirt at the chest, he crossed his arms as if there were a way to diminish his size in front of all those judging eyes. Then a female counselor moved up the aisle. After climbing onstage, she whispered something in Pax's ear. The room went dead quiet. The director's face remained still. Oddly, it was his complete lack of movement that told Toby something was terribly wrong.

"There's been an accident," Pax said, sounding robotic. "None of your children were involved."

A collective sigh came from the audience.

"One of our junior counselor girls has been taken by med-flight to the nearby medical center. Counselors are standing by to take you to your sessions."

"Is she going to be okay?" Toby asked, wondering if it was one of the kids he'd met yesterday.

"I'm obligated to respect the student's privacy. Trust me, everything's under control."

Toby felt bad for the injured kid, but now was his chance to see Ava. Moving faster than he had all weekend, he maneuvered past Pax, who'd come down off the dais to move toward Nan.

"Ms. McEttrick, I need a word with you," Pax said.

Toby was panting by the time he reached the lobby. Ava stood next to a counselor about his age, a guy with a military air about him. He was talking to her in low tones. She stared at the rug, smoothing out the sharp crease running down the center of what looked like a brand-new T-shirt. Neon yellow, the thing hung off her slight frame as if she were its hanger. God, she looked thin. Loose strands of hair framed her sunburned cheeks. Toby couldn't decide if she looked healthy or not. It didn't matter. Seeing her filled the hollow place in his chest. All he wanted to do was wrap her in a bear hug. He stopped himself reaching for her when he remembered Pax's cautionary words.

Don't come on too strong. Take your cues from your child.

"Honey," he said. "It's so good to see you."

"Hi," she said shyly, no edge to her voice but no warmth either.

He wondered if she was still mad at him for sending her here, but he couldn't tell.

"I'm Justice," the counselor said, nearly snapping Toby's fingers off with his handshake. "I gotta say, your daughter surprises us on a daily basis."

Toby didn't like that the guy had his arm around Ava, pulling her close. While she didn't say anything, Ava leaned into him like a solid block of wood. Not a single muscle moved.

"Ava was one of a handful of standouts on our overnight. Moved up an entire level." He elbowed her as if they had a private joke. "A number of students are eligible to get out of their bunk rooms tonight. She might be the lucky one who gets to come up to our special room here at the lodge."

Ava looked at him only briefly before breaking eye contact. In that second that father and daughter connected, her eyes were vacant. How was he supposed to look for the emotion behind the words if she offered him nothing? If she was completely shut down?

"It's a beautiful day," Toby said. "I say we grab a couple of coffees and go for a walk around the lake."

"Coffee's a drug," Ava said.

Justice waved another counselor over. "Maybe later, Daddy-o," Justice said, his friendliness becoming irksome. "You and Ava have a session with her one-on-one counselor. Here comes Honor now."

Ava's counselor was the woman who'd broken the news to

Pax about the accident. Toby could tell she was still preoccupied.

"How's that girl?" Toby asked. "Is she going to be okay?"

Ava moved now, the smallest flick of her eyes, first over to Justice, then back to Honor.

"Kid sure is a daredevil. Loves anything to do with the ropes. Pushed herself too far in an outdoor challenge. I was right there supervising." Justice talked fast, rambling details of what had to be a frightening moment for all of them. "Crazy Mallory—"

"I'm sorry, Mr. Sedgwick," Honor interrupted. "We shouldn't really get into it. We need to talk to the girl's family first. You understand." Her face went pale as she shoved her hands deep into her pockets.

"That's terrible. I think I met Mallory yesterday. You send your child here; you think it's safe."

"It's upsetting to be sure." Honor put a hand on Ava's arm, giving Toby a look that said, *let it go.* "We have a lot to discuss, so shall we?"

Honor led the way down a long corridor; Ava and Toby followed behind. Their group entered a small office and took seats around a table. Toby was relieved when Justice didn't join them. The counselor's tough-guy persona swathed in fake sociability annoyed Toby. And as he recalled from one of Ava's earliest letters, she didn't much like the guy either.

Honor opened a folder already laid out there. "As you know, I'm Ava's one-on-one counselor. And we've met, let's see." The woman seemed nervous as she counted out session dates on her fingers. "Nine times."

Ava stared straight ahead.

Honor blathered on about how she experienced Ava and how proud she was that she'd finally turned herself in on her self-destructive behavior. "It took her some time to own up. But Ava's made progress lately."

"This owning up bit, is this where we get to talk about the things Ava wrote in her workbook?" Toby asked, pointing to the table behind Honor where a stack of them sat piled high. "I'd like to get into that."

"I apologize," Honor said, pressing her lips together. "I inadvertently left Ava's in my cabin. Where we typically meet." She cleared her throat. "Regardless, this is Ava's session. She can talk about whatever she wants."

Toby moved forward in his chair, angling his body so he could see Ava's face. If he could make eye contact, he could better gauge what he should and shouldn't say about what she'd written. The last thing Toby wanted to do was get her into trouble. Say the wrong thing, and he could get her special privilege taken away.

His daughter's face gave away nothing. Ava sat still as a statue next to Toby, her eyes cast down.

"Honey, I don't care about the mistakes you made back in Wellesley. That's all in the past as far as I'm concerned. But we need to talk about your mother. And Poppy. It's time to get the whole terrible thing out in the open."

Ava's whole body stiffened. When she looked up her mouth began to tremble. She shook her head, no, no.

"Going to Thailand was the trip of a lifetime," Toby said. "At first everything was perfect." His words were practiced, as if he were reading from a script.

"So you *were* there?" Honor looked first at Ava, and then back to Toby in disbelief. "Why wouldn't you tell us something so vital to your daughter's well-being?"

Toby's indigestion was back in full force. What was she talking about? He'd told the story more times than he'd cared to. First to the intake coordinator and then to Paxton Worth.

The burning in Toby's chest was as unbearable as it had been the first time that idiot confronted Nan in group. Nan. She wouldn't sit by hemming and hawing about what to do next. Nan would speak up.

"That's it. Ava, let's go." Toby cupped his daughter's elbow with his hand as he stood. She flinched and shook him off.

Honor looked toward the exit. Toby moved one step away from Ava; he opened the door.

"We can leave right now," he said to Ava. "Walk straight out of here. Find our own counselor and go over every last horrible thing that's happened to us."

His daughter finally turned toward him. Toby hated the way she stared through him.

"I love you, Ava. All I want to do is help you."

Ava's hands were folded, clenched tight on the top of the table. They trembled as she spoke. "Mount Hope is helping me reclaim my life." Her breathing was shallow, her voice mechanical, scarily rote, no sign of her signature melodic tone. Ava was as different as Pax had claimed she would be. Except his daughter wasn't polite and calm, she was flat. His Ava would be like Nan. His girl would say what she wanted.

"The program works. Honor's living proof."

"I read what you wrote," Toby said. "I know you're mad at me, but we need to talk about Thailand."

Honor covered Ava's hands with one of her own. The gesture calmed his daughter, as if the counselor knew exactly how to bring her back under control.

Ava was about to say something when Pax appeared, gesturing for Toby to move into the hallway.

"Mr. Sedgwick, please. Is there a problem?" Pax asked, guiding Toby by the elbow away from the session room door. "We don't abide raised voices in our counseling sessions."

"We're leaving. Have someone bring my things to the lobby. I'm taking Ava home," Toby said.

Pax leaned in, lowering his voice. "I'm afraid you can't do that. It's in your daughter's best interest to remain here for the duration of the program. You were right, Mr. Sedgwick, she's been scarred by the horrific events that occurred when she was young. Ava's only begun to benefit from the intensive therapy we offer here. You are ill-equipped. And you simply can't rush this process. In fact, there's consensus among the counselors that her stay should be extended by at least two months."

Toby pulled at his shirt collar in an effort to get more air. "You've got to be kidding. You want me to leave my daughter in your care after you didn't tell her counselor about her mother and sister?"

"Honor's new. Forms get misplaced. These details are neither here nor there. I assure you Honor and your daughter have been engaged in meaningful grief work since Ava arrived here. Regardless, you signed a contract putting me in charge of making decisions on your daughter's behalf. I'm legally obligated to hold you to our agreement."

As Paxton Worth spoke, two burly men moved closer to the session room. The bald one, twice Toby's size and all muscle, made sure to convey their threat was imminent.

"I urge you to spend your energy reconnecting with your daughter," Pax said. "Try to employ what you've learned here so far. Be authentic."

"I want her out. Get me the contract. I want to see what I signed."

"Again with the selfish behavior." Pax practically pushed Toby back into the session room. "What about what Ava wants? Have you asked her?"

Toby's shell of a girl remained at the table. Feisty, talented, capable Ava wasn't in that room. When Pax moved closer to her, asking her what she wanted to do, his daughter turned to Toby, and a single droplet traveled down her cheek. "I'll stay," Ava said, avoiding eye contact with Pax. "I'm staying."

As if the tear burned his own skin, Toby walked over and wiped it. He kissed her head and brushed a stray wisp from her eyes. Backing out of the room, he kept looking at Ava for as long as he could.

Down the hallway into the lobby, he ran as fast as his out-of-shape body would go. Toby stopped at the front desk, ringing the reception bell two, three, four times. He pulled out his cell but there was no signal.

The twenty-something who emerged from behind the saloon-type doors took her sweet time to come to the counter. Once there, she propped her elbows on the desk like she was too tired to hold herself up. "Can I help you?"

"I need to see the admission contract for Ava Sedgwick. I'm her father and I want to see what I signed."

"Sorry, I'm not allowed," she said, her eyes darting around the lobby. "But I can go find our Director. Pax will be able to help you, for sure." Now the girl moved double time, out from behind the desk and down the hall Toby had just traveled.

His actions were a blur, too. He ran past the grand stairs out the entrance to the parking lot. He unlocked his car and started it. No GPS required, he drove down the mountain, his cell phone still glued to his hand. His destination: the first place he could get a signal.

FIFTEEN

Her father didn't just walk away. He ran.

Ava had said she wanted to stay. But he should've known what she really meant was that she wanted to leave.

The director stood between Honor and Ava, his back to the counselor. "Go find an escort to take this one back to the Learning Center. Now."

When Honor took off, Pax shut the session room door halfway and moved closer to Ava, the space between them so small there was hardly any air left to breathe. The back of her neck was all sweaty. Stabbing pains taunted her stomach. Ava looked around the room for a wastebasket; even an empty coffee cup would do.

With one finger, he outlined each strand of her braid, starting around her shoulders, working his way down the length of it, left, right, left, right. This time when he touched it, he wasn't angry; he wasn't threatening to cut it off. Ava wanted to rip out every single hair, one at a time, so he wouldn't have anything to touch. If only she had scissors, she could make him stop.

"You made a good decision for once. There's hope for you yet."

Ava hadn't really made a choice. After all these years of comfortable numbness, in the space of a few minutes she'd been offered two equally terrible options with no time to weigh which was worse.

If she went with her dad—ready or not—he'd take her back to that beach. He'd push and push until she remembered everything, whether she wanted to or not. At Mount Hope, rope challenges and overnights Ava could do. Sleep and water she could easily go without. All at once, looking at Pax, Ava believed she was capable of surviving anything.

"I see you've made progress," he said, his eyes landing on her chest. Ava rounded her shoulders, folding her arms around her waist, wanting to hide.

"A new T-shirt, up one level. That's quite an accomplishment given the circumstances," he said. "Strength under pressure is a sign of good character. See, I don't care what your father thinks—or what anyone else says for that matter. My methods work. A girl like you needs to be broken like a horse. Taken down and built back up."

"Perm to ask." Ava looked past him through the crack in the door. If only Mallory would come around the corner, fine as ever, ready to belt-loop her back up the mountain, then Ava could get that sound out of her head. Rock hitting bone. She could stop seeing red blood spread out over dirt.

"Denied! I know what you want. So I'll tell you how this will go." Pax yanked her braid, arching her back until her neck was about to snap. "I find out you've mentioned her name or discussed what happened—with anyone—and you're back to Level One." He let go of her hair. If there hadn't been a chair right there, Ava would've landed on the floor.

Opening the door, he motioned for her to walk with him through the lobby.

"On the other hand, let me know if any Seeds talk about the unfortunate incident and you'll get extra points." He turned suddenly, straightening her shirt with both his hands. "You'll be a junior counselor before you know it. How does that sound?" he asked, jabbing her so hard in the chest with one finger it would definitely leave a mark.

"Fine, sir."

In the lobby, everything looked normal. Parents sipped coffee looking interested as counselors talked. Teenagers in red and yellow and green stood patiently by, pretending to listen. Happy faces all around—some real, some fake, some forced.

Pax hadn't surprised Ava when he told her how things worked at Mount Hope. She'd already figured out how kids climbed the rainbow, changing their shirt colors by telling on other Seeds. Now that her dad had come and gone, Ava could make up whatever she wanted. She could spin the color wheel and it wouldn't make any difference.

What Ava couldn't do was trust anyone. She walked through the lodge with Pax, a few steps behind. Staring past everyone out the window to the lake, Ava thought: Funny how water had started it all.

That's when she saw Justice.

"Here's the director now," he said to the woman standing in front of him. "He's the one to talk to." Eager to palm her off on Pax, he waved them over. Ava could tell by the way the woman clenched her teeth that she was furious. The lady clutched her shoulder bag like any minute she might belt Justice over the head with it.

Another unhappy customer. Ava wondered how long it would take Pax to convince her to give in to the ways of Mount Hope, to give up on her kid.

"You, come with me," Justice said to Ava.

The minute that creep took her arm, the second Ava saw that smirk, she had something new to strive for. Thanks to one of Mallory's final warnings, Ava would do whatever it took to stay out of OP.

SIXTEEN

Three miles, two hairpin turns, one scenic overlook, and Toby finally had a signal. After hitting Jill's number on speed dial, he breathed into his cell, "Be home."

He hated being this far from Ava, but he had to talk to someone who'd know if the director had it right. Could Pax legally keep his daughter there against her own father's wishes?

"Come on, pick up," he said, unbuttoning the collar of his shirt, trying to take in some air.

"I spoke to you an hour ago," Jill said when she answered, a hint of playfulness in her voice. "You really need to relax about tomorrow's board meeting. You can trust me."

"I'm not calling about work. It's Ava."

When Toby said his beautiful daughter's name, when he thought about her sitting in that room—about him leaving her—he felt pulled into some kind of vacuum. Whatever air was in the car vanished. In a panic, he slapped the buttons on his door, and the automatic windows on the driver and passenger sides came down in unison. Toby stuck his head out, willing the sound the creek made whizzing past his car to calm him.

"Toby, what happened?" Jill asked.

"They won't let me take her home." What had possessed him

to leave Ava there? Why hadn't he just taken her by the hand and walked out the front door? "I need you to find the contract in my desk. Tell me what the hell I signed."

"Slow down. I understand it's a very emotional weekend. You don't want to do anything rash."

"You sound like the director. This isn't about me. It's Ava. She's different—not Ava. It's like she's been brainwashed to say all this stuff they've pumped into her."

"Have you considered that different might be good? She's been out of control to say the least. It's time you looked after yourself a little. Really, they're the professionals. They know what they're doing."

"Look, I've seen her. The place isn't right for us. It's disingenuous, it's extreme."

"Hold on a minute. I don't want to think about what would've happened to Becky if I hadn't sent her to Mount Hope. They saved my daughter's life." Jill's voice was harsh now. Toby could imagine her sitting in the conference room at the head of the judges' table, sounding like one of those Stepford wives.

While he hadn't meant to offend her, he wasn't going to waste another minute trying to sway her to his way of thinking. What he needed was a lawyer. Someone to tell him what he'd agreed to. "Are you going to get the contract, or do I have to ask someone else to help me?"

"I don't need to check it. It doesn't matter what it says. You're her father. The only time things get dicey is when there are custody issues. In your case, there would have to be a mother demanding she stay there, someone willing to pay. They have no legal grounds to keep her against your wishes."

"They're not going to let me just walk in and take her," he said. "Ava says she wants to be there. And Pax has goddamn bodyguards."

"In my opinion, Ava has issues and she belongs at Mount Hope, but she isn't eighteen. If you want to—scene or no scene—you can take her. I'll call local police and tell them to meet you at the lodge, if that helps."

"Do it."

"If you run into problems, call me from the director's office.

Put him on the line. I don't think it'll come to this, but I'll play lawyer and intervene if I have to."

Toby pulled out of the space by the side of the road, turning his car around. He wondered if Jill heard him say he wouldn't make the meeting before the call was lost.

He told himself to stay calm as he drove up the mountain. *Ava will be fine.* The cops will come.

There was no sign of police in the parking lot when he returned to the lodge. Of course he'd made it back before they could get there. He hadn't been gone that long.

As Toby raced up the steps of the porch, he rubbed his arms, trying to warm them against the breeze that came in off the lake. No one stood guard at the door refusing him entrance. Fewer kids, parents, and counselors clustered in small groups throughout the lobby. A quick sweep of the downstairs confirmed what he'd expected. No Ava. Pax must've sent her back to the Learning Center. Though Toby was surprised the director wasn't there, waiting. Did Pax really think he'd give up so easily?

No one interfered with Toby as he climbed the grand stairs, or slipped his key into the lock, or gathered his stuff. In the time it would take him to grab his jacket and zip his duffel, the police would be there. Someone would bring him his daughter. He was minutes away from having Ava back.

Back down the hallway, walking past Nan's room, Toby knocked and the door swung open. Comforter folded down, shades all the way up, the small space filled with midday light. The room was hotel clean. Ready for another unsuspecting parent. While he didn't really expect Nan to be there, he hadn't expected her to be gone either. But of course, Pax was no match for her. Nan had probably already scooped up her nephew and whisked the kid right out of town.

When Toby got to the top of the stairs, he noticed a man in a dark trench coat, a law and order type, enter the lobby, flanked by a female officer dressed in traditional blues. *Good, they're here,* he thought. Toby's pulse shot up and he could feel his neck veins throb. So much for staying calm.

What if the duo didn't believe him? What if Ava insisted she stay? Toby didn't know if he could contain himself if his daughter came out with another one of those Mount Hope tag lines. The only things she'd said thus far weren't her words.

Ava's words were poetry. Like her mother's.

When was the last time he'd told her that? he wondered. Had he ever?

SEVENTEEN

Fringe hadn't been sent to OP from the Ledges. When Ava got belt-looped back from the lodge, there he was, nose to the wall in the Learning Center. Ava couldn't get close enough to Fringe to apologize for ratting him out for something he didn't even do. There were no words to describe how awful she felt for sacrificing him in order to look out for herself, doing what every other kid at Mount Hope did every damn day.

She wanted to ask Justice if Mallory really smashed her head in with a rock or did her crazy brain make that up too? But Ava knew she'd done it. What she didn't know was if Mallory was okay. Was she even alive?

If Ava raised her hand to ask permission to speak—hell, if her chair made the tiniest squeak on the floor—she might end up where she'd vowed she would not go. So Ava didn't take responsibility, or own up, or call herself a misbehaver in front of the rest of the kids. She tried her hardest not to do a single thing to draw Justice's attention as he paced in front of the log wall.

Slipping into a seat next to Cheez, Ava pulled a geography book from the stack in the middle of the table. So mad at her dad, she gripped it with her hands. She still couldn't believe how easy it had been for him to leave her. No wonder Seeds ate poisonous berries and skipped drinking their share of water. Mallory wouldn't be the last kid to try to exit on a medical, figuring it was the only way.

Out of the corner of her eye, Ava saw Cheez tap the page, telling her to concentrate. If she could see that Ava wasn't paying attention, then so might Justice. She thanked Cheez in her head for her random act of kindness and sneaked a sideways glance, flipping to the same page hers was opened to.

The universe was not about to cut Ava a break. On the top of page 236, there was a map of Southeast Asia, bright stars on an ocean blue background. In light pencil, next to the word Phuket, some kid, probably a Benno type, had written ha ha. What an idiot. The name of the little island that lured her father—and ruined her family—wasn't pronounced like a swear. Phuket began with a pure p sound. Like palm tree or paradise or—

She's wearing a sarong covered in exotic flowers, rose, orchid, and thistle. With her black hair framing her face, Mom is a kaleidoscope of color. She looks too pretty to be arguing with my father. "Why do you always do this?" she asks him. "You and your promises."

Poppy yanks the handle of the heavy beach bag we try to carry together. My sister urges me to move faster. "Come on, Ava," she says.

It's not that hard to walk in the sand. I just want to stay back to hear what Mom says to Dad. What he says to her. Then Poppy shouts, "Let's swim."

She picks up the pace, and the strap of my polka-dot bathing suit falls off my shoulder. When I go to pull it up, I lose my grip on the bag. A towel rolls out of it, then another, and another. Towels keep coming, more than could ever fit in one bag. Hundreds of them roll out like carpets. At first they're bright blue and green, then brown and black. The beach, once the color of sugar, is covered in darkness. I can't see anything, but I can hear a chorus. My family's voices. "Rain." "Pick it up." "Swim."

Ava's head was the first thing to hurt when she came to. Groggy, everything blurry, it took her a minute to realize she must've slammed her head into the leg of her chair when she fell. Ava didn't care about her arm, wrenched behind her back by Justice as he pulled her off the floor. Or her face, when he shoved it into the wall. Or her ear, when he screamed right into it. At least things hadn't gotten so bad that he was touching Ava the way he had Mallory.

"I've had it with you. Stop faking. Nose to the wall."

The bump grew bigger and hotter under her hair. Ava thought about Mallory and how much her head must've killed after she bashed it with a rock.

Funny, the worse things got for Ava on that mountainside, the calmer she felt. For the first time since she landed at Mount Hope, Ava might've even smiled. All she could think about was how much she wanted to go back to where she'd just come from. To her life before that punishing water washed everything good away. To her sister on the sand. To her full-color mother—alive.

For once Ava trusted her memory. She lingered on what she could remember, even though it usually upset her too much. Now, after everything bad that had happened, it was weird how good thinking about her mother and sister could make her feel. Ava didn't care that she was standing next to Fringe or that he kept moaning to himself. She couldn't care less that Justice was fuming, talking to someone who'd just breezed into the Learning Center.

"Jesus, I'll do it. Watch my Seeds," he said.

Ava could tell without turning around, it was Honor.

"No," she said. "Stay here. Calm down. Pax has everything under control. I'll take them." Honor had to be talking about Fringe and her. Ava's new plan to stay out of trouble had lasted all of an hour. Fringe was going to OP, and she was heading there right alongside him. Ava tried to imagine OP. Was it a room or a cell? Inside the lodge or out? At least she had a pretty picture of her mother to take with her. Ava kept telling herself it was better to go with Honor than with Justice.

"You're going to hell," Fringe hissed at Ava. "You're going to hell because you killed her."

"Arthur, relax," Honor said, slipping her fingers into his belt loop. "No one is going to hell." She seemed more worried about Fringe than usual, patting his arm, staring at his face like she was looking for something hidden there.

Ava pointed her butt at Honor, waiting to be belt-looped.

"I trust you to be responsible," Honor said. "It's time for you to walk on your own."

In the time it took to work through the bramble, heading toward the lodge, Honor didn't say anything. She focused on Fringe. Three times, Ava almost asked her about Mallory, but every time she was about to, Fringe glared at her, and Ava was afraid to set him off.

Benno was waiting at the bottom of the hill where the path forked. If Honor said it was okay for Ava to walk alone, then why was he here?

When Fringe started dragging his feet, making tracks in the dirt, Benno ran up to grab one of his arms. Honor took her fingers from his waistband and took hold of his other arm. "Arthur's going to be fine. He needs some quiet time and a few extra one-on-ones to sort out—the incident," Honor said, patting Fringe's back as he cried, "No, no."

Ava stood there on her side of the path, trying to make sense of things.

"I'm sorry," Honor said to her. "I should have believed you."

Honor and Benno were aiming Fringe down a trail that led to a low building attached to the far end of the lodge. Ava didn't get what they wanted her to do. Was she supposed to follow them or not?

"Go on," Honor said. "Your father's inside."

If Justice had been standing there, Ava would've known the whole thing was a trick. She saw her father leave with her own eyes. Inching toward the lobby, Ava figured this might be some kind of sick game. Another Mount Hope life-lesson wrapped in persecution. But as stunned as she was that Honor came here as a Seed, then decided to work here, Ava knew she wasn't cruel. It was hard to understand how she could, but Ava knew Honor believed what she was doing was good.

"There she is," Pax said, clutching a stack of workbooks and papers against his chest, standing in the middle of the lobby. Right next to her father. Two other people Ava didn't know stood there too. One of them was a cop.

Something hot bubbled up inside Ava, a soup of anger and

fear. It was a trap. She wasn't going home. She was going to jail for killing Mallory. Pax would make sure no one believed her when she told them Mallory had done it to herself. Ava started to back up, one step, then another. She was startled when the screen door hit her in the back, even though she'd just come through it.

"Ava, come here," Pax said as an order. "Officers, it's like I said. At Mount Hope, you can expect full cooperation."

Wiping her sweaty palms on her khakis, Ava looked around the lodge for an out. She was good at scoping places out without turning her head. Feeling lighter than she had for over a month, it was odd being this close to an open door without someone else's hands on her. The policewoman was shorter than Ava, but had Honor's build. No doubt she would catch her even if Ava had a head start.

Where would she go anyway? Ava had no idea where she was or how far the lodge was from a main road. Her mind was spinning. Her heart racing. Pax hightailed it over to her, pinching her arm as he walked Ava toward the officers. Before she knew it, her dad was next to her too, standing on her other side.

"Take your hands off my daughter," he said to Pax. Then he whispered to Ava, "It's over."

"I didn't do anything," Ava said. "I don't want to—"

"I talked to a lawyer," her father said. "Stay calm, I'll get you out."

He touched her arm, attempting to reassure. As if his hand were on fire, Ava drew back from it. He got this look on his face like she'd said out loud that she hated him. Which in that moment, Ava kind of did. Mixed up didn't begin to describe how she felt about him. Was he just going to hand her over to police without asking what happened?

Then he walked away from her, and like a five-year-old, Ava grabbed his jacket.

"It's okay," he said, lifting her chin. "I'm just getting my stuff." He pointed to his bags piled at the bottom of the stairs. "Come, walk with me."

Gently, he slipped his hand in hers, and this time, Ava didn't fight it. The heat from his touch felt familiar, good.

Her dad got his bags, and they started walking toward the

door to the parking lot.

"It'll be okay," he said. "I'm parked right at the edge of the lot."

Her dad kept shooting the breeze, the way he did when she was little and woke up from a bad dream. The Ava of a month ago would've told him to stop babying her.

Trench Coat Guy and the cop stayed put, talking to Pax. If Ava was in such big trouble, why were they letting her go? This was all so confusing.

They were almost out of the place when Trench Coat Guy called to them. Ava turned to see him step away from Pax.

"Before you go, can I ask you a couple of questions?" He flipped open a small notepad and pulled a pen from behind his ear. "I'm Detective Reilly. You know a student here by the name of Mallory Vincent?"

Ava's throat closed over. Even if she knew what to say, she was pretty sure nothing would come out. Pax gave her one of his stares from a distance, saying, *don't you dare.* Millions of times, she'd wanted to tell Pax to shut it. This time, she had to admit, she wanted him to start talking. No one had given Ava this script in advance.

The detective looked up from his notepad and waited.

The pressure was on.

So, Ava showed everyone how well she'd learned the central Mount Hope life lesson: lie.

"I saw her around," she said. "But my job was to work the program. Focus on my own problems."

"So you weren't there, then? On the overnight trip?"

"I went on the hike, but I didn't see anything."

Pax was a pro at reading lips. From across the room, he pretended to be shuffling the papers he carried, but not before Ava saw that sicko grin he wore when he knew he had someone beat.

Detective Reilly pulled two business cards out of his wallet. He handed them to her dad, along with his pen.

"Keep one of these and write a number where I can reach you on the other. In case I have more questions."

Her father let go of her hand so he could write on the back of the detective's card.

This might be Ava's last chance to find out about Mallory. Everyone was acting like she already knew.

Pax walked toward her. He read Ava again; he knew she was about to go for it.

"You don't want to leave without this," he said, pulling the dirty, tattered workbook from the collection of things he held. "I'm sure you'll want to exercise the same discipline at home. And Mr. Sedgwick, if we can support you in any way, if you feel that Ava could benefit from re-enrolling, don't hesitate to be in touch."

Pax gave Ava quite the send-off, offering up the workbook while at the same time making sure she understood. What happens at Mount Hope stays at Mount Hope. He didn't want her talking to her father about Mallory or anything else. Ava could've told Pax not to worry. Thanks to him, it was going to be a while before she opened up to anyone.

Her dad tucked Detective Reilly's business card in his shirt pocket. "Let's go," he said.

Ava tried to keep calm, politely taking the workbook from Pax. She stayed right by her father, afraid to leave more than a few inches between them.

Through the lobby. Out the screen door. Onto the porch. Down the steps. Across the brick walkway. Past the pine grove, bordering the lake.

The closer she got to the car, the more disconnected she felt from everything and everyone. Was she actually leaving? Ava never felt her feet on the ground. The passenger door opened, no problem. Her dad put his things in the backseat. She got in on her side in silence.

Then he was in, his door closed too. Key in the ignition. Car in reverse. They were driving. It felt like flying. Ava kept looking back, but there wasn't a single person on the porch. No one was going to stop them.

"You okay?" her dad asked.

All she could do was nod. When Ava looked down, she saw two hands in her lap. They didn't appear to belong to her, but they were gripping that stupid workbook.

Now that Pax couldn't see her, Ava told herself she could do it. She rolled down the window and starting tearing pages from the binding.

Watching the wind take her lies wherever they wanted to go, Ava felt the weight of Mount Hope start to come off her.

"Stop the car," she screamed, pointing ahead. "Let me out by the stream. Keep it running."

Her father looked like he was afraid of her, but all he said was "Okay."

When the car came to a stop, Ava got out and climbed over the guardrail. As close to the edge of the water as she could muster the courage to go, she closed her eyes and called up an image of the bunk room. Ava let it go. Then she let go of the Learning Center. The fire pit. And finally, the Ledges. She would not take a single thing from this horrible place. Her mind was a mess as it was.

When flashes of Mallory and Fringe pushed their way in, she whispered *good-bye* and *I'm sorry*. Then, with as much power as Ava could call up, she hurled the workbook. It ricocheted off a cluster of rocks, sliding into the current. This time she'd done it right. One second it was there, the next it disappeared. Ava shook her head to loosen everything she could recall of Pax and Justice, even Honor. She heard her father gasp behind her when she pulled the yellow shirt from her body and let it drop on the surface of a swirling pool. Ava watched the water absorb its color, though it made no move to sink it. Standing there, cold, wearing only a tank top, goose bumps sprang to life all over her arms. Then she felt her father's jacket go over her shoulders, warming her.

Without resistance, she slipped her arms into the sleeves, wrapping the leather blanket around her as her father guided her to the car.

EIGHTEEN

Toby saw the red and white bull's-eye from the expressway in time to pull off the exit and into the Target parking lot. In one stop, he could get everything he needed to stock the house in Maine. After all that had happened back at Mount Hope, he wasn't up for multiple errands. He knew Ava wouldn't be either.

She'd been asleep for nearly the entire ride. He didn't know how teenagers did that, curled up in the most uncomfortable positions. Didn't she have to go to the bathroom? Or ever get hungry?

"Honey," he said, gently touching her shoulder through his leather jacket.

She jerked awake, putting her hands out in front of her like she was going to hit something or someone. He could tell it took her a second to realize where she was, to recognize him.

"I'm going to grab a few things. It won't take long."

Ava didn't say anything.

"You could come. Use the restroom."

"I'm fine."

That was it? His daughter had been in the car with him for hours and all she could come up with was *I'm fine?* Maybe she really hadn't wanted to leave. Toby thought the change of scene, going to their house above the Reach in Blue Hill to set things right between them, was a good idea. After all, Ava had written so fondly of their summer home in one of her letters. Sitting there now, seeing his daughter turn her body toward the window, her back to him, he wondered if his plan to bring her to a place packed with memories wasn't potentially a colossal disaster.

He reached into the backseat, unzipped his duffel bag, and rolled out a pin-striped oxford. "I'll leave this here in case you change your mind. If you want, meet me inside. Or when I'm done, we can ask how far out of the way it is to better stores."

Ava remained silent, her eyes closed tight against him. Toby laid the shirt that could've fit three of her over the back of her seat.

At the entrance to the store, he wrestled a large cart from the corral and shimmied it through the automatic doors. Buttery popcorn invited him inside. Wheeling the carriage by the promotional aisle where pallets of ticketed sale items were stacked, Toby grabbed a box of Wheat Thins. These would tide him over till he and Ava got at least as far as Bucksport.

Up one aisle, down the next, he filled his cart. Aside from last month's out-of-the-blue phone call from the caretaker about a leaky pipe, Toby hadn't really thought much about the place in a while. Now certain items went into the cart without a moment's hesitation. Things they'd need there came back to him automatically. Paper towels, aluminum foil, scissors, tape, a pad of paper, a pack of pens. Other things, specifically for Ava, took longer to choose.

In the women's clothing department, Toby pulled a pair of pants off a shelf. Even before he'd unfolded them, he knew they'd be too big on his daughter.

Toby addressed a large woman wearing a red vest and an employee name tag: Janine. Her job was to refold the merchandise that customers were too lazy to put back on the shelves. "I'm a little out of my element," he said to her, "trying to pick out a pair of jeans for my daughter."

"What size is she?" she asked without looking up.

"Gosh, I don't know. She's sixteen, around five-seven. Rail thin."

"You want Juniors. Come with me."

Janine trudged around the corner, not looking to see if Toby followed. When they arrived in the right section, Toby had even more doubts. Ava wouldn't like all this pink. Everything on these racks was covered in sparkles. No way was he up to the task of picking out clothes.

"You can't go wrong with these," Janine said, reading his expression, handing him a pair of straight-legged jeans. "Plus they come with a belt."

Toby went with the jeans, choosing two different sizes to be on the safe side. He tossed a package of colored T-shirts into the cart. No, wait, Ava wouldn't want those. Remembering how awful it had been to watch her rip off the Mount Hope shirt by the stream, Toby fought back tears. Wearing only a child's undershirt, the bones of her shoulders pushing the limits of her pink skin, it was like Ava was trying to rid herself of the place.

Toby knew Mount Hope was the wrong place for his daughter, but what made him so sure that taking her to the Maine house was the right thing to do? There was that sick feeling roiling around his stomach again. He'd been in the store too long. He needed to get back to her.

Off the racks and into his cart, he threw two plain white T-shirts and a navy blue sweatshirt—the kind that zipped, not the over-the-head Mount Hope kind.

Standing in line at the register, the person in front of Toby nearly finished, he saw Ava wearing his huge shirt, her braid trailing down her back. He recognized her immediately; so tiny was she from a distance. Ava sat at a table in a place the store labeled Target Café. When she noticed him, she offered a halfhearted wave. Toby had hope then, that she might actually have been looking for him. He pointed to his cart and then to the register, telling Ava he was almost through.

"Sorry it took so long," he said maneuvering his way through the food court. Toby put his bags down on an empty chair before sitting down next to Ava. "I bought you some clothes. If you'd rather, I can return them and we could ask someone for directions to a mall. Though I've got to say, we're kind of in the boondocks—"

"That's ok. I don't want to go shopping."

"Well, here then," he said, handing her one of the bags. "You go change. I'll order us a couple of slices. You must be starving."

When Ava was gone a long time, Toby began to wonder if he should leave their food to go find Janine. She wouldn't mind sticking her head into the ladies' room to see if Ava was okay.

As he debated what to do, Ava came out of the restroom. He did a double take and his hand came down on the table tipping over his Pepsi, the plastic lid popping off, spraying soda everywhere. Disregarding the spill, Toby gripped the edge of the table, steadying himself.

Ava's braid was gone. Her hair chopped off at her shoulders, wedged and uneven, was a drastic change. Not the work of a girl having a little fun with her appearance or copying the latest celebrity 'do. Toby held his breath so long he started to get dizzy. He could feel his heart pounding when he remembered the girl. Ava's do-it-yourself haircut looked exactly like Mallory's.

Dear God, what had he done, sending Ava there? And now taking her out?

His daughter acted as if nothing were wrong, handing him the bag filled with assorted items, a tube of toothpaste, the scissors he'd been stupid enough to buy so she wouldn't have difficulty ripping out tags. The new jeans were baggy, rolled up several inches at the bottom. The sweatshirt, also oversize, made Ava look like she was playing dress-up—a child in a grown-up's guise.

Ava sat down, and with a wad of napkins pulled from the stainless-steel dispenser, she started mopping up Toby's spill, her movements robotic.

"Honey, maybe Maine isn't the best idea. What would you think about going—"

She stopped her father speaking by gripping his forearm, digging her nails into his skin. "I'll be good. I'll do whatever you say. I don't want to go back there. And I don't want to go home to Wellesley."

"Okay. All right. We can go to Maine. But you have to talk to me."

Ava tipped her head back and sighed.

Go slow, Toby thought. *Take your cues from your child.*

His hands trembled as he dug through the bag parked next

to him. He placed a blank journal down on the table. Ava stared at it. He couldn't tell if she remembered its significance. Did his girl know how hard it was for him to choose this way of reaching out?

"I loved the lyrics you wrote in your workbook. And the memories of Mom and Poppy." Toby slid it over in front of her. "But in this one only the truth. Okay?"

Ava ran her hand over the orange fabric cover, up the ivy vine dotted with turquoise flowers. Toby walked two fingers over to her across the table. It was a game they'd played when she was little. He'd tease her, making her think he was going to swipe her special book. She'd giggle, pulling away from him, holding the treasure close to her chest, proud of herself for winning, for keeping the thing for herself.

With the lightest touch Toby could manage, he placed his hand on hers, resting on top of a journal stitched with a combination of two sisters' favorite colors.

And for a moment, Ava let it stay there.

NINETEEN

Déjà Vu Hair Salon was sandwiched in the middle of a strip mall in Bucksport, overlooking the Penobscot Narrows Bridge. It was the third walk-in they'd stopped at, after almost giving up hope of finding a place open on a Sunday. Ava agreed to get a real haircut when her dad suggested it, not only because she couldn't stand the pained look on his face every time he glanced at her during the last two hours of the ride but because she hadn't exactly been successful with what she'd set out to do, shearing her hair off in the Target bathroom.

Lucky for Ava, Déjà Vu was nearly empty. Judging from the stares she got walking through the beauty shop toward the stylist's chair, she must've looked even worse than she thought.

"Doll, what were you thinking?" the stylist asked, as she flipped Ava's hair up in the back, over and over, with her fingertips.

Mirrors weren't allowed at Mount Hope, which meant she hadn't seen herself since the night she'd been kidnapped. Back at Target, Ava had taken the plastic bag from her dad, found the ladies' room, and walked right into a stall without looking. When she'd finished removing tags and putting on the new jeans and sweatshirt, she came out to find a skinny girl wearing an unrecognizable face and baggy clothes staring back at her. The auburn hair, a braid longer than it had ever been before, confirmed it. The girl in the mirror was Ava.

She ripped the elastic off the end of her braid, unraveling the three separate strands as fast as she could. Shaking her head, swinging hair in every direction, Ava still couldn't get Pax out of her mind. She shivered then, imagining his finger tracing a path from her shoulders down the length of her back by way of her hair. Remembering how much she'd wanted to cut it—to cut him—back at the lodge, Ava starting humming to drown out his voice. Briefly thanking her father for making it so easy, she reached into the Target bag and pulled out the scissors. The blades made a slicing, sluicing sound working through the hair. Metal slid against metal, resistance then surrender. Ava kept slashing and hacking, letting rich red clumps scatter all over the floor. For the few seconds it took, part of her brain told her to stop, the other part cheered her on, encouraging her to finish what she'd started. Staring at her reflection in the Target mirror, hair at her shoulders, Ava still didn't look like herself. The new 'do reminded her of Mallory.

"Have any idea what kind of hairstyle you want?" the stylist asked, swirling a towel around her shoulders, expertly tucking it in at her neck. "Or do you want to trust me to give you a make-over?"

Through the mirror, Ava could see her dad standing behind her, looking awkward. She was about to tell him to go.

"Mind if I go fill up the tank and grab a few newspapers?" he asked.

Ava shook her head, saying she didn't mind, even though the pizza and soda she'd eaten back at the food court suddenly started to disagree with her.

He's not leaving you for good in a hair salon, Ava told herself.

"I'll be back here in half an hour," he reassured. "Anything she wants," he said to the stylist, "doesn't matter the cost." Then he was off.

Ava gathered as much of her hair as she could, pulling it back so she wouldn't have to see the result of her Target freak-out. She watched her eyes get teary like Fringe's used to, the way Mallory's did before she went ballistic in that ravine.

"I don't know about going shorter," Ava said. "Maybe just a

trim."

"Look, honey, I don't know why you gave yourself a hack job, but obviously you think it's time for a change. Sit back and relax. You're in my chair now. Trust me, with a good haircut, you'll be a new woman."

The stylist was right. A warm-water shampoo, the aroma of mint and honey conditioner, and Ava was feeling a little like herself again. Even though the stylist occasionally massaged the sore spot left on her head by the Learning Center floor, she could close her eyes and not be afraid.

Like a magician, the woman pulled strands of hair through her comb and then her fingers, snipping and trimming, some hair feathering down, and what was left of it framing Ava's face. Without effort, the woman marked her passage from the old Ava to the new.

Just as she spun the chair around so Ava could admire the transformation, her dad walked into the shop. Ava saw him through the hand mirror she held to look at the back of her hair. He put a hand to his chest clutching his newspapers tight. When his mouth opened, a single word flew out. Ava couldn't hear it over the blow dryers or the stylist asking her if she liked her new do. But thanks to Mount Hope Ava could read lips.

Then he said it again, loud enough for everyone to hear. "Rain."

LYNNE GRIFFIN

PART TWO
THE REACH

TWENTY

Herrick House, Maine
Journal Entry #1

May 14

The last time I was inside Herrick House, I was eight, my sister about to turn seven. In the eight years since—when I dared revisit this place in my mind—memories didn't come whole like wide open sailcloth. More like snippets and swatches, bits of things I couldn't always piece together into something pretty. Sometimes little scraps would work their way free, at odd times, like yesterday, when my dad called me Rain in the hair salon. Short for Lorraine, it was the name he called my mother when they weren't fighting.

My dad told me my new haircut made me look older, more sophisticated, that he could see a resemblance to her in the shape of my face, in the angle of my chin. That's the most he's said about her in as long as I can remember.

Then this morning, another memory came crystal clear. No haze, no need to dig for details. The last time we spent the summer in the house around the corner from where my mom grew up above Eggemoggin Reach, a place my sister once called Egg McMuffin Peach, I remember building a fort in the attic with Poppy.

It was Mom's idea. I was probably driving her crazy, complaining about how many days in a row it was stormy, moping about not being able to play croquet on the side lawn or take the canoe out on the pond. Mom was in the sunroom, curled up in front of the fireplace, on that lumpy green sofa, the one that came from her old house. A log snapped as she put her book of poems down and pulled her legs out from under her. Mom took Poppy's hand, then mine, a child on either side of her. She marched us down the hallway, with its wide-planked floors, up one flight, then another, the second set of stairs steeper and more crooked than the first. "You girls have to learn to use your imagination. When I was your age, I'd stack my books, position a couple of chairs, use a few sheets, and voilà! A secret paradise to play in."

The knock on Ava's bedroom door made her drop her pen, slap her new journal shut, and yank her bedspread up around her neck, all within seconds flat.

"I know you don't drink coffee anymore," her father called from the hallway. "But how about a cup of herbal tea? There's a tray in the sunroom." He didn't say anything else, but she knew he was still standing there. His feet blocked the light that crept in under her door.

She would've loved a cup of coffee—even settled for the tea—but she didn't really want to go downstairs. What she wanted, was to be alone. To call up her own soothing memories of her mother and Poppy.

Ava had this new theory, that if she forced her mind to focus on only the good stuff, the nicest bits she could remember, then her crazy brain wouldn't get stuck on bad things. Mind control by Ava, not by Mount Hope or her father.

She waited until he left, then crawled out of bed, still fully dressed in baggy jeans and sweatshirt. She followed the smell of food.

Aside from some of the rooms being smaller than she remembered, Herrick House was exactly the same. In springtime, a fire was always lit in the sunroom fireplace. Bright light filled the space overlooking the Reach, and the table by the window was set with two mugs and a plate bursting with sandwiches. Ava wondered who'd removed the white sheets that were draped over the furniture as of last night. Looking at the old sofa, she blurred her eyes, trying to imagine her mother there, curled up reading her favorite poems out loud.

"Hungry?" her dad asked. "James brought us a few things till I can get some groceries delivered. Turkey, ham and Swiss. There might be chicken salad." He pointed to more food on one plate than Ava had seen in over a month. For a second, she thought about hiding some in her pocket for later.

Ava wanted to ask who James was, but not being up for chatting, she went with neutral conversation. "What time is it?" She shook her head. At times it still surprised her how short the stylist had cut her hair, though she did love how free it felt.

"Two," her father said, glancing at his watch, pretending he didn't already know. "That overnight hike wiped you out, huh? A woman I met at the parent session said it's tough terrain up there." He took a sip of his coffee, looking at her over the rim.

Her father was fishing. Like she wasn't going to notice him bringing up something about Mount Hope, thinking she'd spill her guts about the prison without bars he'd just sprung her from.

Right then, Ava felt like doing a little trawling herself. "Yeah," she said. "Things got crazy after that girl—you know." Ava slid a half of a turkey on rye onto a smaller plate sitting next to the mug of tea meant for her. "Hope she's okay," she said, taking a bite, watching her dad for clues.

"I don't mind telling you, I almost had a heart attack when the director told us a girl was MedFlighted to Plattsburgh."

Yes! Ava had her first concrete detail about Mallory. The way her father said it, Plattsburgh had to be a hospital.

When the back door squealed open and heavy boots hit the hardwood—one, two—her sandwich went flying, sending a tomato slice across the table. Splat.

Then, strangely, the boots and whoever they belonged to retreated.

Her father leaned forward, trying to see who was in the hallway. How safe did she feel? They had an intruder and he didn't even get out of his chair.

"James, is that you? Come on in," he said. "There's someone I want you to meet."

"Sorry, Mr. Sedgwick. Gonna have to remember to knock." The kid named James ducked as he came into the sunroom, into their ancient, low-ceilinged house. If she'd had the energy to care, Ava would've been mad at her father for inviting someone in when she looked so terrible.

"Ava, this is James St. Croix, our caretaker. James, meet my daughter."

He was older than Ava, but she couldn't tell by how much.

"Hey," James said, whipping off his wool hat. It was the patterned kind, with flaps over the ears and braided strings. He didn't smooth his hair down, just let it stick up and out in a bunch of different directions.

"Don't like tomatoes?" James pointed to the one that had escaped from rye. The kid's eyes were big and brown and kind of droopy, so it was hard to tell if he was teasing or not. Ava couldn't stop staring at the two scars that ran along the same diagonal plane on his face. The dramatic one through his left eyebrow pointed like an arrow to the faint one that zigzagged from his nose to his upper lip.

Her father pushed a napkin toward her, telling Ava with his hand to pick up the wayward fruit. His eyes told her to stop being rude too.

"I'm not really a caretaker," James said, walking over to the fireplace. "Just filling in."

If James lived in Wellesley—whether he was smart or not—he'd be in college, working at some upscale place at night or on weekends, being groomed to work for someone like her father. Instead, as a Maine year-rounder, here he was, counting on them to pay him to take care of a house they never came to.

"I meant to tell you earlier how sorry I was to hear about your uncle passing. How's Biddie holding up?" her father asked.

"Some days better than others. I bet she'd like it if you stopped in to say hey."

"I will. It's been too long. I've got a few things I need to do in town. Phone signals drop all over this property. I've got to get the landline reconnected, and wireless too. Frank doesn't still have that pay phone in the back of Bucks Harbor Market, does he?"

James pulled three pinecones from a bowl on the mantel. He tossed them into the fire and stoked the logs. Back at Mount Hope, Ava had thrown pinecones into the pit without a second thought. It wasn't until James did it in that room—the sappy fragrance released into the air—that she remembered. At Herrick House, that was something her mother liked to do.

"You can get a good signal outside Bucks or you could use mine. I've hooked up a phone in the boathouse," James said.

"Good to know. But I don't want to disturb your things," her father said.

"No problem. It's your place. You sure it's okay I'm still out there now that you're back?"

They were like two old ladies going back and forth. For God's sake, there were five bedrooms in this huge house, and her father was making the kid sleep in the boathouse? Clearly her father had a pattern of banishing kids outside. Any bunkhouse, log cabin, shack or shed would do.

"Later," Ava said, pushing her plate away, pulling her legs out from under her like her mother used to. Back to her room, back to her happy memories. She'd had enough of real people for one day.

TWENTY-ONE

*I'm standing inside the boathouse on the side lawn of Herrick House,
looking out one of the bay windows. It's a blue-sky day and the ocean is
glass. I get the idea to go down to the dock to dangle my feet. When I turn
around, suddenly I'm in the bunk room at Mount Hope. Cheez is standing
there, holding a geography book like a teacher. With the eraser end of a
pencil, she's pointing to a map of Southeast Asia. Tapping the page, again
and again, in two-four time, she chants to a drumbeat. "Phuket. Phuket."
She walks toward me. The closer she gets, the louder she yells, until she's
screaming. The veins in her neck are bulging. I back away from her, covering my ears, but that only makes her shout louder. When I bump into
something, I whip around to find Mallory. Her hair is wrapped in a towel
like she just got out of the shower. She crowds me too. I'm trapped between
both girls. "You didn't tell your father, Ava. You didn't do what I told you
to, and now look what happened." With one hand, Mallory yanks the
towel, and her head tips onto her shoulder, it rolls down her arm, it's about
to hit the floor—*

The images were so jumbled and crazy that Ava knew right off it
was a nightmare. Frantically panting, she gripped her sheets and
looked around the room. She felt lost.

No log cabin walls. No Justice. She wasn't at Mount Hope.

No couch against the window. No guitar. She wasn't in her room in Wellesley.

Ava tried to shake those images from her mind, willing things to come clear. Slowly, even in the dim light, the bamboo shades came into focus. She recognized the sloped ceiling inches from her head and the old blueberries-on-cream bedspread pulled up to her chin.

There was no way she dared go back to sleep with the things that lingered there. The tiny clock by her bed was hard to read. God, let it be morning, she thought, as she pulled open the blinds. She finally took a breath when she saw the sun working its way up over the Reach.

The house was quiet. She listened at the top of the stairs for voices. If her dad and James were yakking in the sunroom, she wasn't going down there, especially since she was wearing the same getup as yesterday.

With no place to shop for clothes within walking distance, Ava needed to hunt down old things that had belonged to her mother. It was no good to take baths and showers only to keep putting back on the same Target jeans and sweatshirt.

Bare feet on hardwood, she walked as quietly as she could along the back hallway, away from the stairs, toward the other bedrooms. The one next to hers was her sister's, and Ava walked right in. Nothing about the room seemed familiar. Aside from the watercolor painting, splashes of blue flowers with black circle centers—blue poppies. These were the flowers her sister loved, not the standard orange blooms. These were the flowers Ava remembered flooding her mouth and eyes and ears, overtaking her in one of her freak-outs. Poppies mixed up in a memory from a painting in a kid's room. *Nothing to be afraid of,* she told herself.

Trying to tease something nice from the mist and fog that was her brain, Ava touched Poppy's spread, ran her hand over the arm of her chair; she picked up her pillow and squeezed it. Poppy wasn't a scaredy-cat kid who begged her sister to sleep in her bed on stormy nights. Ava's sister wasn't afraid of anything. And they didn't play in here. They spent their days outside or in the attic.

The room next to Poppy's belonged to their parents. Ava's

father wasn't staying in there though. After they climbed the stairs on Sunday night, dragging themselves toward sleep, she'd watched him lug his bag to the guest room at the far end of the hallway. He didn't slow his step or touch their closed door; he didn't even turn his head when he'd walked by it.

Dark wood, nothing mysterious on the outside, the glass doorknob was cool to the touch. Ava opened the door to the room, half hoping that like in Poppy's place, there'd be nothing there for her.

Since she'd been back, Ava had noticed most of the rooms in Herrick House didn't hold their personal things. Aside from a few books, lamps and furniture, the stuff that made the house a summer home—that said real people lived there—was gone. Ava and her father hadn't been inside the place for eight years. Which in a way made it more annoying that he made James sleep in the boathouse.

Her parents' room was no exception to the new house rules. Their wedding picture wasn't on the nightstand, and neither was the one of two sisters sitting in the rowboat, with their lips stained by cherry Popsicles. No bottles of lavender perfume were there to uncork, to help her call up her mother's scent. Bureau drawers were empty. The wardrobe stood vacant.

Then click. There's a picture in Ava's mind of her mother reaching behind her back to zip up a fancy dress. Poppy's jumping on the bed. Click again. Her mother turns from the mirror to wipe Ava's tears, saying, "Be a big girl. Set a good example for your sister. Daddy and I won't be gone long. I'll come home as soon as this silly fundraiser is over."

"Ava. You up here?" Even from the farthest end of the hallway, Ava could hear worry in her father's voice.

"I'm in Mom's room. Looking for clothes."

When he stepped into view, she could tell by his face that he didn't want to come anywhere near that room. He stared hard at her, like it would hurt more to look anywhere else.

"I should've done a better job with the shopping," he said.

"You know, some of your mother's things are in the attic. I'll ask James for the key. Or I could give you some money to go in town."

"Whatever." Ava turned her back on him, taking her sweet time to close the wardrobe.

"It's hard. For me. Being here. You?"

Ava hated it when he didn't speak in complete sentences.

"It's all right."

"I've got to go pick up groceries. Get the mail forwarded. You could come."

"No thanks."

It was strange to feel so mixed up about him. Ava walked by her dad, wishing she felt brave enough to brush against him. To make a little contact with someone who wasn't hitting her in the head or smacking her in the face. Except she still blamed him. For sending her to Mount Hope. For being so hard to talk to about Mom and Poppy in the first place.

He followed her, hanging on the threshold of her room.

"We could go to Blue Hill or as far as Ellsworth if you want. Check things out together. See what's the same and what's changed."

"Maybe later," Ava said, crawling back into her bed, pulling her spread over her head.

Her dad didn't stomp out of her room into the hallway or down the stairs like he was angry. His feet said he was hurt. His lonely steps took him right out of the house, leaving her alone again.

Under the covers, the sharp edge of her dream found her.

Mallory wasn't even in the room and she was making Ava feel guilty for not telling her dad about Mount Hope and why she did what she did. What Ava couldn't figure out was whether bashing her head in had been Mallory's plan all along, or if the place finally made her lose it? Ava and her father would need to be speaking in paragraphs before they could talk about that. The least she could do was find out if her roommate was okay, and according to James there was a working phone in the boathouse.

Hunting for her socks and boots, Ava found a pair of old flip-flops shoved in a corner under her bed. They were too small for her, but not by much, and something from Maine was miles better than anything from Mount Hope. Ava crammed the boots into her wastebasket and went downstairs.

Whether on a mission or not, she was ready to get outside. The quiet house spooked her. The breeze coming up from the Reach made her shiver, but the dew on her toes felt so familiar, so good. The hedges that fenced in the side lawn were overgrown, not flat and cut short the way they were when she and Poppy played hide-and-seek there. Back then it was a maze of a place decorated with petal-layered peonies and color-by-number roses.

Standing there by herself in the middle of May, looking at the tips of those neglected plants starting to turn green, Ava remembered a day when she was lying on the grass staring at clouds, searching for hidden pictures with her sister. Ava and Poppy wore shorts over their bathing suits like they did most summer days. Poppy was loving all things plaid and Ava was stuck in a polka-dot phase.

"There's a bouquet of goldenrod and a bunch of black-eyed Susans," Poppy said, pointing to a white ball of nothing.

"You can't say you see specific flowers. Clouds don't come in color," Ava said, trying to decide if the glob of fluff she had her eyes on looked more like an elephant or a butterfly.

"Can too," Poppy said. "It's an imagination game, Ava. I'm using mine is all." Poppy leaned her shoulder into her sister's, encouraging her not to be so serious. "When I grow up," she said, "everyone in my family is going to be named for a flower. Like me. I like Zinnia for a girl, don't you?"

Mom had been reading two chapters every night of Chasing Redbird. Ava liked the main character too, but not enough to name a kid after her.

"What about your husband? Boys aren't named after flowers, you nut."

"I'm going to marry a guy named Salvia. I'll call him Sal for short."

There was a pause, and then both girls started laughing. Holding their stomachs, bumping into each other as they rolled around in the grass. Ava and Poppy scrambled to their feet and started running after each other through the garden, in and out of the hedges, down the path to the boathouse.

Now eight years later, walking through the same yard, Ava remembered coming to a dead stop when they saw their parents arguing. Mom was yelling, her face all red and tight. Dad held on to her arm. Neither of them noticed the girls standing there.

"Please go," he said.

Mom's shoulders were hunched, and she bit her lip, trying to pull away.

And then, like that, the memory went dark.

In front of the boathouse, Ava closed her eyes, hoping she could dig up something more. She lifted her head, breathed in through her nose, desperate for some smell to glide in on a breeze, bringing another detail along with it. One minute, then two, she waited. But nothing came.

It felt weird trying to work things loose after spending so much time trying to push them back where they came from. At home in Maine, it felt like the only place in the world where Ava could trust the memories would find her, and that when they did, she'd be ready.

The boathouse was more weathered than it had been when she was little. Shingles were missing in places, and the windows on the coast side had masking tape Xs, meant for storm winds.

Being on the side with the best light, Ava leaned up to the window, putting a hand over her eyes to block the sun. It was hard to see in through the grime. Zany shapes and their playmates tricked her eyes. She couldn't make out what was inside. Inching along the building till she came to the front, Ava tried the door. It took some effort to push it open.

"If you wanted me to show you around, all you had to do was ask."

The deep voice startled her, and she turned to see James standing there holding a brown paper bag with red lettering.

"You scared the shit out of me," she said.

"Didn't mean to. You're the one who came to pay a visit."

"I'm not visiting. I need to use the phone."

"Coulda asked to do that too." James moved into the boathouse and pulled a string dangling from the ceiling in the middle of the room. A bright bulb lit up the place, and Ava still had no idea what she was looking at. Her hands and feet started to go numb the way they did when she was getting sucked into one of her blackouts. The urge to run was fierce, but Ava couldn't move. James didn't look anything like Justice or Benno, and his vibe was a lot calmer, and still she didn't feel like being alone with him.

James pushed aside a giant pair of gloves and a sci-fi kind of helmet so he could put the Ace hardware bag down on a long metal table. It reminded her of the ones they had in science lab at Wellesley High.

A crazy collection of things lay this way and that, top to bottom, all over the boathouse. Copper leaves attached to plumbing pipes hung from the ceiling. Coils upon coils of metal circles, like a Slinky gone haywire, sat on a square wooden platform on the floor. A mangled blue bike had been mounted on the wall.

"I'm a sculptor," James said, pulling more pipes from his hardware store bag.

"It's a studio," Ava said, as more of a fact than a question.

"When my uncle got sick and I took over the caretaking, your dad offered to let me work here in exchange for helping out. I live with my aunt over by Walker Pond."

She wanted to go in and look around, to keep taking in all his cool stuff, but it was smarter, safer, to stay where she was, to keep her eyes on the guy.

James took the phone from its base and walked halfway to her. Stopping in the middle of the cluttered space, he seemed to know not to come too close. "If I put 911 on speed dial and let you have this, will you come in and close the door? Squirrels have a thing for my space." When he glanced at her feet in those little-girl flip-flops, he smiled.

There was a sliver space between his two front teeth and a tiny hollow in one cheek. Not deep enough to call a dimple, more like a dent he might make in one of the pieces he was working on. All his imperfections, including the two scars, should've added up to a face not much worth looking at. But somehow, all put together, James was some kind of beautiful.

Ava didn't take the phone. After closing the door, she walked toward a torn seat that came from an old car. A metal stick figure sat there, her arms empty, as though she were waiting for something to drop.

James took his time putting his supplies away, while Ava circled his sculptures one by one. Every few feet she stopped to take in the ordinary junk that James had turned into remarkable pieces.

"How do you know what'll look good together?" she asked, touching an iron woman's hand.

"I went to art school for a year and a half. Now, mostly, I get a feeling and I trust it."

"Something inspires you and somehow you know what to do with it. You relax and the piece comes to you."

James nodded, but he didn't say anything else. Maybe he was superstitious when it came to his art. Sometimes talking about what inspired something wrecked it. Ava didn't tell him it was the same with her music. With writing her songs.

"I've got a few things I need to do for your father," he said, trying once again to hand her the phone. "Stay as long as you want. When you're done, shut the light off and close the door, okay? You can leave it unlocked." There was that smile again.

"That reminds me," Ava said. "Do you have my dad's key to the attic? He said you'd know where it is."

"I gave it to him on my way out. Saw him put it in his jacket pocket."

Ava needed that key. She felt ready now to go up to the attic. Happy memories would be waiting for her there.

TWENTY-TWO

Toby couldn't remember the last time he stood in Biddie Purcell's kitchen. Stuck in a time warp, Lorraine's best friend from childhood used steady hands to pour coffee from a percolator.

"Don't just stand there," she said. "Make yourself useful."

Toby reached into the hutch and pulled two of her mother's plates out, setting the chipped china down on the plank-top table, scratched and stained. Biddie cut slices of cranberry loaf right out of the cast-iron pan, putting a sliver in front of him.

"You don't look surprised to see me," he said. Disappointed with the size of the piece on his plate, nonetheless Toby took a large bite of the buttery bread.

"It's Maine," Biddie said. "People been talking 'bout you since you drove 'round Walker Pond Sunday night. I knew you'd come when you were good and ready."

Biddie's name had never suited her; it belonged to an old lady. Bridget Cornish Purcell was Toby's age, and even she wouldn't use the word *lady* to describe herself. Rough around the edges, her hair pinned up in a sloppy bun, she wore a pair of overalls that could easily have come from the closet of her recently deceased husband. Biddie was as plain as the house she lived in. Yet there was nothing modest about the view from her window. Her home sat spitting distance from where Lorraine's family home had been, nearly two miles from Herrick House on a parcel of land off North Deer Isle Road overlooking the part of the Reach called the Punch Bowl.

"It's hard to believe Charlie's gone," Toby said, taking a bite so big it nearly choked him. He took a swig to wash it down. "Sitting here, I almost expect him to bang through that door, smack me on the back and tell me a story about some annoying summer person."

"I miss that Charlie too," Biddie said, tucking a stray piece of hair behind her ear. "He wasn't like that for some time. You wouldn't have recognized him. Awful to say, but it was a blessing when he passed."

Toby rearranged the napkin on his lap, trying to draw less attention to his gut. Giving up, he leaned forward, putting an elbow on the table. He wondered if Biddie recognized him after all these years. The summer before Toby took his family to Thailand, he hadn't been protected by a shield of extra flesh.

"He looked like a skeleton." Biddie stared at Toby over the rim of her mug. "Couldn't do a single thing without help, which a-course he hated. Thank goodness James dropped what he was doing to come live with us and help me out."

"I'm so sorry," Toby said.

This would be where Lorraine would touch Biddie's arm, rubbing the sleeve of her flannel shirt, soft and worn. Certainly now would be the time to bring up Biddie's other loss, of her other nephew and James's cousin—little Bobby Carmichael. Toby just sat there.

"I couldn't handle coming over here, after—" He couldn't say *Lorraine* and *Poppy*. Their names burned in the back of his throat. "No excuse," he said. "I should've at least come to see you when Charlie got sick. Some friend I turned out to be."

Toby used a finger to press one crumb on top of the other on his plate. He was afraid to look at Biddie, for fear there'd be some sign she held a grudge.

"For godsake, take another piece," she said.

He looked over to see the same bland expression she'd had on when she'd met him at the back door, as if she'd seen him just last week. Biddie had a history of being quick to lose her patience with Toby. But after all this time, she was calm with him. Detached in a similar way to Ava.

Toby always told Lorraine that Biddie didn't like him. She held him personally responsible for Lorraine leaving Maine. And she resented him for his money. The last time he'd seen her, she'd come right out and said so.

It was Labor Day weekend, and the Sedgwicks were sharing Sunday supper with the Purcells. Toby leaned back in the porch chair next to Lorraine. Errant spikes of loose wicker poked him from behind. Trying to get more comfortable, he propped his feet up on the railing. Flakes of paint fell onto the deck as he crossed his legs at the ankles.

"Toby, look at the mess you're making," Lorraine said. "You'll hurt her feelings if she sees that."

"It's not my fault. I'm not the one who needs to get out here with a paintbrush."

He took his feet down and blew the chips through the slats, never taking his eyes off his girls and Biddie's nephew, Bobby. All three children played tag in the side yard, weaving in and around Charlie's rusted-out truck. Toby felt bad for the boy with the Coke bottle glasses strapped tight to the back of his head. Geez, the way the poor kid ran was awkward as hell. Back at Herrick House, he'd meant to ask Lorraine why the boy had stayed on longer than usual this summer. Amid the commotion of getting ready to come here, he'd been sidetracked by Ava begging him to help her find her flip-flops.

Bouncer started in on his nonstop barking. Once Charlie's Doberman got going, he didn't pause for a breath. Poppy was standing two feet from the end of the dog's chain, waving a tennis ball, jazzing the dog up to play a game with her. Bouncer got more excited with every circle he completed.

"Poppy, don't tease the dog," Lorraine said.

"I'm not. I want to play with him, don't I, boy?" Poppy kept waving the ball.

"Bouncer, quiet," Biddie shouted through the screen. She carried a full tray of gin and tonics and was trying to maneuver the door with her elbow. Toby was about to get up to open it for her when Ava scrambled onto the porch and jumped into his arms, landing full force in his lap.

He rubbed his daughter's back and patted her shoulder in the time it took to catch his breath. "No one's taking Bouncer off the chain while we're here," he said.

Lorraine hopped up to get the door for her friend, holding it open to let Charlie through too. He carried a platter loaded with top-notch steaks; Toby's contribution to the meal.

"Kids, you've got about twenty minutes to ride them bikes," Charlie said. "I'll ring the bell when the chow's ready."

Ava hesitated to go down the steps toward Poppy and Bobby. "Go ahead," Toby said. "Bouncer can't reach you."

In seconds, Ava was on her bike, riding down the lane to catch up with Poppy and the boy.

"You'd never know those two are sisters. One fearless. The other afraid of dogs, bears, and thunderstorms," Toby said to Charlie. "And you should see Ava near the water."

"Who can blame her?" Lorraine asked. "After falling out of that boat the way she did. It's all my fault." Toby's wife rubbed her arms as if overtaken by a chill.

"By the end of the year, Ava could be swimming like a fish without an ounce of worry, if you'd agree to come with me," he said, putting his feet back up on the railing a little too loudly. Paint flaked off again, this time sprinkling down on the deck right in front of Biddie.

"I'd only spend a couple hours a day checking in on the Thai projects and the rest of the time I'd be with you and the girls," Toby said. "We could stay as long as you like. It's a perfect place to teach her."

Lorraine didn't say anything.

He could've kicked himself for rambling, for bringing it up yet again. This time in front of friends. So he tried to make light of it. "Charlie, you up for a trip to paradise if I can't convince Lorraine to go?"

"Dinner's almost ready," his wife said, pushing out of her chair. "I'll go get the children." Lorraine changed the subject by leaving. Now if Toby had done that, he'd get a ration. She'd accuse him of shutting her down.

"You can't make Lorraine happy by promising to take a little time off," Biddie said. "One vacation with the wife and kids isn't going to change what she wants."

Without looking at Toby, Biddie brushed the paint chips from under his feet off the deck with her bare hands. Clapping them together, as if to say *I'm done with you*, she started humming "Can't Buy Me Love."

Toby knew what Lorraine wanted. For him to work less. For their family to live more simply by moving back to Maine. That's all she ever talked about.

Eight years later, the two remaining friends were quiet with each other. Sitting at Biddie's kitchen table, the only sounds came from Toby chewing in unison with the buzz and bubble of the filter inside the fish tank over by the hutch. Watching the unremarkable guppies make lazy circles around their boxy home, Toby resolved to walk more now that he was faced with free time and great views. He was tired of people checking him out, never in a good way.

Trying to distract himself with things like food and fish and coastal views wasn't working. After that Sunday supper at Biddie and Charlie's, Toby and his wife put their girls to bed. When the girls were tucked in, Toby followed Lorraine into the sunroom where she'd begun tidying up, packing boxes with the toys and books Ava and Poppy would want back in Wellesley. The Sedgwicks would spend yet another Labor Day in bumper-to-bumper traffic, getting home in time for the first day of school.

"Please talk to me," Toby said, taking a stack of books from her hands and placing them inside a cardboard box.

Lorraine busied herself, dusting tables, closing drapes, acting like he wasn't even there.

"Okay, I get it," he said. "I'm not paying enough attention to you and the girls. But you know the Foundation is on the verge of going global. We're doing great things for whole communities, Rain. It's not like I'm wasting my time doing something trivial."

"Like I am writing poetry and taking care of our family."

"God, no. You know I didn't mean that. Come on." Toby stood in front of Lorraine, blocking her efforts to fill boxes. "I'll try harder to be home more."

"You've said that before."

"This time it'll be different," Toby said. "My first priority when we get back to Wellesley, is to hire someone to share the workload. Please come with me on the trip. Let me show you I can change. At least promise me you'll think about it."

Toby's head pounded as he went back over things, sitting across from Biddie. Her eyes were on him, and as a result he felt tension spread down his neck and across his shoulder blades.

Biddie slapped another piece of cranberry bread on his plate. "You want to know what people are saying about you and Ava being back?" she asked. "That she got in some kind of trouble, and you couldn't handle her." Biddie nipped a corner of her bread and popped it in her mouth.

"I'll always be the bad guy up here, huh?"

"It's Maine," she said. "Everybody talks, no judgment."

Toby laughed. "You don't believe that for one second. If Charlie were here, he'd say 'Once a summer person always a summer person.'"

"And if Lorraine walked through that door, she'd say you were never a bad guy."

If only Lorraine would walk through that door. "Jesus, Biddie," he said. "I've made a mess of things." Toby threw his napkin down on the table. "Everybody told me the same thing. That Ava's being out-of-control had nothing to do with what happened. She was drinking, doing dangerous things, and I was out of my league. So I sent her to a place her teachers and one of my colleagues swore by. What a disaster. I went up there for the parent weekend and I knew Ava didn't belong there. Next thing I know I'm driving here."

Biddie didn't say anything. Toby was glad she didn't fill the air with platitudes the way Jill so often did. Jesus, Jill. He'd forgotten to tell Ava this morning that she was driving up with files from the office and things from home for her. Would he never learn? He'd been back in Maine less than forty-eight hours, and already he was repeating history, bringing work—with all its baggage—to Herrick House.

"You must've come back for a reason," Biddie said, refilling her mug.

"I don't have a clue what I'm doing. The girl needs a mother or a counselor. Probably both. I think she's starting to remember the whole damn thing."

"No one can replace Lorraine. I'll give you credit for not having done that already. But for chrissakes, tell me the details and then send Ava over here and I'll fill her in. After we talk, I'll put her to work in the garden. A little real work might do a Sedgwick good."

No surprise Biddie wanted to know exactly what happened; it was like her to ask straight out. But Toby couldn't risk anyone else knowing the whole story before his own daughter. He'd tried a few times to open up to Ava about that day, but she looked so fragile, so cut off from him. He couldn't bring himself to do it. Things were getting better between them by inches, not miles. He needed Ava to trust him again. He'd need to be patient and wait for the right time.

"I don't know how long you're sticking around, but I got a friend who works with kids in Bucksport, if you want to go that route."

Biddie reached over to grab a pen and notepad off her cluttered countertop. After scribbling down a name and number, she tore the paper from the pad and handed it to Toby. "My gut tells me it's okay for her to talk about it," she said, looking wistful. "Maybe it's time everyone did."

The minute Biddie finished speaking her piece, Toby knew she was right. He'd known as much after a few hours at Mount Hope. Even though, all along, Ava knowing every detail was exactly what terrified him.

Biddie got up and started clearing the table. "Look, unless you got something else to say, I got work to do 'round here."

He picked up his dishes and brought them to the sink. Thanking Biddie, he walked onto her back porch. Toby paused making a mental note to pay James a little extra to put a fresh coat of paint on those damn railings.

TWENTY-THREE

Toby stood outside Bucks Harbor Market but he wasn't taking in the boats lolling about, moored in rows to the dock. He wasn't people-watching hoping to see a blast from his past. There was no need to run through the checklist in his mind. Between yesterday and today, his errands were done. The groceries were in the backseat, the phone and Internet scheduled to be hooked up at Herrick House tomorrow; he even felt good about reconnecting with his old friend. Though after talking with Biddie, Toby regretted asking Jill to come to town. For some reason, she set his daughter off, and he couldn't jeopardize the progress they were making. It had only been hours ago that Ava and Toby had had a minor breakthrough.

Last night after supper, he'd been sitting in the sunroom reading the paper when he heard creaks coming from the back stairs.

"Hi honey, you feeling better? Sure are catching up on your rest."

"I wasn't sleeping. I'm playing around with some lyrics." Ava turned her back to him to browse the sparsely lined bookshelves next to the fireplace. Her delicate finger slid up and down the spines.

"I'm glad you like it," Toby said. "The journal, I mean."

"I do. Have you seen that small tan book with the palm tree

on the cover? It was Mom's." Ava paused after referring to her mother. "I want to know who wrote the poem 'One day I'll swim, beside your boat, something, something sweet sixteen'?"

Toby suddenly felt guilty for packing up the best volumes. If it weren't so late, he could've shown Ava where he'd put the rest of Lorraine's poetry collection. Instead he got up from his chair and moved next to her, hoping what he did have to offer wouldn't send her back to her room. He reached up to the highest shelf and pulled down a hardback book, its ratty cover frayed top and bottom. "How about this one?" he asked, handing it over.

His daughter flipped it opened, revealing page after page of colored crayon shapes. Sketches of rainbows and tulips, rudimentary shapes of birds and suns, a bunny popping out of a black hat. "Mom was really pissed at me when I drew in here," she said.

"No, honey. Poppy did this. Your mom was upset with her, not you. She couldn't believe that your six-year-old sister didn't know any better, that Poppy thought it was okay to color in one of her treasures. That night after dinner, she was sent to her room without dessert. We found you on the back stairs sneaking Poppy a bowl of ice cream."

"So Mom wasn't mad at me? I don't remember it like that."

"When you mentioned it in one of your letters, I thought as much. But I'll bet you remember that Bucks Harbor Market has the best black raspberry in town. That's still your favorite, right? We could go now, if you want to."

Ava closed the book, holding it tight to her chest. Toby could see her knuckles turn white from squeezing it. "Yeah," she said. "Okay."

Toby grabbed his keys before Ava had the chance to change her mind. Even if all they talked about was scenery and town gossip, it would be a start.

One day later, Toby stood outside Bucks, well aware he was about to screw things up. Yet again. He needed to call Jill's visit off.

He could meet her on the main road to explain his dilemma. Ava was on edge and he didn't want to upset her. Toby dialed Jill's cell.

"Hey, where are you?" Toby asked, barely able to hear her. Her responses all broken up.

Given when he'd last spoken to Jill and where the signal usually got lost on the trip, he tried to figure out where she might be.

"—house," Jill said.

"About that. Can you hear me?"

Toby waited and listened, but all that came through was choppy speech. All he could make out was the word *there*. And then, *already there*.

How the hell did she get up to Maine so fast? Toby got back in his car and raced home, slowing down only on the stretches of single-lane road where cops liked to hide.

Jill's car was in the driveway, but when he came through the front hall, he didn't hear a single sound. Entering the kitchen, he didn't see a thing out of place. It wasn't until he threw his jacket over the back of a chair that he saw them. Jill was sitting in the sunroom staring at Ava. His daughter was turned toward the window.

"If I didn't know better, I'd think you flew here instead of drove," Toby said, looking at Jill, forcing a laugh. Ava held her arms tight; her legs were crossed too. With one foot swinging, her child-size flip-flop made a slapping sound. It might've been Morse code for *I-hate-you-Dad*.

"We appreciate you bringing everything up here," Toby said to fill the void. "Ava and I are going to stay put for a while. I knew she'd want some of her things. Especially her guitar." Toby hoped the mention of his daughter's music might help her to lose the attitude.

"How long?" Ava and Jill said in unison. They'd both turned their heads so fast in his direction he wouldn't have been surprised if one of them got whiplash. His daughter might have had the hint of a smile on her face. Jill most certainly did not.

"For once in my life, I'm going to play it by ear. Ava, will you get the groceries out of the car? Jill and I need to talk a little business. Then I'll make some dinner for the three of us."

Toby felt less ambivalent than he thought he would in their presence. After all, he was the parent and the boss.

Ava dragged herself off the couch and sighed as she trudged out of the sunroom, taking the side door to the lawn.

"Wow, you weren't kidding. She looks awful," Jill said, after

Ava slipped through the screen door. "I think you're out of your league up here. Why don't you let me put you in touch with Becky's therapist? The woman's got a practice in Boston right around the corner from the office."

Toby could no longer see his daughter which meant neither could Jill. She rose from the couch, smoothed out her tight skirt, and walked over to him, standing by the doorway. "Let me help you," she said.

Her voice low and sultry, she caressed his upper arm. With her face inches from his, Toby felt absolutely nothing. Now that he'd made a connection in his mind between her and Biddie, Jill's delicate cologne and the tasteful blouse ruffled around her breasts, much lower than anything she'd worn to the office, did nothing to entice.

Toby backed away and circled behind Jill, taking the lone chair next to the couch.

"I'm in an awkward position here," he said. "I'm grateful to you for coming all the way up here. But I'm not really sure what's going on with Ava. Don't know if I'm doing a single thing right, but something tells me I shouldn't do anything to mess with our routine. I've booked you a room at a terrific B and B in town."

"She doesn't like me."

"That's not true," Toby said, hoping his face didn't betray him.

Situated on the corner cushion of the couch, as close to Toby's chair as was physically possible, Jill slid her hand a little too high on his thigh. Jesus, if Ava came back now, the gap he'd been slowly closing between them would crack wide open.

"You give Ava a lot more power over your life than I think you should," Jill said. "What I learned when Becky was at Mount Hope was that I needed to be her parent, not her friend. I hate seeing you make the same mistake I did."

"Look," Toby said, taking her hand and putting it back on her own knee. He was more than a little annoyed to hear the name of that place. "You've been a terrific friend to me. I don't know what I'd do without you at the office. But I'm not in a good place." Toby stuttered; God, he sounded like he was twelve.

Jill took a throw pillow from the couch and placed it in front of her, covering her blouse, squeezing the perfect square tight. A hard look replaced her seductive one of moments ago. "Of course, I'm only trying to help," she said. "No one knows better than I do what a tumultuous time this is for you. Whatever you need me to do. Say the word."

"One thing I am certain of is that I need you to keep things running smoothly at the office while I get my family act together."

"You're right, this is a bad time. The focus should be on Ava. I want you to know I'm here for you."

"Things are difficult, but that doesn't excuse my selfishness. I shouldn't have dragged you up here." Toby shifted nervously, knowing he needed to be straight with her. "I'm sorry if I've sent any signals that I want more than friendship. Ava is my first and, right now, only priority. But it wouldn't be fair to let you think my feelings are going to change."

He was almost through his truth-fest when Jill got up, smoothed out her skirt, and opened her briefcase, pulling a stack of legal documents from it.

"If you'll sign these, I'll be on my way. I really should be heading back." Jill was all business now, handing him the papers and a pen. He signed one contract after another, torn between looking to be sure they were the same projects he'd endorsed via phone and trying to think of something kind to say, a more effective way to apologize. He wondered if Jill would stand by him work-wise. He couldn't blame her if she quit. He could see now, that he'd been complacent where she was concerned. Self-centered. He had enjoyed their easy way with each other at the office; their dinners after work were pleasant enough. Still, everything he'd told Ava about Jill remained true. He didn't care for her in a romantic way. They weren't dating now, nor would they ever be. So why did it feel as though he'd just broken things off with her?

His cell phone rang inside his shirt pocket, making him scribble a stray line across one of the contracts. He checked the number, and though it wasn't one he recognized, he answered it. He mouthed *sorry* to Jill.

"Toby Sedgwick?" a woman asked. Her voice was familiar, though he couldn't quite place it. "I met you at that hellhole. It's Nan McEttrick."

The call went in and out. Regardless of the poor signal, he wouldn't have been able to hear anything over the racket Ava was making in the kitchen, dropping grocery bags, slamming cabinets. Toby had no idea if Nan could hear him either.

"Mine got more bars over there," Jill said, her mouth tight, her words terse. With a forceful gesture, she pointed out of the sunroom. Anybody looking on would've thought she was ordering Toby out of his own home. Conversely it was a good sign, her offering him even a minimal assist under the circumstances. He hadn't botched things completely.

He started walking toward Ava. "Listen," he said to Nan, "I'm going to hang up. Give me five minutes and I'll call you back from my caretaker's landline."

Toby ended the call as he stepped into the kitchen.

Late afternoon sun streamed in through the window overlooking the Reach, outlining Ava in light. She had Toby's leather jacket over her arm. Standing there so still, she reminded Toby of all the times she'd played freeze-tag with Poppy.

In one hand Ava held the key to the attic, in the other she gripped a slip of paper. He froze too when she turned it around to show him. Bordered in blue, the run-of-the-mill name tag Mallory had given him had a crease down the middle, its edges crumpled from living for two days in Toby's jacket pocket.

Written in black Sharpie, it said, *Get us out before someone dies.*

TWENTY-FOUR

It was Mallory's handwriting for sure. Ava had watched her bunkhouse roommate write in her Mount Hope workbook enough times to recognize it right off. It gave her chills to read those words scratched out on that slip of paper. Her dad looked like he was going to steal one of her moves, ending up on the floor. Ava pulled out a kitchen chair and motioned for him to sit. There was no way he'd be in for an easy landing.

"Mallory's fine," she said. "I called the hospital in Plattsburgh a few hours ago. She's in stable condition." As soon as Ava said it, she felt less confident than when she'd been talking to the nurse, surrounded by James's artwork. She'd been so glad to find out Mallory was alive that she didn't stop to think about what that sentence meant.

"That's good, right?" she asked.

Her dad nodded, reaching out to take the name tag. Ava couldn't tell if he was saying yes to her question, or if he was onto her. "You know her, don't you?" he asked. "You lied to the detective."

He bent over, putting his head as close to his knees as it would go.

That's when annoying Jill came in. Ava wasn't about to spill things in front of her. Why did she have to butt in, especially up here in Maine? Wearing that stupid blouse and enough perfume for three people, could she be any more obvious that she was after her dad and his money?

"Oh, God, are you all right?" Jill asked, acting all fake. She bent down to get a better look at his face, feeling one cheek then the other with the back of her hand. Ava wet a few paper towels and smoothed them out over the back of his neck. Jill must've heard him accuse her of lying, because when he wasn't looking, she shot her a glare that rivaled one of the ones Ava used to get from Justice.

"You don't look well. I'm calling an ambulance," Jill said.

"No, no, I'm all right." He slid the note from Mallory into his wallet, right in front of the detective's business card. Patting his face with the paper towels, he stood. "See what happens when I skip lunch." He rubbed his stomach, trying to make a joke. "Really, I'm fine, just wiped out from everything."

By everything, he meant Ava.

"Mind if I rescind my dinner invitation?" he asked.

Jill looked pissed. Ava wanted to thank Mallory right out loud for doing her such a huge favor, sending Jill on her way.

"Your color's awful," Jill said. "I wouldn't feel right leaving you. Why don't you let me make you an omelet or something?" She pointed to the carton of eggs on the counter, which, at that very moment, Ava decided to step in front of.

"He won't be alone," she said. "I'm here. And our caretaker's right out in the boathouse. The kid works late every night. Dad, I'm going to make pancakes, okay?"

Her father took advantage of Ava backing him up, by putting his arm around her. "Perfect. With blueberries, please." He smiled and thanked her with a squeeze.

In the beginning, when he'd first hired Jill, Ava was young and she didn't pay any attention to her. Later, when her father spent more time with her, supposedly doing business, something about Jill bugged her. Once her father asked her why she didn't like Jill, so Ava told him straight out how she gave her dirty looks when he wasn't looking. How she always brought up her psycho daughter, Becky, telling Ava how great the girl was compared to her.

Standing there now, looking at Jill, Ava had no trouble pinpointing exactly why she hated her. She had to be the one to tell her father about Mount Hope. Ava had heard so many kids tell their stories during The Circle that she started to see things clearly. Jill wanted her out of her way so she could have her father to herself.

"I'll walk you out," he said to Jill.

As she turned toward the sunroom to go get her things, Ava overheard her say, "Please know, I'll do whatever I can to help you."

Her father stopped on the threshold separating the kitchen from the sunroom. He pointed a finger at Ava, warning her to be nice or to wait there, she couldn't tell which. Either way, she knew she was in trouble.

"Thanks for bringing my guitar," she called after Jill.

Five points to Ava for being polite.

It had been almost an hour since Jill brought her guitar case into the sunroom. When Ava first saw it, all she wanted to do was flip open all four latches and pull the instrument onto her lap. But she wouldn't play it in front of Jill. She wouldn't share that part of herself with the person who'd tried to get rid of her.

Now that Jill was out of there, Ava could hear the music calling her. Lifting the guitar from the velvet lining, she didn't even take the time to sling the vintage strap over her head. The strings burned her fingers as she strummed. One splinter from Mount Hope was still lodged in her finger. She didn't care. Finger-picking one of her songs, a river of emotion rushed from her.

It was the perfect tune for how she felt. The chords, the dynamics, even the lyrics, came back to Ava as if she'd played it yesterday. In the middle of singing—*you are silent rain, I am paralyzed*—she sensed her father there. Ava covered the strings with her palm to stop them from vibrating. When she dared to look up, the afternoon light had to be playing tricks on her. Her dad never cried.

"I promised to return that call," he said, pressing his lips together. "Then we need to deal with some things."

Obviously, the things they needed to deal with involved Mount Hope and the detective.

Jill had one thing right. Her dad did look terrible. Ava wondered if he still didn't feel good or if he was freaked out by Mallory's note.

"It's a nice night. Walk with me," he said.

Ava put her guitar back in the case and went to him.

"I'm sorry I sent you there. It's obvious to me now, you didn't belong there with those kids. Mallory seems like a very troubled girl." He held open the door to the lawn. "And I should've told you Jill was coming. I wasn't trying to keep it from you, or even surprise you with your guitar. All I can say is sometimes I'm clueless."

Ava brushed past her dad, letting their sides touch. Not one foot apart, they took the path to the boathouse. When he owned up to making mistakes, she could relate. Away from Wellesley and out of Mount Hope, Ava could see she was partly to blame for the mess they were in. Maybe he deserved another chance.

She was about to tell him that no one belonged at Mount Hope and that the detective should take a closer look inside the place, when her dad pulled her toward him. He kissed her on the forehead. "I'm glad we came to Maine," he said.

Like a scene out of a fairy tale, his kindness broke the spell that evil place had over her. Suddenly, standing above the Reach with her father, it was easier to pretend Mount Hope never happened.

TWENTY-FIVE

While her father took care of business, making his call, Ava went back to her guitar. Sitting on her mom's couch in the sunroom, she played her favorites. Songs by legendary writers Ava knew by heart and some songs she'd written herself a long time ago. It was getting harder to play with that one finger throbbing, calling to mind Mount Hope. It was as if Mallory were sitting next to her, taunting her, telling Ava to go back out to the boathouse and tell her father everything she knew about the place.

As Ava mulled things over between songs, she heard a knock. It felt weird to be proud of herself for not jumping.

"You're good," James said, pointing to the fireplace. "Mind if I work in here?"

It was his job to close the house down for the night, and right then it bothered Ava that she and her father made him do it.

"Sure, go ahead."

She didn't have the guts to keep playing in front of James, so she bought time tuning her guitar, turning the pegs, plucking the strings. The sliver, wedged deep in her finger, wouldn't cooperate, finally making her wince.

"You okay?" James turned from stoking embers. Before Ava could say anything, he walked toward her, sat down on the couch, and asked without words if he could take her hand to inspect it.

"You wouldn't believe how many of these I get, working with the things I do," he said.

James turned her finger side to side, massaging it, seeing if he could coax the stubborn thing out. Everything about him was warm, his fingers holding hers, his knee touching hers, his voice. A prickly feeling that usually frightened Ava radiated down her arms and legs. Her heart beat light and fluttery but it didn't knock on her chest from the inside out like it did when she was about to freak out.

"I could take it out," he said. "Be a shame to have something so small keep you from playing."

All Ava could do was nod. James went into the kitchen. She could hear him opening and closing drawers. As the water ran, the ancient pipes made an embarrassing racket. When he came back he had exactly what he needed. James knew where things were in Herrick House better than she did.

The bowl of water, a box of matches, and the Band-Aids didn't slay her. The miniature first aid kit that belonged to her mother, covered with Poppy's heart-shaped stickers, would've knocked her down if Ava hadn't already been sitting.

Without James telling her to, she put as much of her hand in the bowl of sudsy water as she could. He pulled a long needle from the kit and lit a match. The burnt smell made her dizzy. Or maybe James did, when he took her hand and patted it dry with a towel.

Laying the needle lengthwise across her skin, below the deepest end of the splinter, he pressed down, slowly rolling the needle upward. The pressure beneath the sliver and the upward motion prodded it to inch forward. James was patient and gentle, and when that wasn't enough to work the splinter free, he pierced her finger, exposing only enough skin so he could give the piece of wood a tiny push.

"It'll be tender for maybe a day, but it won't hurt as much as before." He removed what was left of the splinter with a pair of tweezers and wrapped the Band-Aid around her finger. Ava didn't want the operation to be over.

"I haven't played in a while," she said. "It'll take a few weeks at least to build calluses."

"That's something you want, right?" James turned her palms up, and with one of his paint-flecked fingers, he touched them. It felt electric. Ava told herself she could handle it if he kissed her.

"I should get going," James said. "Got more to do 'round here before I do some work of my own."

James collected the bowl and the towel. Ava picked up the first aid kit, trying to remember the last time she'd seen her mother use it. Had it been on her?

Ava didn't want James to go. Her father would be back from the boathouse any minute, and she wasn't sure she wanted to talk to him now.

James moved through the downstairs closing windows and pulling drapes. He called back over his shoulder, "See ya, Ava."

After he let himself out, Ava remembered the key to the attic. Earlier she had found it exactly where James said it would be, inside her father's coat pocket. Right next to Mallory's note.

As much as Ava wanted to head up there now to get a look around, she couldn't make herself do it. Bats came out at night. And like Mallory had said, the dark's the worst. Sick of always being so afraid, and liking that right then, thanks to James, Ava felt calm, she'd put it off till morning. Not about to take chances, she'd wait for the sun.

TWENTY-SIX

Ava pulled her boots back out of the trash and laced them; she grabbed her old tennis racket. The steps to the attic were sturdy, the floors solid. Nothing creaked as she climbed. Without cobwebs, it wasn't like she'd stepped into one of those scary movies, but it wasn't pretty either. Plastic containers filled with her mother's things outlined a path. Electrical cords dangled, swinging rafter to rafter. Screens for windows of all sizes fit snugly under the eaves. Rolls of pink fluffy stuff she and Poppy had been told never to touch were stacked in a corner.

It was hard to know where to start.

Ava went straight for the window on the ocean side of the house, hoping light could give her some direction and calm her nerves. Stretching her hand out to yank the pull of the shade, she jumped back, ready to swing if she had to. Armed and afraid of bats in the attic, Ava's mind slipped back to Mount Hope. The noise the shade made hitting the casing reminded her of that morning in the bunk room when Mallory let go of theirs by accident, sending Cheez popping up, her hands stretched out ready for battle.

Thankfully the light illuminated a familiar box. The capital letters written on the cardboard invited her right over. Suddenly Ava wasn't worried about finding clothes or hunting for memories.

All she wanted to do was open the box marked BOOKS to find her mother's copy of *Blueberries for Sal.*

The spine crackled, and a mildewy smell wafted out from the inside. Ava took her time turning the pages, running her hand over the picture of Sal holding her tin pail in one hand, a blueberry to her lips. And like that, Ava was far away from Mount Hope and safe at home. The memory of her mother reading to her didn't come by way of a dream or as part of any freak-out. It was as clear and real to her as the book she held in her lap.

Mom sat on the lumpy green couch in the sunroom wearing shorts over her bathing suit like Poppy and Ava always did. The book lay in the hollow her legs made. There was no fire in the fireplace. It was August, and they were taking a break from the intensity of the midday sun. Mom was in the middle, Poppy on one side, Ava on the other. It didn't matter how many times she read those books to them, or that they were capable of reading more difficult ones on their own. There was magic in the words written by the man who was practically their neighbor. Robert McCloskey lived over on Scott Island, a short boat ride from Bucks Harbor Landing. Poppy and Ava had never met him, but Mom and Mrs. Purcell sure had. His signature was in every one of her books to prove it.

"I have an idea," Mom said, pausing on the page where Sal's looking behind a big rock. "You girls remember picking blueberries on Caterpillar Mountain, over by Walker Pond?"

"Is that the place I fell down and ripped my jeans?" Poppy asked, trying to turn the page.

"That was last week," Ava said, placing a hand over Poppy's, not wanting her to read ahead. "We haven't picked berries yet this summer."

"I have," she said, putting her fingers over her mouth, her eyes shifting toward our mother.

Ava's sister was one of those kids full of surprises; you never knew what she'd do next. Dad said her name suited her. Poppy— the wild flower.

Mom gave her a worried look.

Poppy smiled big. "Kidding." Lowering her voice, Poppy tried to sound like Dad, parroting something else he was always saying.

"Never pick and eat anything without showing it to a grown-up."

Mom playfully elbowed Poppy, then tapped the book. "Some people say this story took place on Blueberry Hill," she said. "But Mr. McCloskey told me, Caterpillar Mountain was the real inspiration. I say we pretend to be Sal and her mother. Let's go there to act out the story like a play. What do you girls think?"

"What about the bears?" Ava asked, trying not to sound anxious.

"We'll use our imaginations," Poppy said, reaching across their mother's lap to elbow Ava the way her Mom had just elbowed her.

Ava didn't ask about bears on that mountain because she'd be disappointed if they weren't there. She worried they would be there.

"I'll go tell Dad," Poppy said. "He'll want to come." She slipped off the couch and went running toward the dining room where their father was working, even though he was supposed to be on vacation.

"There's only one girl in the story, and there aren't any dads," Ava said.

Mom closed the book and tidied the stacks piled on the floor, as if she hadn't heard her. "He'll be too busy. It'll just be us," Mom said quietly, talking to herself.

Mom had been right.

Carrying tin pails and pretending there were bears on that hillside turned out to be fun. Poppy kept trying to get the *plink-plunk* of a blueberry landing in her pail to sound exactly the way Mom said it when she read from the book. Ava filled her pail with perfectly ripe berries. They decided to go home when Mom's eyes wouldn't stop watering. "Too much sunlight," she'd said, even though Ava knew those tears had something to do with Dad.

Ava couldn't remember much of the rest of that day or if Mom read to them that night. What she could remember was having bad dreams about bears. The next morning, she was wiped out from having spent hours running in circles and trying to find good places to hide on the side of Caterpillar Mountain.

Poppy leaned on her door. A muffled "Good morning" came through cotton as she struggled to get her sweatshirt over her head.

"Need help?" Ava asked.

"I can do it myself," Poppy said. Once her head popped out, she tipped her nose up and breathed deep, sniffing the air like a puppy. "Mmmm good."

The smell of bacon lured the girls downstairs. It got stronger the closer they came to the kitchen. Dad stood at the counter chopping potatoes. Poppy and Ava turned their heads, looking at each other, puzzled. Eggs weren't sizzling in a skillet, cooked by Mom. Instead bacon and onions were hiding in the bottom of the giant pot she used for making chowder.

"You girls had so much fun yesterday, I thought we'd surprise Mom today by acting out her favorite McCloskey story."

Poppy jumped up and down in the kitchen, twirling around shouting "Yay!" *One Morning in Maine* was everybody's favorite.

All these years later, sitting on the floor in the attic, Ava could've paused the memory right there, happy to have called one up without sweating, choking, or fainting. Closing one book, she could've turned off the movie, saving it to watch another time or not at all, the choice was hers. With her eyes wide open, Ava dug into the box looking for that much-beloved story. Flipping through its pages, even with some part of her not wanting to, Ava felt brave enough to go back to that day.

Before Mom had taken three steps into the kitchen, Dad poured her a cup of coffee and kissed her on the lips.

"Happy Mother's Day, Rain," he said, pulling out a chair, setting the mug down on the table. "Who says it has to be celebrated on a certain day in May?"

Dad retied the loose strings around and around his waist. Wearing Mom's flowery apron over his shorts, his skinny legs stuck out underneath, making him look like a Popsicle.

"As I recall you worked that Sunday." Mom didn't sound mad. Her smile told everybody she was kidding. She held her mug in one hand and stuck her other one out to protect her coffee, afraid it might get knocked over because Poppy wouldn't quit spinning.

Dad took her sister by the hand to a chair and put a glass of milk in front of her. "Not today, I'm not," he said.

At first, it bothered Ava that they weren't acting the story out exactly as Mr. McCloskey had written it. In *One Morning in Maine,*

Sal and her father do the clamming. The mother and sister stay home, counting out the milk bottles to go to Mr. Condon's store. They'd skipped that part and went straight to the shore. Bored with digging, Poppy skipped stones across the water. She said she wanted to pull out a tooth and lose it in the muck like Sal did. Mom told her she was to do no such thing. Teeth came out when they were good and ready. When Poppy wasn't looking, Dad handed Ava a flawless seashell he'd found on the beach. "It's perfectly fine for Sal to have her story, and for you to have your own," he said.

Less than an hour later they got into Dad's boat to head for Bucks Harbor. They were going to eat ice cream before chowder. Mom hopped in and started the motor. She loved to rev the engine. He buckled their life jackets and then one by one lifted Ava and Poppy into the boat.

"I want to sit on that bench," Poppy said, pointing to the one her sister had taken nearest Dad.

"Sit near Mom for now," he said. "You and Ava can switch on the ride back."

"That's fair," Poppy said cheerfully.

Ava leaned into Dad, hugging him a little, happy to have him all to herself. Mom angled the boat out and away from Bucks Harbor. She turned her face into the wind, letting her hair fly in the breeze.

"Hey, where are we going?" Ava shouted above the noise the wind and motor made.

"I'm taking us for a spin around Scott Island, including Mr. McCloskey in our perfect day," she said.

It was hard to see his house from the water, but the idea of circling a real author's island seemed pretty great to Ava. Cruising in and around Bucks Landing made their story a little more like Sal's. Ava reached into her pocket to make sure the shell was still there. Mom and Dad kept tossing happy faces back and forth across the boat, finally looking the way people should on vacation. Dad scoped out the shoreline. Mom watched where they were headed. Ava closed her eyes and invited the sun to rest its rays on her.

When the boat leaned a little, Ava's eyes popped open but there was nothing to worry about. Mom was swinging them around, pointing the boat toward the landing. Time for ice cream.

That's when Ava saw Poppy on her feet, making a move toward the front bench. She must've thought it was time to switch places. Ava leaned forward to reach out to her sister. All of a sudden it was Ava being lifted from her wooden seat, raised up by the wind, tossed into the air. Seconds later her body slapped the surface hard, and the ocean sucked her down and down.

Heavy footfalls echoed up the stairs to the attic pulling Ava from her unpleasant memory. "You up here?" James asked.

She managed to choke out, "Over here."

Before he could duck under the eaves and sit down on the floor across from her, Ava shoved the books back in the box, feeling bummed that she hadn't had the chance to dig a little deeper for Mom's poetry.

"Find anything?" he asked.

"Some old books." Out of breath and sweaty, Ava brushed her hair off her forehead. "My mom's."

She wiped her hands on her jeans, hoping James hadn't noticed how bad she looked.

"You okay? You look sick like your dad did last night when I found him in the boathouse."

"Thanks," Ava said.

"I didn't mean to insult you." He got up to open another window.

"Watch out for bats," she shouted, scrambling to her feet. With the tennis racket held high, Ava backed away from him.

"Doubt there's any up here. My uncle Charlie took pretty good care of your place."

Ava lowered the racket, trying not to look crazy. Just call her Fringe.

"Sorry about your uncle." Ava wished she could've come up with something more original to say.

All she remembered about Mr. Purcell was that his skin was leathery and that he grilled every time their family came over for dinner.

James kept his gaze out the window.

"Sure is hot up here," she said.

"Fresh air will cool it down," he said. "In the meantime, I could drive you to town, if you want. Your dad said you need to buy stuff."

Ava wanted to go with James, and she told him so. It would be nice to get out of Herrick House for a while.

"I'll meet you at my truck," he said.

After James left, Ava reached back into the box. She pulled out *Blueberries for Sal* and *One Morning in Maine*. With Mom and Poppy gone, they were hers to keep.

TWENTY-SEVEN

Toby paced in his caretaker's makeshift studio, rehearsing how to tell Ava they were going back to Mount Hope.

He stopped short in front of a disturbing piece. A stick-figure mother made of metal, holding a stick-figure baby, both of them parked on a remnant car seat. James had told him the sculpture commemorated the woman who died after having a random seizure and crashing into a guardrail on a road off Route 3 in Ellsworth. Her two-week-old infant had been found dead, strapped in his car seat. To be sure it was a beautifully rendered sculpture, a heart-breaking reminder of how fleeting life could be, but Toby didn't see how it would help the father who'd commissioned it.

Ava would be up soon, which meant he needed to stop wasting time trying to make sense of the boy's hodgepodge art work and start thinking of a good way to explain what he planned to do.

He took a seat in front of the work bench. Back-to-back sheets of sticky adhesive trapped shards of pottery inside. The smashed-up mess hadn't been there last night when he'd come in to use James's landline to get in touch with Detective Reilly and return Nan's call.

After leaving a message for Reilly, telling him about the note and asking about Mallory's condition, Toby dialed Nan.

He couldn't believe her impeccable timing, tracking him down at the exact moment Ava had found the haunting note. Strange how after knowing Nan only two days, Toby missed her pluck and spunk.

Right from the start, she'd been someone he could talk to. As ineffectual as he was with Ava, Nan didn't judge him. Looking back on things before Mount Hope, Toby had been going through the motions, working at the Foundation, raising his daughter the best he could. The night the police brought Ava home from the train tracks, something in him broke apart. When he enrolled her at the camp, Toby truly believed he was doing the right thing. But after those parent sessions, and watching Nan go to battle for her nephew Arthur—a boy not even her own child—well, it knocked sense into him. He'd finally found the courage to go up against Pax, to follow his gut and take Ava out.

She picked up on the first ring.

"I found a note," Nan said, her voice cracking. "Under the wiper blade on my car. It says: Get Arthur out, he needs a hospital."

Toby slid the name tag he'd been given out of his wallet. What the hell was going on? How many warnings did the girl give before having her accident?

"You've got to help me," Nan said. "Between my selfish brother, that arrogant director, and a detective who claims his hands are tied, no one will let me take Arthur home. He's still there."

The injustice of Nan's predicament drew him in. He couldn't refuse her. As tough as the whole thing would be on Ava, he wasn't about to leave Herrick House without her. If he explained things right, Ava would see the good they'd be doing. Father and daughter banding together for a good cause. To get Arthur out. Ava knew the ins and outs of Mount Hope and which counselors could be counted on to help them. He had the means and the money. So while listening to Nan, Toby snapped into action. With a confidence he rarely felt when dealing with Ava, he told her, "Yes, let's meet at Bar Harbor Airport."

He heard a truck start up. By the time he maneuvered through the cluttered space to look out the window, James was backing out of the driveway. There was someone in the passenger seat, but from this distance, Toby couldn't be sure it was Ava. Plus she would never be up this early.

Out of the boathouse, down the path, across the side lawn to the sunroom. "Ava, you home?" He took the stairs to her room.

The door was partially closed or halfway open, depending on how he chose to see things.

Resigned to the idea that, ready or not, he would have to come clean, Toby knocked lightly. "Ava?"

She wasn't there. Her hiking boots were crammed into her wastebasket. A tennis racket leaned against the bureau. The clothes he'd bought her at Target were all over the floor. Things were starting to look like home.

Then he noticed her bed, perfectly made, not the usual tangled mass of sheets. Her blueberry-covered spread was tucked in severely where pillow meets headboard; everything about it was neat and tidy.

He undid the spread. As if the edges of those books were knives, he pulled Lorraine's childhood favorites—his daughters' too—from their secret place beneath her pillow.

Years ago, one book had started an argument between husband and wife, while the other, because of his stupid idea to enact it, put Ava in harm's way.

Thinking about how much his girl had been through filled Toby with fresh guilt. Eight years after she fell from that boat, after she'd lost her mother and sister—all thanks to him—what did her so-called protector do? Made everything worse.

An expert at helping other people, Toby had the ability to set this right. And that's what he intended to do. He'd tell Ava they were leaving Maine to make a difference. For Nan. For Arthur. Toby placed the treasured books back under her pillow, tucking in the spread, making it look as close to the way Ava had arranged it as he could. His daughter would see her father's plan was noble. She'd want to help too.

TWENTY-EIGHT

James didn't talk much, but when he did, not a word was wasted.

"What was the camp like?" he asked.

Ava stopped in front of a bronze Native American sculpture parked in the middle of the sidewalk on Main Street in Blue Hill.

"My dad hired guys to drag me out of my bed, shove me in a car, and take me away. They wouldn't tell me where I was going. For hours neither one of them said anything. I still don't get why he did it."

And Ava didn't know why she spilled the things she did to James either. Except he radiated the kind of calm she hadn't known in a friend in a long time. During those last months she'd spent in Wellesley, the kids she'd hung out with weren't peaceful. They were empty inside. And at Mount Hope, one kid after another was even more messed up than she was.

James listened to the stories Ava told about Mount Hope, about spending more time with loneliness and desperation than she had since she was little. As they went in and out of those shops collecting clothes, Ava using the credit card her father left on the sunroom table along with a note that said, *use as you please*, she told James she didn't want to be mad at her dad. Things were better now that they were in Maine, but still there were times when Ava couldn't help resenting what he'd done.

She told him about Mallory. A kid so hopeless, she smashed her head in to get herself out on a medical.

James didn't rush to say stupid things or nod like mad, acting like he knew what Ava had been through. He just kept his pace in line with hers. He walked steady, the rhythm of his steps slow as a ballad. The creases on his forehead were proof he was paying attention. Ava could tell by the collection of contours and curves that showed up on his face as she spoke, lines deep and at the ready, that James had some practice listening to sad stories.

Once, out of the blue, his hand flecked with copper paint touched hers, sending streaks of heat up Ava's arm.

While she hit the fourth store, James waited for her on a street bench. When Ava came out, wearing funky striped cargo capris and a V-neck T-shirt that said FOLK THE WAR, a peace sign where an O should be, a guitar for the L, he looked up from texting.

"Way more you," he said.

The soft fabrics tingled where they were tight against her skin. The clothes felt nice on her body. The new canvas flats felt good on her feet too, not at all like the Mount Hope hiking boots or the Herrick House flip-flops.

"Hungry?" James pointed to a vegan café on the corner of Cross Street. The measured way he spoke didn't bother Ava in the same way her dad's clipped version did. She got the sense that she could ask James anything, and that he'd answer—honestly and completely—even if things came out in short sentences or single words.

His truck was parked in the opposite direction. Ava was about to ask for the keys, so she could run back and throw her stuff in, when he reached out, offering to take the bags off her hands. Waiting at the crosswalk, Ava decided to test her theory about him.

"Are you ever going back to school?" She punched the signal button, once, twice. On the third time, he covered her hand.

"Won't change any faster 'cause you keep pushing."

She didn't want him to let go, but he did.

"Probably not," he said. "I found the kind of sculpture I love to do and I'm getting paid to do it. Sweet deal, don't you think? Caretaking in exchange for an oceanside studio."

"What do you call what you do?"

Ava had taken more music than art classes at Wellesley High, but she'd seen enough paintings with melted clocks and broken faces to know that what James did had a name.

He didn't cross, even though the light flashed WALK. All he did was turn toward her. "Some people call it trash art or junk art. Think it's not really sculpture."

As James talked about his work, his whole body woke up. It was like her question flipped a switch and suddenly he was animated. The bags started swinging as he waved and formed things in midair. Ava could almost see the things he made back at the boathouse—all metal, wood, and glass.

"It's been around for centuries. Gained notoriety in France during the early nineteen hundreds. They called it objet trouvé—found art. Beautiful, huh?"

Ava could've listened to James talk about twisted pipes and broken plates all day. The café they stepped into was full of people—not one table free. She jumped when a phone rang even though it was in his pocket not hers. James put one finger out in front of him, telling Ava to hold on, then stepped outside to take the call.

A waitress a few years older than Ava, with a bird's nest for hair and flour stains all over her shirt, took her name and eyed James through the storefront glass. "Table for two?" she asked.

"Ava?" James walked back in, coming up behind her. "It was your dad. He wants us to meet him for lunch. You up for that?"

She wanted to say no. With James, Ava was having the first real conversation in weeks, maybe months. Why couldn't things stay the way they were? She liked the sound of table for two.

Then the tiny dent in his cheek caved in when he smiled.

No questions asked, she climbed into James's truck and let him drive her to her father.   Ava didn't think anything was wrong until after James turned off Route 3 into the Bar Harbor

Airport parking lot and the terminal building came into view. When Ava and Poppy were little, Dad used to bring them there to watch the planes take off and land. There wasn't any place to eat inside.

"What's going on?" Ava looked at James, trying to gauge how

much he knew about why they were there. It never crossed her mind that this was a trick, that it wasn't about lunch.

"Just said to meet him here." James looked toward the terminal entrance. He was as calm as could be.

"Is he leaving?" Ava asked, banging her hand against the passenger door. "To go back to work?"

"Don't know," James said. "He didn't say."

Ava wasn't going into that airport. She wouldn't give her father the satisfaction of saying goodbye, giving him permission to leave.

Suddenly she didn't want to stay with James either. He'd given her no real reason not to trust him, but now she was wary. Not knowing what to do, Ava gripped the door handle. She felt stranded. Then she heard a sighing noise as James slid his hand across the vinyl seat. When he took hold of hers, he whispered, "Sometimes you gotta ask."

James and Ava walked to the airport entrance. Her dad was sitting in one of those bucket seats, deep in conversation with a woman, the two of them yammering back and forth. The waiting area was filled with more staff than frequent flyers—they were the only two in their row.

"Ava." When her dad stood up, he knocked over a paper bag that had been parked on top of his suitcase. "This is Nan. We were in the same parent session at Mount Hope."

As soon as her dad said where he'd met her, Ava placed her. She was the angry one yelling at Justice in the lodge lobby, and then later at Pax.

Ava's body responded to the recollection. Her skin prickled head to toe. Her chest hurt from not being able to catch her breath. Geared up to run, her feet refused to cooperate. The new canvas flats were stuck to the floor as if she'd landed on a wad of gum in the high school cafeteria.

"Sit here. Come now." Her dad picked up the brown paper bag and pulled a few deli sandwiches from it. "You too, James." He placed them on a table. "Take what you like. That one there's vegetarian."

"Can we stop with this?" Ava didn't care about meeting his friend or eating his lunch. "What are we doing here? Why did you make me come?"

"I need your help," Nan said, toggling her thumb back and forth, aiming first at Ava and then at her dad. "Something's not right at Mount Hope. I want to fly you and your father back to upstate New York to help me get my nephew out."

"You're his aunt," Ava said. When Fringe kept repeating the phrase *Nan can fly* over and over on the Ledges, she'd thought he was just stuck on one more crazy-ass thing. Except right there, through the plate glass window, sitting lonely on the tarmac, was a plane not much bigger than James's truck. "Is that yours?"

"I know this is asking a lot," her dad said. "But we need to get Arthur out and you know the place better than we do."

Ava couldn't believe what he was saying.

"The police need to hear things straight from you. It's the right thing to do." He kept on talking. When he got close enough to Ava to take hold of her elbow she remembered Justice's threat. He'd warned her that eventually her dad would find a way to send her back.

"You're right, you're asking too much." Ava didn't know where to go or what to do. It was getting harder to stand.

Nan marched over, shaking a piece of paper at her, raising her voice so loud that the few people scattered through the terminal turned to look. They probably figured Ava was a brat and Nan her self-sacrificing mother. "Someone left me a note," she said.

Ava didn't have to read the thing Nan waved under her nose to know it was another one of Mallory's notes.

"What if you were still there? You'd want someone to come." Nan's eyes welled up, exactly the way her nephew's did. "Think of how awful you'll feel if anything happens to Arthur. I can't do this by myself," she said. "I've tried."

Ava pointed beyond her to where her father stood. "How do I know you're not going to dump me there again?"

He bent down and unzipped the front pocket of his suitcase. Out came the journal with the turquoise and tangerine cover, the one he'd bought her at Target.

"Because when I gave this to you, I made the same promise you did. No more keeping things from each other. God, Ava, I wouldn't leave you there." He held it out to her. "And so you know,

I didn't read it."

James walked into the circle, taking the journal from her dad. When Ava accepted it from him, it felt like they were playing some kind of game Poppy might've invented.

Nan's words kept ringing in Ava's ears. *What if you were still there?* It was all too overwhelming. It was her fault Fringe got sent to OP in the first place. But go back to Mount Hope?

Ava didn't think she could do it.

"I could come. If you want me to." James cupped Ava's elbow with his hand, and there was that feeling again, warmth traveling throughout her body. "Say the word and I'll get your stuff from my truck."

With barely a nod from her, James pulled his keys from his jeans and took off to the parking lot. She couldn't believe he was willing do that for her.

As soon as he was out of sight, even with Nan right there, Ava walked up to her father.

"Ok, I'll go. I'll talk to the detective. But it's up to me whether or not I go anywhere near that place. I decide what I do and don't do. Understand?"

He hugged her tight while she remained stiff in his arms. "Absolutely," he said.

In the time it took James to collect Ava's stuff and her father to drag his luggage outside, Nan had settled things at the flight desk and started the engine. Walking toward the plane holding only her journal, Ava realized it had been eight years since she'd last flown.

Seconds later, the ground shook under her feet, the same way it did the night she'd lost it on the railroad tracks, starting the downward spiral that brought her to Mount Hope the first time. Vibrations traveled up Ava's arm, across her shoulders, into her neck; they hovered over the top of her head. Her father stood next to her, urging her to climb in. James was already in the back, patting the seat and shouting above the noise, "Next to me."

But Ava couldn't let go of the door. Awash in dread, she looked at her father and tried to form the words, to tell him she was disappearing. Nothing came out.

"Are you all right?" he shouted. "James, quick, help me lay

her down."

Ava felt their arms encircle her waist. And then she didn't.

My feet are on the ground in Maine, but I'm flying in a plane with my father. There is no pilot. No matter how many times I blink, I can't stop seeing random things. Images I know don't go together. Pink batik. Fringe rocking against a boulder on the Ledges. A sandcastle. Benno grabbing the rope to climb the concrete wall. Blood from Mallory's head spreading out over dirt. A little girl skipping on a beach—

TWENTY-NINE

Toby motioned for James to help him ease Ava down on the cool pavement. He wrestled with his jacket, and when it was finally off, he rolled it into a makeshift pillow. James lifted her head gently, supporting her neck, so that Toby could position the jacket under her shoulders. Nan shut down the plane and hopped from the cockpit, completing the crowd around Ava.

Toby felt sick to his stomach, looking at his daughter lying there. He touched the tattoo his daughter had gotten in memory of her sister. As he rubbed Ava's arm, he was filled with overwhelming sadness. It being yet another thing father and daughter had never discussed.

It took a few seconds for Ava's breathing to become regular and her eyes to flutter open. Toby had mixed feelings about sending James to call an ambulance. The color came back into her cheeks, and fire would surely follow if he embarrassed his daughter with sirens.

"I'm fine," she said to no one in particular. Weak and trembling, she asked them to help her up. As Ava smoothed her hair down, front, back and side, Toby thought it oddly adolescent that she cared about her appearance under the circumstances. Then he saw her run her hands over her shoulders, along each arm.

Brushing pretend dirt off her pants, she pressed her thighs and knees as she went. His daughter was making sure nothing was bruised or broken.

"Has this happened before?" Toby asked.

Ava wouldn't look up. Toby watched James lace one hand in hers. All business, Nan bent down to collect Toby's jacket.

"Last time was at Mount Hope. Right before you got me out," Ava said.

"Is that what happened the night on the train tracks?"

Ava nodded.

Toby had gotten things horribly wrong. The night he'd walked in on Ava leaning over the back of her couch, her skin pale, her hair damp, she wasn't high or coming down off drugs.

"Why didn't you tell me?"

Ava adjusted her shirt. When she finally looked at him, her expression told him everything. He'd let her down. Ava found it impossible to confide in him.

"It must've been the plane," Ava said. "It happens if I get upset or remember something. I freak out. Sometimes black out."

After everything Ava had been through, how come he'd never suspected she suffered flashbacks? Standing there on the tarmac, he remembered that terrible trip out of Phuket International. His beautiful girl strapped into her seat, leaning on him, gripping his arm, chanting over and over, *Mommy, Poppy, Mommy, Poppy.*

"Some things are hard to talk about," James said.

The boy had such a calming presence that at times Toby forgot he was there. Then James would say something thoughtful, or do something kind, and Toby couldn't imagine him not being there.

"I thought I was going crazy."

"You're not," Toby said. "But we need you to see someone. You could really hurt yourself."

"I'm fine. Let's just go. I'm getting better at controlling it."

"No, no," Nan said. "I'm being selfish. I can't ask you to do this. Look, Toby, you take care of your daughter. I'll go fight the good fight on my own."

"Whatever money you need, it's yours," Toby said. "My associate's put in a call to a great lawyer. I'll do whatever else I can from here."

"You've done a lot already. I owe you." Nan's smile was forced. She turned to Ava and put a hand on her shoulder. "You, too. Thanks for being willing to help."

Toby wondered how long Ava would allow Nan's hand to stay there. If Jill had tried that, she would have shaken it off.

"Mind if I ask you something?" Nan's voice quavered, reminding Toby he had seen her this way before.

Ava acted all timid, but she nodded okay.

"Paxton Worth told me Arthur didn't want to see me. I don't believe him. Do you know if he saw Mallory's accident on the overnight? Was he okay the last time you saw him?"

Ava looked from Nan to James. His daughter had only known him for a few days, and yet the two shared a knowing glance.

"Mallory didn't have an accident," Ava said, staring at Nan. "She bashed her head in with a rock to get out of there. And so parents would start asking questions. I saw her do it and so did your nephew. I got bumped up a level, basically bribed so I wouldn't tell. He got sent to OP."

"Jesus. What's OP?" Nan asked.

Toby knew by the way Ava said *OP* that it wasn't any place good. Then he remembered that military-looking counselor touting some special room kids got sent to, making sure Ava knew she was in line for the so-called privilege.

Ava swallowed hard. She wouldn't look at Nan or Toby, or even at James.

"It's the place they take misbehavers. I never went, but the kids who did said it was hell. They hurt you even worse when you're in there."

For a second no one said a word. Toby reached out to steady Nan. She closed her eyes, but not before the tears came.

"It's worse than I thought," Nan said.

"Dad, you should go with her. Get her nephew out. I'll help from here. I'll tell you where things are. I'll even talk to the detective if you want me to."

"I can't," Toby said. "I won't leave you."

"Ava can stay at Biddie's," James said. "My aunt won't mind."

"It's okay this time," Ava said. "I'll be fine. Go. Really."

When Ava said *this time* it was as if she were drawing a distinction between all the other times Toby had left her. Standing there, he felt something deep inside him tighten.

"No," he said. "It's not right. You passed out."

"Look, I know I've got stuff to deal with. It wasn't easy telling you what I just did. I'll see someone when you get back."

"Toby, please," Nan said. "I don't have the same power as a parent with Mount Hope. But my brother will cave if someone other than me confronts him. He's so close to letting Arthur go, I can tell. Together you and I can browbeat the detective, and get him on the horn with Ava. I'll fly you back here any time you say the word."

Turning to Ava, Nan wagged a finger at her, the gesture both motherly and playful. "You have to promise to stay at Biddie's place and stick with James. You'll need to keep in touch."

Toby was stunned to see his daughter respond to Nan's no-nonsense approach. He didn't like the thoughts creeping in. Of Pax and Jill's allegations—that Ava desperately needed a parent.

"Dad, if you want to make things right with me, you'll get on that plane. I've been selfish. I should've said more before now."

In the charged silence, Toby wondered if he could ever do enough to earn Ava's forgiveness.

"Do it for me," she said. "Tell the detective to collect the kids' workbooks. Everything written in the first few days is the truth. After that they punish you if you don't make stuff up."

So there it was. His daughter had been coerced into writing those lies and her letters. Nan was right. The goings on at Mount Hope were worse than they could've imagined.

"On one condition," Toby said. "I want you to make an appointment to see Biddie's counselor friend today."

When Ava said she would, Toby liked how it felt to be assertive—to firmly and confidently take charge. He hugged his daughter as tightly as he dared, and before Ava pulled away, he kissed her cheek. "I'm going to make things right between us," he said, holding her shoulders. "I'll start with Mount Hope, but I'm coming back. You and me—we're going to figure everything out, here in Maine."

With Ava's particular kind of sweet shyness, she smiled. It was as if Toby had given her a gift she'd secretly wanted. Staying in Maine. The same one her mother had always longed for.

Unable to say anything more, Toby shook hands with James and got on the plane. It felt so right and so wrong to trust the capable woman beside him to taxi him away from his daughter. Minutes later, they were flying. Toby looked out his window to see Ava staring skyward, watching him go. As Nan circled the airport, heading the single-engine aircraft in the direction of Mount Hope, he saw her wave.

THIRTY

≈

James called his aunt on their ride home from the airport. Ava kept her gaze out the window, watching the plane get smaller and smaller. In no time, her father and Nan were out of sight. From the way James explained things, Ava was relieved. Mrs. Purcell didn't mind that she was coming, and James didn't make her sound like a whack-job either.

The house was as she remembered it, though smaller and a little shabbier. The weathered shingles were darker gray, the shrubs tangled and tall. It struck her that once Mr. Purcell, and now James, took meticulous care of Herrick House at the expense of their own waterfront ranch. Their house wasn't much to look at, but their pretty-as-a-picture view of the Punch Bowl was as beautiful as the Sedgwicks was of the Reach.

With James's truck parked in the driveway, Ava could see a person's shadow inside the screen door. Ava hesitated to get out, remembering the Purcells had a dog. When she was a kid, their Doberman would growl at her, showing off his sharp canines. He terrified Ava, so she'd run to their house clinging to her dad, or gripping Poppy's hand. Sitting there, taking in that yard, Ava could almost get a whiff of his stale breath.

"I don't hear the dog," she said.

"You remember Bouncer?" As James spoke the dog's name, he smiled, flashing that space between his teeth and the hollow in his cheek.

"That dog used to scare the shit out of me," he said. "He's been gone a long time. Biddie doesn't have any pets. Unless you count a couple of fish."

"Poppy was a year younger than me, but when Bouncer would run up to us, I'd start shrieking and my sister would start whistling. He'd realize it was her and start digging in the grass for a tennis ball."

"When I was over here, my uncle would have to take Bouncer to work with him so I could play outside without freaking out."

"I wonder why we never met when we were kids."

"I didn't come over much back then."

A squeaky screen door opened, and Mrs. Purcell came down the steps. Talk about strange. She might've been wearing the same jeans and flannel shirt she wore the last time Ava had been here.

"It's been years and I can't wait another minute to get a load of Lorraine's girl."

Ava stepped out of the car and without meaning to, glanced around to make sure James was right about Bouncer.

At the sound of her mother's name, Ava choked out the word *hi.*

"It's you." Mrs. Purcell took Ava's hands and held them out. "You've got different coloring for sure, but you look just like her."

"Thanks," Ava said. "For letting me stay here."

"James, get her things. Put them in the front bedroom."

It was easy for James to take her stuff inside in one trip. All Ava had was what she'd bought earlier in town. Mrs. Purcell waited until the screen door slapped shut before she spoke again.

"Are you okay with your father leaving on his—trip?"

"It's complicated. I wish we had nothing to do with that place. But I'd want someone to do something if I were still there."

Ava wiped her eyes with the back of her hand. James didn't need to always see her acting so emo.

She heard him call to his aunt through the screen. "Sorry, I gotta eat and run. I've got to deliver the Linden piece this afternoon. Ava, do you want to come? We could get you a phone on the way back."

"Sure," Ava said.

"There's tuna for sandwiches in the fridge," Mrs. Purcell said. "Make 'em hearty. This one needs a little meat on these bones" She pretend to pinch Ava's arm. "And no need to waste money. Ava can have Charlie's phone."

She knew Mrs. Purcell was trying to be nice, but Ava didn't like her drawing attention to how skinny she was, not in front of James. And though it was a generous offer, she didn't want to be walking around with a dead guy's phone in her pocket either.

"No, I couldn't do that," Ava said. "My dad wants me to get one so I can call him. He told me to put it on his bill."

"Yes, Toby would want that," she said. "James, ring the dinner bell when you're ready. Ava and I are going for a little walk."

The worn path was familiar, though nothing sharp or crisp came in the form of memories. Nothing flickered through the leaves the way the sun did. Mrs. Purcell and Ava were quiet as they walked through the arbor of spruce. Ava started to wonder what they were doing meandering this trail. Fewer trees, lapping waves, the woods ended where a cluster of rocks began.

"Pretty," Ava said.

"Come, let's go down to the dock."

Ava planted her feet firmly in pine needles. "Here's fine."

"A-course," Mrs. Purcell said, shaking her head, pursing her lips.

Ava willed the woman not to talk about her mother. She wasn't ready.

"You haven't been a fan of the water since the time you got tossed overboard. Your mother felt terrible, so you know."

"She talked to you about that?"

"Lorraine talked to me about everything. We were as close as you were to Poppy."

"I found some books in the attic the other day," Ava said. "The ones Mr. McCloskey signed. Leafing through those pages, everything about the day I fell out of the boat came back to me."

"Lorraine said it was all her fault. Shoulda been more careful with her girls."

Mrs. Purcell pointed to a huge rock lodged in the water by

the shore. "See down there? Lorraine and I used to sit on that thing, talk ourselves blue for more hours than you are old. I don't know how many times she'd imagine being rich enough to live on an island, spending her days writing books. Your mother wrote poetry. Grew up through that clearing there. Her house is gone now or I'd show it to you. Wasn't much different than mine."

There was a brief moment of silence.

"How old was she when she met my dad?" Ava asked.

"He came here summers. We always knew him, but Lorraine and Toby didn't become an item till he finished college. Whisked her away from Maine, he did."

"Mom loved it here. I don't remember her liking Wellesley very much."

"Hated it actually. Always wanted to live here year-round. But your dad wouldn't have it. He had work." Mrs. Purcell said *work* like it was a swear. The face she made confirmed it. Mrs. Purcell and Ava's mom did talk about everything.

Ava jumped when the bell rang through the trees, trilling down the hill. James was ready to roll, and she was glad. She'd only been gone five minutes, and already she found herself missing him.

"Efficient and responsible, that James. Don't know what I'd do without him." Mrs. Purcell put her hand out to stop Ava from heading up the path. "Before you go, I need to tell you. Your dad called me from his airplane." She said *airplane* the same way she said *work*, which told Ava she might not have been best friends with both of her parents.

"It's his friend Nan's."

Suddenly protective of her dad, Ava didn't want Mrs. Purcell getting the wrong impression about him taking off.

"Right, well, here's the thing," she said. "He wants me to be sure you make an appointment with my friend."

"I told him I would."

"Now, see—did you know my friend's a head doctor?"

"I figured."

"I don't need to tell you, your father's an expert at telling other folks what to do. I'm not about to make you call her, and I told him so. Unless that's what you want to do."

Ava lifted one foot to brush dirt from the top of her new flats. "I think I want to go. Once anyway."

"Enough said. I only wanted to be sure. I'll call her for you while you're gone with James, if you like."

Dusting off the other shoe, Ava nodded. "I'd appreciate that."

"I know we don't know each other well. At all really," she said. "But whatever you need, don't you hesitate to ask. I'm happy to talk about your mother anytime you want. I miss her something awful."

"Thanks again for letting me crash here, Mrs. Purcell. I don't mind spending time alone at Herrick House, just not at night."

"Call me Biddie, everyone does. You're welcome to stay as long as you like. James says you're real nice to be around. Speaking of James, be a good friend to him. Boy's been through a lotta heartache." Looking up through the trees at her cottage, she paused. "Well, haven't we all."

Trudging up toward Biddie's, though the hill was hardly steep, Ava got a flash of hiking the Ledges. It felt good to get to the top and see James holding two sandwiches wrapped in plastic, waving her over to his truck. She was happy to jump into the passenger seat, ready to head to James's studio, a.k.a. her backyard boathouse. It wasn't that Ava wanted to get away from Biddie. She liked her, she did. She knew a lot about Ava's parents, about her and Poppy too.

But spending time with Biddie was like skimming SparkNotes, when Ava was pretty sure she was ready to read her story on her own. At least maybe a little at a time.

THIRTY-ONE

It didn't take long for Ava to pack a few more of her things and grab her guitar. The warm sun and calm air invited her to wait for James on the hill outside the boathouse. He could take as long as he wanted to put the finishing touches on the sculpture they were about to deliver. Ava would never rush an artist.

At first, lying on that grass, she tried to call up memories of Poppy, but nothing solid came to her. Probably just as well. When something started off good for her, it didn't always end that way.

Halfway between awake and asleep, Ava let herself think about James.

He's holding my hand. It's not heat or pressure I feel, more like he's a string keeping me from floating away, from getting too high, too far off the ground. We're walking toward the dock, and this time I'm not afraid to go near water. He bends down to take off my shoes, one and then the other, placing them away from the waves that lick the shore, ripple, ripple, kiss. I sit down on the dock and stick my feet into the sea like a brave person; it chills me all the way up to my knees. James sits next to me and places his hand on top of mine. I slip my hand out from under his and place it lightly on top. He does the same, and then I do it again, careful, so as not to get splinters;

it's a silly game we play. He laughs, but there's no sound. We haven't done that yet, laugh together; I don't know which notes he sings. When he turns to me, I ask him where his scars came from. Using one finger, I trace the one through his eyebrow, then keep going, down his nose, through the faint line above his lips. "Ava," he says. "We can go now."

James shook Ava awake. When her eyes flew open, she searched his face. Could he tell she'd been dreaming of him, wishing he would kiss her?

"Sorry it took so long," he said. "One of the pieces needed welding. It was tough loading it onto the truck. You still up for going?"

Ava got up off the lawn and reached for her guitar case. "Yeah, no, I want to come. I can help you get it out of the truck."

As James drove for twenty minutes, he didn't say much. Neither did Ava. Feeling all self-conscious, and fearing he could get inside her head and know what she was thinking, she filled her mind with meaningless things. Ava read signs. Ellsworth. Frenchman Bay. Acadia National Park. Preoccupied, it took her a while to figure out what the thing was and where they were taking it.

It wasn't until James pulled off Route 3 and parked his truck on a busy side road that she realized. The wire figures parked on the vinyl car seat were a mother and her baby. James was bringing the likenesses of real people to the exact place where they'd died.

Removing the sculpture from the truck was the easy part. James didn't warn Ava that they were about to do something hard with their bodies and their hearts. He didn't expect her to act weak or whine that it weighed a ton. So she didn't. They worked together to secure the sculpture with metal bolts and locks into the ground. She didn't lose it until he pulled the silver and gold painted sign from an ordinary plastic shopping bag and staked it in the dirt.

Amelia & Liam.

"It's the most beautiful sculpture I've ever seen," Ava said, letting her tears do their thing.

"I think it turned out fine."

In the few days she'd known James—when he was quiet

205

with her—Ava got the sense that he was shy. Seeing him leave his interpretation of this mother and her baby there, she understood. James saved his energy for times like this.

"I started memorializing people after my cousin died," he said. "I took a random bike, painted it white, sketched his favorite things on the handlebars, the seat, the frame. His bird. A few stamps. The names of his books. Then I left it near where he was killed. People called it ghost art. They started asking who'd done it."

James took a few steps away from the sculpture, up a mound of grass overlooking his piece and the road. When he sat, he wrapped his arms around his knees. It wasn't until he patted the ground that Ava joined him there. The confidence that came from hard work, and the lullaby the cars sang, urged her to sit as close to James as she dared.

"What happened to your cousin?"

"Bobby visited Maine every summer, but he didn't move here until his mom died. No one could find his dad. My mom said it was better for him and me if she and my dad took him in, instead of Biddie. My mom was the oldest, so she got her way."

While James talked about his cousin, Ava put it together. Biddie, Bobby's mother, and his, were sisters.

"Bobby was a cool kid, even though he liked different things. Before he came here he had this bird named after a rain forest. He taught Daintree to hold a book and repeat stuff he whispered, so it looked like the bird could read. Other kids thought Bobby was weird. He got teased a lot. I was in high school and he was at the middle school, so it was hard for me to protect him, you know?"

James stacked twigs on top of rocks, pebbles on top of stones. Ava had so many questions, but he seemed to be partly there on that stretch of road overlooking his artwork, and partly somewhere else. She wouldn't get in the way of a memory, especially one that didn't belong to her.

"The night before he died, Bobby came to my room to ask me to meet him after school out behind the cafeteria. He wanted me to scare those kids into leaving him alone. I believed him when he said the other kids were mean, that they treated him badly. But if I'd known how bad things were, I never would've stayed after class. I never would've been late."

"By the time I got to the middle school, Bobby wasn't there. I looked all over school grounds and then decided to drive the route he usually took to our house. Bobby rode his bike everywhere. Other kids knew it too."

"A few streets from where we lived, I saw two boys following him, banging into the back of his ten-speed with theirs. Bobby's bike shook back and forth, but he kept his balance, he kept heading for home. I could see he was standing on the pedals, pushing the bike as fast as it would go. I beeped and beeped, but he wouldn't turn around, just kept riding. When I got close enough, I stopped my truck and jumped out to yell at those kids. I told them to take off and leave him alone. They sped up and rode around Bobby. I shouted out to him, letting him know it was me. He panicked. Bobby turned his bike and rode straight into traffic."

"Everything flipped into slow motion. The way he rose off his bike, twisting in the air, rolling up onto the hood of that car. Over the roof. Onto the ground. The way his bike tried to follow. When I got to him, I pressed my shirt over the gash in his neck. It wouldn't stop bleeding. And then it did. Even before the paramedics told me, I knew. Bobby died right there on the side of that road."

Ava could see James's story as he told it. What happened to Bobby—and James—was shocking and sad, so hard to believe. Ava laced her hand in his.

"When I was little, my mom told me about the time she met Robert McCloskey. He told her he thought in pictures. That only after he'd sketched his drawings would he fill in the words to the story. I think some things are like that. Other times there aren't any words to fill in."

"That's why I do this," James said, his eyes focused on his sculpture. "I can't change what happens. But I can make people remember."

"The bike on the wall in the boathouse. It's your cousin's."

James turned to Ava and nodded. He let her see his tears, making no apologies for parking his sadness right there between them.

"Crazy, huh, hanging it there, using it as my inspiration?"

"You're asking me if I think you're crazy?"

And then, there it was, his laugh. The rhythm and cadence exactly as she would've written the melody, if Ava was the artist, and James was the song.

THIRTY-TWO

With Nan's papers finally in order, Toby gunned their rental, driving in the direction of Mount Hope. After spending thirty-six hours traipsing from lawyer meetings to courthouse to judge's chambers—after pleading with her brother to finally sign custody papers—Toby felt as though he'd known Nan much longer.

"I can't believe all that's happened since we met," he said. "Never thought I'd say this but I can't wait to get back to Maine."

"I'm so glad Ava's doing better."

Toby leaned into Nan, bumping against her shoulders. "She might only be good because I'm not there."

"That's not true. You said she's more relaxed with you. Look how much she's helped us. It gives me hope for Arthur. I'm counting on the experts being right about kids and resilience. But I gotta say, after this mess, it won't be easy to trust any of those fools again."

"Don't say that," he said. "Ava's first appointment is this afternoon. I'm feeling guilty enough for not being there."

"I'm not saying this to make myself feel better that you're here with me, but Ava told you she wanted to do this on her own." Nan swung her body sideways, her knees brushing Toby's leg.

"I know," he said. "She told me three times. But I want to

meet the counselor myself this time—even if she is Biddie's friend. I'm not going to be so trusting this time."

"I can't thank you enough for helping me," Nan said.

"I told you, this doesn't begin to cover what I've got to do to make amends."

Toby let Nan think he meant atoning for sending Ava away when what he was really thinking about was his family. He realized then that it would never, ever be easy to talk about Lorraine and Poppy with anyone, even Nan.

"Do you ever get a gut feeling that you need to see Ava right this second or you'll die?" Nan asked.

Toby had felt it, that sinking feeling.

"I've had a connection like that with Arthur since he was a baby," Nan said. "I can pretty much fly out of any airport, so I moved every time my brother and Arthur's mother did. I had a feeling from the start that someday he would need me. Really need me."

"Ava was always cautious. Anxious around dogs and strangers. And God, the water. But never in a million years did I guess things would turn out like this. Clueless dad."

"I don't see you that way at all. People like Paxton Worth go after vulnerable people. Parents at their wit's end with their kids. You saw my brother. There's a father who couldn't care less. It was like he didn't want anything to do with Arthur until I wanted to care for him. He acts like his child is some kind of possession."

"I keep going back over it, wondering what part of me thought relinquishing my daughter to that place was a good idea. I can't believe I got sucked into all their promises. Their 'success' stories."

"It's like Stockholm syndrome. The parents and kids need to find some meaning in their terrible experiences, so they rave about it."

"Well, when I get home I'm going to make sure Ava believes me. I didn't know what I was getting us into." As Toby spoke, the guilt wormed its ugly way in again. All he wanted to do was get this thing done. Get Arthur out and have Nan fly him back to Maine. Driving toward the overlook where he knew there'd be a signal, he'd have to settle for his daily phone call to Ava.

"I despise that place with a white-hot passion, and trust me, if you repeat this, I'll deny it," Nan said. "But I did learn some things about myself."

"What, you wanna be more like me?"

Nan laughed. "I'll give you some of my aggressive if you give me some of your passive."

He pulled the car off the road at the exact place where he'd called Jill, and where Ava had winged her workbook into the water, disrobing in front of him, trying to leave Mount Hope at the water's edge.

"I want to tell you about Ava. Why she's having so much trouble. About my wife and younger daughter," Toby said. "Someday, okay?"

"You can tell me now." Nan leaned in. Shoulder to shoulder, without hesitation, she rested against him.

"We're about to spring your nephew. Let's focus on you for now." Toby pulled out his cell and hit speed dial. "There'll be time enough for us to talk once we have Arthur back."

Ava picked up. "Hey Dad." The lightness in her voice was a relief to him and still he was hit with the feeling Nan had just described. Toby wanted to go home.

"We're almost there," he said. "The detective is going to meet us. Our plan is to head straight to OP. Where is it exactly? It doesn't show up on the property map."

"It's behind the main lodge. But it'll be locked and guarded. Probably by Justice. I'd go find Honor first. She's been trying to get him out since she got there. Plus she'll have keys."

Ava sounded good. She was better, happy. He told her to go to her appointment with the counselor and not to worry. He'd be back before she knew it.

He recapped Ava's directions for Nan, while she scoured the Mount Hope map.

"I wonder why Reilly won't tell us what's going down up there," she said. "Why can't he arrest them for treating kids the way they do?"

"If Pax has the upper hand legally, or he's good at hiding things, there isn't much Reilly can do about it. It's Ava's word against Pax's. Or if charges are coming, Reilly won't jeopardize things by tipping everyone off, including us."

"If I hear someone say teenagers exaggerate one more time, you'll have to restrain me."

"I'm guilty," Toby said, raising his hands up in mock surrender. "I used to believe these kids push the envelope."

"No one deserves what those counselors are dishing out—" Nan went silent when over the rush of the stream and their conversation sirens wailed. Toby started the car and shifted into first. "Something's wrong. Let's go."

At the entrance to Mount Hope, a half dozen or more police cars sat with lights flashing. At least two news crews were setting up cameras.

"Why the hell didn't Reilly warn us?" she asked.

Nan and Toby rushed past two uniformed officers who stood by bumper-to-bumper police cars. Two sedans had their back doors open.

The lobby was chaos. Groups of girls Ava's age were crying hysterically—clinging to each other on sofas lined up against the walls. Two police officers were making their way through the lobby with boxes on carts. Brimming with files as evidence, the carts were none other than the ones that had delivered food to the parents during the weekend the director had had them under his thumb.

"There he is," Nan said. "Over there."

Toby turned, expecting to get his first glimpse of Arthur, but Nan was pointing to the detective. When Reilly shifted left, Toby was stunned to see him putting cuffs on Paxton Worth.

"Come on," Nan said. "He'll know where Arthur is."

She pushed her way through the crowd of kids and police milling around the lobby. Toby did his best to keep up.

As they approached Detective Reilly, he finished reading Pax his rights. Then he motioned for a policewoman to come to where he stood. Reilly slapped Pax on the back and told the officer, "Get him out of here."

"What's going on?" Toby asked.

"We've been investigating the place for some time, long before you contacted us. Had an officer undercover for well over a month."

Nan stepped in front of Pax before he could get far. She shouted over the commotion. "Where's Arthur?"

Her agitation made Toby's heart race, and beads of sweat began dripping down one side of his face.

Pax glared at Nan, a menacing look worse than the one he'd given the detective.

Toby recognized an older boy by the registration area. He was one of the students who'd helped with the parent session. "This is bullshit. Such bullshit," the boy said. With each swear, he kicked the desk.

Hurrying over to him, Toby interrupted the boy by touching his shoulder. "Where can we find Arthur McEttrick?" he asked.

"Locked up, man. Good luck getting him out now."

Nan came up behind Toby. "Please tell us where he is."

"I know where he is."

Toby and Nan turned to find Mallory standing there. She pulled Nan by the sleeve. "Come with me."

"You're a snitch, Mallory," the boy shouted. "Don't think I won't tell."

"Hurry. This way," she said.

Toby couldn't take his eyes off the shaved patch on the girl's head, and the gash, a thick red rope around one ear. He'd been told she'd been discharged from the hospital, but never imagined she'd be sent back here.

Checking over her shoulder, Mallory seemed to be as much running toward something as away from something else.

"Is Arthur okay?" Nan asked.

"I haven't seen him in a bunch of days. But I know where he is, and who has the key."

Toby and Nan followed Mallory down the corridors off the main lobby, beyond the conference room where they'd spent the weekend getting chastised for being horrible parents. Past the session room he'd sat in with Ava—the place where he'd almost been duped into believing that they were in counseling, and that his daughter wanted to stay.

The door to the director's office was open. Inside, two police officers were loading more files into boxes.

Toby thought he was seeing things when Ava's counselor,

Honor, started placing cuffs on Justice.

"What are you doing?" Nan asked.

Toby still couldn't comprehend why Mallory was back, never mind why one counselor would be handcuffing another.

"Detective Cass Logan," Ava's counselor said. "Excuse me while I take great pleasure in arresting this lowlife."

"I want a lawyer," Justice said, spit collecting on the sides of his mouth.

Mallory's feet were glued to the office threshold. Toby had the urge to protect the girl somehow, though she was doing a terrific job all on her own. He could see she refused to look anywhere near Justice. But he kept staring at her, as if by sheer will he could pull the girl's eyes toward him.

"Miss McEttrick needs to find Arthur," Mallory said.

"Kid's a loser," Justice said.

Nan looked like she was about to belt him.

"Where's the boy?" Toby said.

The detective held Justice by one arm as another officer moved in to restrain his other side. It was time to get him out of the office, and still she was holding him back. The officer had no intention of walking Justice by the girl.

"Take them to OP," Cass said, tossing a set of keys to Mallory. "Tell any kids you see on the way to go straight to the lobby and wait for their parents, or stay with the officer they've been assigned to. No one leaves the camp without talking to me. I want a record of where everyone lands."

Toby couldn't tell if she was playing Mount Hope staff member or had assumed her official duties.

"God, what a mess," she said. "This was supposed to go down smoothly. Someone leaked the investigation to the press, and now it's pandemonium."

"Do you know if Arthur's okay?" Nan asked.

"Like I said in my note, he's going to need a hospital. This place has been real rough on him." Cass Logan stared at Justice with hate in her eyes.

"You left the note? I thought you did," Nan said, pointing to Mallory.

A puzzled look crossed Cass's face.

"I passed a note to Mr. Sedgwick during the parent session," Mallory said. "Telling him to get us out. I was sure Justice found out I did it and I was headed to OP. That's why—" As Mallory reached up to cover her ear, Nan put a hand on her shoulder to calm her.

"Mallory, I'm sorry," Cass said. "I did my best to protect you kids from inside. I worked as fast as I could to collect enough evidence, not just to get Pax arrested but to bring the whole place down."

"It's no use," Justice said. "You can close Mount Hope, but Pax has partners. They'll just find a way to open another camp, and name it something else."

Cass pulled Justice's hands tighter behind his back. "Look, I've got to get this piece of crap out of here, and make rounds. There are a few high-risk runners I don't want to get lost in the shuffle. You'll be okay with Arthur?"

After agreeing to touch base with Cass before they left the lodge, Toby and Nan looked to Mallory. The girl couldn't get out of the office fast enough, exiting the back door, moving toward a low building at the edge of a trail leading up the mountain. Toby fell behind. Rocks and tree roots made it difficult for him to navigate the narrow path. Nan and Mallory were practically running. Toby's knee touched down as he tried to get out of the way of a hefty girl with oily hair. He leaned on a nearby tree for support.

"Hey, Mallory," the girl called out. "Did Justice really get arrested?"

"Yeah," she said, pausing to wait for Toby.

He wondered how many of the students knew that Honor was undercover. Toby waited to see if Mallory would be the one to send the rumor spreading around the mountain.

"Your parents coming?" the girl asked.

"Nah, I'm transferring. To Narrow Lake."

"Good luck with that," the girl said. "Gotta be better than this place." She backed away from Mallory like she had a contagious disease, then turned and lumbered in the direction of the lodge.

Nan stopped in her tracks when she heard Mallory say she was moving to another facility. It hadn't occurred to Toby that not all the kids would be going home. Guilty as he was of being blind to Ava's problems, what kind of parents looked at that poor girl's scalp, heard what went on at Mount Hope, and didn't drop what they were doing to come rescue her?

"Do you want me to call your mom and dad?" Nan asked. "I could explain things."

"Don't worry about me. I'll be fine," Mallory said. She wiped her eyes with the hem of her orange T-shirt. "Come on, Arthur's in here." She opened the door to a darkened hallway.

It took a few seconds for Toby's eyes to adjust. The metal door straight ahead was closed; a heavy padlock hung from its hinges. Mallory fiddled with one key after another until she found the one that fit. Unlocked and opened, the room was no brighter than the hall they were standing in.

"Arthur, your aunt's here. To take you home," Mallory said in a low voice. She wore the same clunky boots Ava had stuffed in her wastebasket back in Maine. Gingerly, the girl placed one step after careful step on the concrete floor, making her way toward a shape lying on a bare mattress.

"Nan can fly," Arthur said.

The thin shadow moved abruptly, pressing his back to the wall. Even from the doorway, Toby could see the boy was a wreck.

"I'm here. We're getting you out now." Nan's voice cracked with every word.

"Let's take it slow." Mallory kneeled to one side of Arthur, hooking her arm under his. Nan did the same on his other side. She, too, was tentative with him, acting as though he were a frightened rabbit.

"I want to go. But I can't," he said, shaking his head, pointing at the door. As Arthur scrambled toward the wall again, he banged his head. That's when it occurred to Toby: the boy was alarmed by his male shadow standing in the entranceway.

"I'm Ava's dad. Do you remember her?"

"Ava needs to be saved."

"No, kiddo," Nan said. "Ava's dad took her home already. She's in Maine."

"You're not Justice?" he asked Toby.

"Justice is gone," Mallory said, helping the boy up. "Outside you can see everything clearly. Come on."

Toby took this as his cue to move out of the building, to wait for them on the trail in the sunlight. He couldn't blame Arthur for being afraid. Poor Nan. How was she ever going to help him? He seemed so much worse off than Ava, or even Mallory. When Cass Logan had suggested Arthur needed a hospital, Toby had been foolish enough to think dehydration or broken leg. Now it registered that the police officer masquerading as a counselor had meant a psychiatric hospital. If a place like McLean in Belmont were right for the boy—and Toby wasn't convinced that it was—would Nan be strong enough to leave Arthur somewhere else, again?

Mallory, Nan, and Arthur came into the light. It was painful to watch the boy tremble at the sight of Toby standing there. God only knew what Justice and Pax had done to him. Toby shuddered then, wondering exactly what they might have done to Ava.

At that horrid thought, everything went hollow and dark inside. Toby didn't mean to be selfish, but suddenly he needed to be with his daughter. He couldn't get back to Maine fast enough. He didn't know how he would do it, if Nan decided not to fly.

THIRTY-THREE

The visit to Biddie's counselor friend reminded Ava of her one-on-ones with Honor back at Mount Hope. The rocking chairs, the boxes of Kleenex everywhere, the ceaseless questions. Here in Blue Hill, the session didn't take place on a cabin porch. No one escorted her unwillingly by her pants. Ava walked in all by herself, through one private door and fifty minutes later, out another. This time, it was her choice to go.

Ava didn't really get why people called psych doctors shrinks. Sure, she'd been a little leery, not certain she'd be able to look at things more closely. Ava wanted to be a regular kid with no reason to be there. But after rehashing as much as she was ready to talk about, her head didn't feel any smaller. Her mind felt open, less cluttered. Her thoughts a little clearer.

When Ava landed back in the waiting room, Biddie was there, pretending to read a magazine. "Sarah's nice, huh?" she asked, popping up out of her seat, tossing the Time back on the side table.

"She's okay."

It had been a relief when Biddie offered to drive her to the appointment. Even though James probably would have, that didn't mean Ava wanted him to. She wished Biddie could've stayed put in her car or used the time to do errands.

"Did you make another appointment?" she asked.

"Yeah."

"When's that?"

"I wrote it down."

"Okay, I get it. You don't want to talk." Biddie jingled her keys in her coat pocket.

"You want to grab a coffee?" Ava asked.

"That'd be nice. Feel up to making a couple stops here in town first?"

Ava wanted to go meet James but didn't say so. She stood without moving. It was a trick she'd learned at Mount Hope.

"Won't take long," Biddie said. "I think you'll say the detour was worth it."

Biddie drove the single-lane road while Ava stared out the window. Gullies brimmed with wildflowers, the mountain crest stood mighty in the distance. Blue Hill was right out of a storybook.

"That sculpture there is the first one James did," Biddie said, slowing down as much as she could with the string of cars trailing behind them. The ghost bike was parked in the grass on a carpet of blue violets.

"James told me about his cousin. Your nephew," Ava said, turning back to look at the artwork for as long as she could before the car started going full speed. In the last second, she noticed a plaque that read: BOBBY CARMICHAEL.

"Can you believe nothing happened to those hooligans who tormented that dear, sweet boy? I hope their consciences never let them rest," Biddie said.

"Wait, James's cousin was Buggy Carmichael?" Poppy and Ava played with a boy off and on one summer, but she hadn't put things together till now. The boy she knew wore thick glasses with a string holding them around the back of his head. Like the goggles James wore when he was working, they made his eyes look three times their normal size. He looked really funny when he rode his bike like crazy down the lane.

"Don't let James hear you call him that. Any kind of teasing, no matter how little, sends that boy over the edge. Can't say I'm one for nicknames myself. I've hated mine my whole life. It's an old lady's name. Though I suppose the older I get—"

For the first time, it really hit Ava how nicknames could hurt. "Sorry," she said. "About your nephew. I don't know why I called him that."

"Don't worry. You and Poppy were always real nice to Bobby whenever he spent time at our place." Biddie reached over to pat her knee. "We've known far too much tragedy, you and me."

Ava was quiet for the rest of the trip, not being one who liked to discuss all the catastrophes she'd been introduced to. A few miles down the road, Biddie pulled into a parking lot. The funky red barn had the words MUSIC LIBRARY on a carved wood sun that hung above the door.

"This place is famous all over the world for lending sheet music. Want to go in?" Biddie asked.

"Are you kidding? Can I?"

"Open weekdays, ten to four. Go ahead."

Ava had never seen anything like it. Rows and rows of bins housed music cataloged by style and period. The place smelled of old paper and wood. A tabby cat curled up by a window, her eyes closed against the streaming sun.

Choral works. String quartets. Madrigals. Motets. Ava wasn't much interested in chamber music, but the library was impressive all the same.

"Can I help you find something?" a woman asked, from behind the counter.

"I'm a singer and I play guitar."

"Classical or contemporary? I'm Mary, by the way." She stuck her hand out to shake Ava's as she came down off the raised platform. "Welcome to Bagaduce Music Lending Library."

"Contemporary, I guess." It was a wonderful kind of overwhelming, standing in the company of thousands of notes waiting to be played. Ava could've stayed there all day.

Biddie hung by the window, stroking the cat's back. The tabby lifted her head, nestling into her hand.

"Let me show you to that section," Mary said. "Do you like folk or popular? Maybe both?"

The works of artists Ava had never heard of, and some she had, were cataloged alphabetically. Ava hummed softly as she turned the pages, reading the music. Amazed by how much of it she could play, Ava wanted to borrow the whole bin.

Biddie was patient and Mary helped Ava choose good pieces to start with. "You can come back anytime you like. The music isn't going anywhere. Well, out and back in. After all, we are a library," Mary said, laughing at her own joke.

After Ava opened a membership and logged out the things she wanted to borrow, she thanked Mary and left.

The door to the barn wasn't even closed before, clutching the music to her chest, she hugged Biddie.

"You're welcome, sweetie. Imagine the likes of Copland and Bernstein, even Mr. Yo-Yo Ma, having a hand in getting the library off the ground."

"I can't believe it's right near Herrick House," Ava said. "I never knew this kind of place existed."

"There's something else you may not know about. Up for one more stop?"

Biddie could've taken Ava anywhere after clueing her in to the music lending library. "Sure," she said, climbing into the car and buckling her seat belt in a single motion.

Minutes after passing the Fish Net and Blue Moose restaurants, driving through the historic part of town, Biddie pulled into another parking lot. It was a library kind of day.

"Come with me," Biddie said.

Ava followed her into the Blue Hill Public Library, by the circulation desk, past the children's room, through the reference section. The place was pretty with its dark wood shelves, comfy seats and windows galore. Ava stopped breathing when, from the doorway of the alcove, she read a sign that ran the length of the back wall bookshelf.

THE LORRAINE WHITE SEDGWICK POETRY COLLECTION.

"Did you do this?" Ava asked, moving into the space, unable to take her eyes off her mother's name.

Even as she spoke, Ava knew it wasn't Biddie's doing.

"Your father can be one exasperating person, and then he'll do something so nice that it makes everything all right. For a time."

"When did he do this? Why didn't he tell me?" Ava thought back to the night she had asked him about one of Mom's poetry books. The night he'd invited her out for ice cream. Did he try to tell her then? Had she shut him down?

Ava walked up to the bookshelf, sliding a random volume from the stacks.

"Two years after your trip, your dad came to Maine to pack up her things. He asked Charlie if he'd mind being caretaker of Herrick House. Apparently he stopped here to talk to the head librarian about this. Being Maine, a-course, everyone knows everyone. Alice called me the minute Toby left. Said, he'd loaned your mother's books to get it started, and donated the money to add to it and keep it going. Always was good at throwing the dough around, your dad."

Ava opened a delicate book by an author whose name was its own poetry. Flipping through pages, she landed on "Myth."

I was asleep while you were dying.
It's as if you slipped through some rift, a hollow

Ava could only read two lines before the tears came.

Biddie leaned forward, patting a chair next to hers. "You can talk about it, sweetie. Eight years is a long time to keep things bottled up."

"I don't know how. All I remember is in pieces," Ava said. "You know that kids' toy, the View-Master? It's like I've got a bunch of separate pictures. There's one of Poppy on the sand. One of me holding my mother's hand. It doesn't matter if I'm wide awake or dreaming, none of them string together right."

"I remember things too. I helped your mom pack a whole bunch of pretty clothes for that trip. We went shopping for weeks before, picking out bathing suits and those funny things you wrap around yourself a million ways."

"Sarongs."

"That's it. Lorraine had a whole rainbow in that suitcase. 'Toby's taking me to paradise,' she told me."

"The village was beautiful. Our room was right on the beach. We could see the ocean from every window. The sea was so clear my mom said we could get a sunburn even if we stayed under water. That was for Poppy's benefit. She didn't like sunscreen. I did what I was told. I wasn't much for swimming."

"Your mom thought that was the trip you'd get over what happened to you in the boat. If your dad said it once, he said it a hundred times, you were going to learn to swim by the end of the year. Personalized lessons, he called um."

"He did teach me. I got pretty good too, but Poppy, little as she was—she was the fish."

"Nothing you could do but love that girl," Biddie said, shaking her head, then gathering stray hair and shoving it behind her ears.

"That day, Poppy begged me to go swimming. I remember taking my towel from our beach bag."

Biddie got up and came over to sit on the arm of Ava's chair.

"I don't remember what happened next. There's a huge chunk of my memory that's just gone. The next thing I know I'm alone in a hospital. Barely anyone spoke English. I was so scared I couldn't talk."

"Oh, sweetie. You poor thing."

"I don't know if it was hours or days before my dad came to get me. Last week, when we were at Bar Harbor Airport, getting ready to leave here, I remembered flying out of Thailand. We were in a small plane flying over the island. My dad told me not to look down. But I did. I remember, I did. This is how it happens. Things come back to me. I get a piece out of the blue, and then it's up to me to figure out how it fits into the bigger picture."

"Why don't you ask your dad to fill in the parts you don't remember?"

"When we first got back, I couldn't. It's weird how I blocked it all out. Whenever I missed Mom and Poppy, it hurt too much to talk about them."

Biddie took the slim volume of poetry from Ava and reached over to hold her hands, squeezing them once, then quickly letting go. Her brief touch left the memory of warmth on Ava, like when the sun goes behind a cloud and you begin to wonder if it had ever been sunny to begin with.

"A few months ago, something came back to me. A silly promise I made to Poppy. The summer before we left, we were lying on the hill at Herrick House and she asked me to give her a huge party for her sweet sixteen. Right before Christmas, she would've been—"

"And once you remembered that, you started to remember other things? Did you tell that to Sarah?"

"Yeah. She said that's how it happens sometimes. Things are all tucked away nice and neat until one memory cracks everything open."

"It's happening to me now. With you all back here, I'm recalling things big and small."

"Sorry I'm having that effect on you."

"No, no, not you."

Biddie moved back to her seat.

"You don't like my father, do you?"

"Forgiving isn't always easy to do."

"It wasn't his fault."

"They could've stayed here to patch things up. He was always going on some trip somewhere. He kept pushing Lorraine to travel. She was like a sister to me and he took her away. Why couldn't he let her be happy? Here. All she wanted was to stay here."

Ava wasn't sure she wanted the rest of Biddie's memories. She had plenty of her own to sort through. Right then, sitting in front of a poetry collection her mother would never see, Ava felt ready.

THIRTY-FOUR

The artistic vibe the studio gave off made it easier for Ava to spend time in the boathouse. After she learned to ignore the whoosh and beat of James stirring up grout to finish the concrete piece and got past him wearing a helmet to hammer ceramic plates, she sort of got into it. Two artists sharing space.

Ava wasn't playing guitar or singing. Or writing her lyrics. In the back corner of the studio, leaning up against her family's boat, with James there, she felt comfortable enough to open her journal and position her pen to start going back over it.

"I'm almost done with the breaking," James said. "Might need to crack a piece here or there, but I promise to tell you if I need to make noise."

Ava like the way James respected her jumpiness. "Who's this one for? Or would you rather not talk about it till it's done?" She looked up at the banged-up bike hanging on the wall, the one that belonged to Bobby. James's source of encouragement inspired Ava too, now that she knew what it stood for.

"This old guy who lives out on Flye Point, Andy, commissioned it. His wife died suddenly. He asked me to come out there and help him figure out a way to keep her memory alive. We walked around the place, but nothing came to me. Then he asked me in for a cup of coffee."

"Is that the lady's china you're breaking?" Ava asked.

"It is. Andy didn't need any convincing when I told him my idea. He's got one son; the kid lives in California and doesn't want his mother's stuff. Edie loved her pretty plates and platters. Andy said this'll be perfect."

"What's it gonna be?"

"A garden sculpture. We'll put it down by the water. Everyone sailing by will be able to see her."

"Where do you get your ideas?"

"I don't try too hard. I mostly learn to make friends with patience."

When James talked about the way he worked, how he thought about art, he sounded much older than Ava. Still, he never came off like he was telling her what to do or how to be. So Ava didn't ask more questions, she just settled back against the boat and tried to take his advice.

Ava hadn't written in the pretty journal for days. The doctor reminded her yesterday that free writing was a good way to call memories from their hiding places. She'd started off using her Mount Hope workbook that way, until she was slapped into realizing it was only meant for lies. In Honor's group, she'd hated sharing those made-up entries—consoling the other kids after they told their tall tales. But after visiting her mother's poetry corner at the library, Ava could see how using the journal the right way—to put what she knew in order—might help.

Dad, Mom, Poppy, and I eat breakfast at a round table outside, across the street from Patong Beach. A pink, orange, and blue umbrella shields us from the sun; it almost matches Mom's sarong. Poppy is eating her eggs too fast. I take small sips of my yummy-tasting juice, trying to make it last longer. I'm stalling. I don't want to go any closer to the shore. Dad wears shorts—not a swimsuit—which means he's going to work, not staying with us. If he isn't going in the water, neither will I.

Watching Mom stare out to sea, I wonder if she's seen what Dad is wearing. Or is she focused on the pretty things she'll write about today? Her leather-bound journal sits next to her plate, a pen lounges on a blank page.

I look across the beach, through the parade of coconut palms, trying to see what she sees.

"I've got an idea for a poem," I say, hoping to distract her from Dad. "The beginning goes, 'Crystal, air, foamy, blue.'"

"Here," Mom says, sliding her journal toward me. "Write it down before you forget. Isn't it wonderful, Toby? Another poet in the family."

"Oh, no. Not another poet," Dad teases, walking his fingers across the table, pretending he's going to take the journal from me. I giggle, pulling it away from him, holding the treasure to my chest, proud to keep the pretty book for myself.

Three rhymes later, Poppy is out of her chair, begging to go to the beach. The table shakes. My guava-papaya mix sloshes on the place where my mother has written "Ava's Poem."

I don't think it's right for him to leave Monopoly money on the table to pay for breakfast. He smiles when I say so and tells us to collect our stuff. He'll get us settled on the beach, then go to his meeting.

"You said you were finished with work," Mom says. "Why do you keep making promises you don't intend to keep?"

Mom and Dad argue about his meeting, while Poppy keeps moving away.

"Ava, hurry up."

"Shhh," I say, trying to keep track of what Mom and Dad are saying. Trying to figure out what I might do to make them stop.

"It's an interview," he says. "I'm hiring someone. Isn't that what you want?"

Poppy and I try to lug a heavy bag together; she has one handle, I have the other. My sister is shorter and I'm trying to hold Mom's journal, so it isn't easy. Poppy's always too fast. She practically drags me until Dad tells her to slow down.

"You've always got an excuse," Mom says.

My sister starts skipping on to the sand, begging us to go closer to the water.

"Come on, Ava. You can swim good now," Poppy says.

"Well," Mom corrects her. Then looking over to me, she says, "It's true."

I shake my head, happy to hide behind my need to write poems. The way my mother does.

We stop at a long row of beach chairs. Out of the beach bag comes my blue towel, the polka dot one that matches my bathing suit. I use Mom's journal to anchor it to the sand while I dig through the bag for sunscreen.

My memory wants to stall here. But I feel safe and strong in James's studio. Leaning against the hull of this boat, I tell myself there's no water here. I can let myself see what comes next. I let the images flow from my head, down my arm, and out the end of my pen.

Like an optical illusion, I watch as the sea inches back from the shore. There's an Asian man taking pictures. Click. Click. Click.
"Toby make your choice," Mom says. "Right here, right now."
Except for people pointing, everyone on the beach is standing still, even Poppy.
"Come on, girls," Mom says grabbing our hands. "We're going in."
As she marches Poppy and me toward the sea, my breakfast rumbles in my stomach, singing out some kind of warning.
I look back over my shoulder. "Daddy, please," I say.
He does not move. His feet are firmly planted in the sand.

Whiz, zip, crash.

Ava didn't mean to scream when she heard something clang to the floor of the studio. James shut off the torch he used to heat metal and cut steel. He dodged and weaved through the tight space over to the boat. "I'm sorry," he said. "I asked if it was okay to make noise. I thought you heard me."

"My father just stood there. She begged him to choose us and he didn't. My mother walked us right into the water and he did nothing." Ava stood up and began pacing the cluttered boathouse.

Between concrete totems and brass signs, she didn't know where to go or what to do.

"My mother and sister drowned." She placed a hand to her chest, willing her lungs to fill with air.

"I know," James said.

How stupid could she be? Of course, James knew. Everyone in Maine had to know the Sedgwicks' story. The only one who didn't seem to was Ava.

Her father must've been more than happy to keep her in the

dark. No wonder he always avoided talking about what happened. And as soon as she started to remember, he'd gotten rid of her by sending her to Mount Hope. Her father didn't want Ava to know he stood by and did nothing.

Ava choked back sobs. Covering her ears, she started to hum, trying to block out the memory of horrible sounds.

James put his arms around her.

"I can't believe he didn't do anything," Ava said.

"Maybe he panicked. People don't always think straight when awful things happen."

Ava couldn't believe what James was saying. She couldn't stay another minute in that stupid boathouse. Not if he was going to take her father's side. Ava was almost to the door when she remembered her journal, lying on that chair. Marching back to get it, she hit her head on a collection of copper wind chimes that hung from the ceiling. Dissonant notes were the soundtrack to her moving toward the boat, reclaiming the journal her father had insisted contain nothing but the truth.

THIRTY-FIVE

Toby left the airport and drove as fast as he could to Biddie's. Ava wasn't answering her phone and he was desperate to see her. He parked next to Charlie's old Buick, a car that magically kept on running. He couldn't believe Biddie still drove it, rust and all, around town. Feeling nostalgic, Toby tapped its hood as he walked by it.

It was his second visit to Biddie's place since he and Ava had returned to Maine. No one met him at the screen door this time, so Toby knocked once and then let himself in.

"Hey, where's Ava?"

Biddie stood right where he'd left her, staring out the kitchen window. With her shoulders tense and her chin jutting out, Toby could tell she was furious. She shook her head back and forth like a disapproving mother. No offer of coffee or a buttery slice of cranberry loaf was forthcoming.

"It took longer than I thought to settle things. I didn't factor in an investigation. The place was a house of cards," he said. "I owe you. Pick the night. The Arborvine's still the place to eat, right? My treat."

"It won't work this time," Biddie said. "When are you gonna learn you can't buy people off?"

"What are you talking about?" Toby took a seat in the chair

Charlie used to sit in.

"Ava told me. I know." Biddie slammed a half-filled mug on the table. Coffee slopped up over the rim.

Toby's mouth went dry. He was unable to swallow. Or breathe. To speak or move.

"Wellesley wasn't far enough? You had to drag her away on one of your fancy trips. I thought Lorraine was nuts when she agreed to go with you. And then, when she needed you most, where were you?" Biddie was shouting now, banging her fist on the table with each word. "Ava's lucky to be alive, no thanks to you."

Toby didn't need Biddie to remind him it was his fault they'd all been there.

He put a hand over his mouth. Oh, God, how much did Ava remember? "Where is she? I need to explain."

"You want to know what I told Lorraine that summer? I told her straight out to leave you." Biddie shook her head again. "If Lorraine had only listened to me, she'd be here now." Using the sleeve of her flannel shirt, Biddie wiped her face. "You know what she said? That no matter what, she never would."

"Well, in the end, Rain did leave me, now, didn't she?" Toby didn't care that Biddie was crying—something he couldn't remember ever seeing her do. He stood so abruptly that his chair tipped back, crashing into the hutch, sending china cups bouncing off the shelf into the fish tank.

"It's your fault," Biddie yelled.

"You don't know. You weren't there."

"Ava said you just stood there."

"Tell me where she is." When Biddie said nothing, he kicked the chair out of his way. Toby wasn't halfway to the screen door when in on a sea breeze came the soft notes of a familiar song.

He didn't bother to keep the screen door from banging. All he wanted to do was get to his girl.

On the far end of Biddie's property, a little over a mile from Herrick House, stood a cluster of pine with a wooden swing perched above the Punch Bowl. Toby followed the sound of the chords.

Walking toward Ava, seeing how small she looked rocking on that swing, strumming her guitar, Toby realized this was why he hadn't come clean a long time ago. He was a man who found what had happened to them impossible to comprehend. How could he ever justify talking about it with a child?

"I missed you," he said, sitting next to her.

Ava stopped playing, and in a clumsy gesture, she rearranged her guitar so she could push off the swing. Pine needles under foot made her skid as she moved away from her father.

Toby caught her by the arm. "I can explain."

She wrenched it free, turning her back on him. "Now you want to talk?"

Ava's words were harsh, and in that instant, Toby felt faint-hearted and weak.

"You have every right to feel betrayed," he said. "What happened to you was unimaginable."

"You just stood there." Ava spun around to look at him. She banged the neck of her guitar against the chain sending discordant notes out between them.

Toby looked down the slope in the direction of the dock.

Waves rippled toward the shoreline, the glassy serenity severed by a passing boat.

"I remember you guys fighting," she said. "Were you going to divorce her? Was the trip a last-ditch effort to stay together?"

"Your mother was a wonderful person. She loved you—."

"Answer my question," Ava said, raising her voice.

"Okay—yes, we had problems. She hated Wellesley and wanted to move back up here permanently. Rain thought this was a better place to raise you girls. But it wasn't anything we couldn't have figured out."

Ava held the guitar tight to her chest.

"I never wanted a divorce. Sometimes I thought your mother did. But I was just talking to Biddie. She said your mother told her, she'd never leave me. I'm telling you the truth. We were working it out."

Toby wanted to reach out to comfort Ava. Put a hand on her shoulder, ask her to take a seat next to him. The right gesture could be the bridge between them.

He didn't move. Ava stood there staring blankly up at the pine trees, taking in their lilt and sway. Or maybe she was holding her head up to keep the tears from falling.

"I can't handle being at Herrick House with you," she said.

Ava fiddled with her guitar strap, winding an errant thread around her forefinger. "I asked Biddie if I could stay here for a while and she said I could."

"Come on, Ava. I'll give you your space at home. I plan on working as little as possible, and from here. We'll stay in Maine. Forever if you want. We still have a lot we need—to—"

Toby spun his wedding ring round and round, realizing it hadn't been this free moving in years. He had so much to tell Ava. About Nan and Arthur. Mount Hope. But Toby had to be careful. Anything he said now could make things so much worse.

In the time it took to gather his strength, to muster the words, Ava had had it with him.

"I gotta go," she said. "James is delivering a sculpture this afternoon and I want to catch up with him before he leaves."

"We need to talk about your mother. Whether you want to or not."

Ava held her hand out, gripping the neck of her guitar with the other. "Please stop pushing me. I can't listen to you right now."

"Then I'll make an appointment for us with that doctor you like. I'll go as often as you want. I'll sit there for the rest of my life if that's what it takes." Toby let out all the breath he'd been holding since he started to speak. "And then there's Mount Hope."

Ava's eyes widened. "What? Did something happen when you were there?"

"We can talk about all of that with your counselor. Okay?"

Toby saw his daughter tremble. He wanted to pull her close to hold her, whether she rejected him or not.

"Look, Dad, tell me now or forget it."

"The place was under investigation. Late yesterday, they shut it down. Pax and Justice have been arrested."

Ava looked at Toby like he'd completely lost his mind.

"While Nan and I were there, we found out some things about your counselor. Honor's an undercover cop. She was there on a mission to close the place."

Ava stared at the collection of pinecones scattered at her feet as though she weren't really seeing them.

"Did she really go there when she was my age? Was the part about her being a seed true?"

"Her real name is Cass Logan. When she was sixteen, she spent almost a year at Mount Hope. Since she's entered law enforcement, it's the second wilderness camp she's worked to shut down."

"I never saw her hit a kid. She took away points real easy and acted tough, but she never hurt anyone."

Toby paused. There was no perfect segue. "Mallory was there."

"At Mount Hope?"

"When she was released from the hospital, her parents sent her back to finish the program. They said the events of the overnight proved she needed more help than they could give her."

"What kind of people are they, to make her go back?"

"By the time Nan and I got there, everything was a mess. Kids were trying to leave. Reporters everywhere looking for interviews. Pax had been arrested. Mallory overheard us asking about Arthur. She said she knew where he was and could help us get him out."

"OP."

"We got the keys from Honor—Cass. And on the way over to get him, a girl asked Mallory if she was going home. Mallory said her parents weren't coming. That if she wanted to get her son back, she had to cooperate. She was being transferred to Narrow Lake.

"Nan offered to call her parents to explain how bad things were, to convince them to bring her home. Mallory said not to worry, she'd be all right. In the middle of it all, she was so calm and confident, I didn't give it another thought. Arthur was really shaken, and Nan was preoccupied with getting him out of there. Cass told us to wait in the lobby until someone could take a look at Arthur and officially release him. All the commotion was making him more anxious. Nan was getting riled up by the minute. It was taking too long. After an hour, I decided we should head to town and have Arthur seen at the local hospital."

Ava didn't move. She didn't blink. The way she stood, waiting for him to continue, reminded Toby of the way she'd looked at Mount Hope. Shut off, closed down. He couldn't finish.

"Something bad happened. I can tell," Ava said taking a step toward Toby.

"It's a lot to process. I think your counselor will really be able help us to make sense of all this craziness."

"Dad, tell me now or I'm leaving."

"We made it to the parking lot, one of us on either side of Arthur. That's when I saw an ambulance stationed out front. None of us had heard it arrive. There'd been no siren. When the three of us came down the steps of the lodge, Cass ran up to us, urging Nan to get Arthur back inside. Paramedics wheeled a stretcher out of the clearing. Cass pulled me aside to tell me. After helping us get Arthur out of OP, Mallory walked into the woods, climbed the rock wall, and hanged herself by the ropes."

"No!" Ava's guitar fell to the ground with a twang. Pine needles flew in all directions. "You're lying. Mallory wouldn't do that."

"Honey, you know better than anyone what Mallory did on that overnight. I'm so sorry, but she did."

Now Toby was up, moving toward her, determined to find a way to comfort his daughter.

"Why don't you ever know the right thing to do? Couldn't you tell she needed you?"

"Ava, come on. Everyone—even you—said what she did on the Ledges was a tactic to get out of Mount Hope. When I saw her, she seemed sensible. She knew where to find the keys and Arthur. Look, you're my daughter and I love you, and still I missed things with you. There was no way I could've known Mallory was desperate enough to do that."

Ava pointed to her guitar. "Bring it to Biddie's. I'm going to Herrick House to get the rest of my stuff. I'm moving out. For good."

"Please don't. We can work this out."

Ava climbed down the slope, only as far as the trail.

"At least let me drive you," Toby shouted after her. "The walk home will take over an hour, and you'll have things to carry. I won't try to change your mind. But we still need to talk about your mother."

Ava spun around, anchoring a hand on her hip. "What else could you possibly have to say?"

Once again Toby hesitated a moment too long. Ava stormed off. Leaving him alone in the woods.

THIRTY-SIX

Five minutes into the walk to Herrick House, Ava wished she had let her dad drive her. She could've hummed a song, run lyrics in her head, done whatever it took to block him out on the ride to get her stuff. Then she wouldn't have been so jangled, making her way through the woods.

Ava kept telling herself, *this is Maine, there's nothing to worry about, you've been through worse than this before.* But after hearing about Mallory—the trail and the trees, the noises the woods made—everything reminded her of Mount Hope. Wearing canvas flats instead of hiking boots made it harder to dodge patches of mud left over from yesterday's rain. Ava stumbled over stones on the path. With every snap of a branch, she could hear Justice's voice: *If you're not throwing up by the end of this hike, I haven't done my job.*

Ava started jogging. She was afraid to turn around. If she did, and Arthur was there, falling down on that trail, begging for water, crying for a break, shit all over his pants, then she would know she'd finally lost her mind. Even looking forward with her eyes wide open, Ava could see all kinds of horrors. Justice punching him in the head at the fire pit. Mallory bashing herself with a rock. Then Mallory again, climbing the rock wall, dropping down the braided rope—

"Moons and Junes and Ferris wheels, the dizzy dancing way you feel."

Ava sang random lyrics to keep pictures of Mallory hanging herself out of her head. All she had to do to prove to herself she was in Maine—to erase any comparison to that horrible camp—was take the trail down toward the ocean. As if she could go closer to the water to feel safe and less scared.

Ava didn't mean to shriek when a chipmunk crossed her path. If he hadn't startled her, forcing her to jump back a foot, slapping a hand on her chest so hard it stung, Ava might've thought the little thing was cute with his hunchback, his black and white twin stripes running down both sides. Ava hadn't caught her runaway breath when she heard a noise behind her. Whipping around quick, it was only a pair of chickadees in a tree. She might've laughed, if she wasn't already crying.

The more she tried not to think about Mallory, the more she did. Ava couldn't believe she was dead. How could anyone do that? Mount Hope was awful, everything about it bad. The counselors were evil—the ones who weren't cops—but nobody knew how to work the program like Mallory did. It was only a matter of time before someone let her out. Why wasn't her baby enough to keep her from doing it?

Hiking through the woods with no one belt-looping her, it was easy for Ava to say. It seemed like forever since someone hit her, spit at her, or touched her without permission. Sure, her dad ticked her off when he told her stuff, and made her mad when he didn't. He'd only just gotten back to Maine and already they were fighting. She was pissed at him for telling her about Honor being Cass and about what Mallory had done. How could he not know how many terrible moving pictures and silent films she'd already stored in her head?

Ava had given up hope of ever being able to control her mental slide show. And apparently her father wasn't finished. She could tell by the look on his face there was more.

Biddie, on the other hand, was nice enough, but she always wanted to talk about Ava's mother. Digging up memories, pressing Ava to remember whether she wanted to or not.

But as annoying as both of them were, between her dad and

Biddie, Ava had her choice of houses to sleep in and all the food she could eat whenever she wanted to eat it. She could come and go as she pleased. Mallory couldn't do that anymore.

As Ava got closer to Herrick House, all she wanted to do was find James. Right then she felt bad for storming out on him. She pushed aside the twinges in her shins and the cramp in her side, hoping she could move fast enough to get to the studio before he did. Ava knew if she showed up ready to help James deliver the garden sculpture to Flye Point he'd act like nothing had happened. James was a forgive-and-forget kind of guy.

When she came out of the canopy the woods made, the sun warmed her. It also put a spotlight on her dirty shoes and mud-splattered pants. Ava could only imagine how bad her hair looked, sweaty and stuck to her scalp. Maybe she had time for a quick shower before grabbing the rest of her things. The boat-house stood between her and Herrick House. The sun was so bright, Ava couldn't tell if the lights were on or off inside. She hoped James wasn't ready to go yet. Shading her eyes, Ava peered in the window. He wasn't there.

Rounding the boathouse, Ava moved toward the door. She'd stop inside to leave him a note, telling him not to go to Flye Point without her.

The only light in the place came through small windows, casting shadows on half-finished projects. Ava pulled the chain that hung from the ceiling, lighting up the concrete sculpture James was set to deliver. Accented with the old lady's smashed-up platters and plates, it stood over six feet and had the rudimentary shape of a woman. The replica was beautiful. Boaters would definitely smile seeing her parked on the shoreline. Before long Ava heard a squeak come from the back corner near the boat. She was out of there if a squirrel had found its way inside off the trail.

All Ava could find were scraps of graph paper on James's workbench. No pencils. The place was messier than he usually left it, and Ava was making it worse. The copper wind chimes that hung from a hook on the ceiling tinkled. The noise stopped her mid-rummage. With no open windows, the movement she made couldn't account for them swaying.

"Ava's home," a voice said.

Before she turned around, Ava told herself it had to be her imagination. She'd been slowly losing it, and now her brain was finally blowing out in one giant short circuit. He couldn't be there. What the hell would Arthur McEttrick be doing in her boathouse?

He sat in the corner leaning up against the boat, exactly where Ava had the day before, when she'd had her most memorable flashback. Wearing regular jeans and a sweatshirt, his hair clean, no strings dripping down his forehead, Arthur looked almost normal. Except he was rocking side to side.

Never in a billion years did she think her father would fly back here with Nan, and then invite her and her nephew to stay at their house. Couldn't he just have bummed a ride?

If Ava wasn't so out of her mind seeing Arthur there, she might've tried to picture what the last few days were like for him, trapped in OP, not knowing when he'd be able to come out. She wondered if he knew about Mallory.

"What are you doing here?" Suddenly she felt guilty for all the times she'd called him Fringe, for all the other nicknames she'd made up, from Buggy Carmichael all the way to every last kid at Mount Hope. Thinking about Bobby, Ava glanced at the wall. That's when she noticed his bike no longer mounted there.

When she thought her heart couldn't take another jolt, Arthur stood up and started moving in slow motion toward her. He held the damaged bike by one handlebar, dragging it along with him.

"Can you leave that there?" she asked. Her hands were stop signs in front of her.

Arthur gripped the crooked seat, knocking things over as he moved through the boathouse. Pieces of wood, sheets of pressed aluminum, a collection of pipes, all different sizes, made a racket as they rolled to the floor. Ava wanted to protect James's things, but getting closer to Arthur wasn't something her feet seemed willing to do.

"What if I need it?" he asked, turning to look behind him as if someone were going to steal the thing. When he stared back at Ava, his forehead was all lines and worry. He hung on to the bike even tighter. "To get away."

"You won't. Need it, I mean. It doesn't work anyway. See?"

They both looked at the mangled bike. God only knows what

Arthur saw.

"Mount Hope is closed," he said. "Justice is bad. He's in jail."

"My dad told me." Ava took a step toward the door, wanting to get away from him. Arthur was creeping her out. He moved closer to the door too, standing between her and Herrick House. Sad for him and scared for herself, Ava couldn't move past him to get outside.

"Mallory's dead," Arthur said. His tone was flat, his mouth turned down. All signs pointed to the fact that he could lose it any second.

"I know."

Wow, that was brilliant. The only person she'd formed an alliance with was gone and Ava couldn't think of anything to say. She wasn't very good at keeping Arthur calm like Mallory could.

"It's a sin to kill yourself," he said. "She shouldn't have done it. Now she'll have to live in hell."

"Mallory's not going to hell, Arthur. It wasn't her fault." Ava reached for James's phone.

Why wasn't he here by now? Ava didn't care about her filthy clothes and messed-up hair, she just wanted him to pull his truck into the driveway and see the light on in the studio and the door open the way she'd left it. Ava would even give her dad a happy hello if he tracked her down in here.

Then it hit her, Nan must be up at the house. She wouldn't have left Arthur alone in Maine.

Ava pressed her home number and put the phone to her ear. In the fastest move she'd ever seen Arthur execute, he lunged for her, knocking the receiver out of her hand, sending it sailing. "Don't hurt yourself, Ava," he said, trapping her in the corner with the bike.

Ava's back ached from being shoved against the workbench. "It's just a phone," she said, lowering her voice. "See?"

"You shouldn't hurt yourself. Even if they tell you to."

"I'm not going to hurt myself."

"Mallory did. She took a rock and—" Arthur took his open-palmed hand and hit the side of his head over and over again.

"Arthur, don't." Ava put her hand on his head to stop him from beating himself. His hair was fine, like Poppy's was a long time ago. In that instant, Ava didn't know which emotion would win out, feeling bad for him or sick for herself.

"I'm sorry I blamed you for throwing my workbook off the Ledges. I made a mistake."

"Saying sorry is good." He closed his eyes and nodded.

All she could picture was him rocking against the boulders on the Ledges while Mallory climbed down into that ravine.

"I gotta go," he said. "They say it's not enough to be sorry."

Arthur headed toward the door, still pushing the busted bike. His bony body pressed against her as he moved. Ava tried to get out of his way, and when she did, she knocked a couple tools off of James's workbench. Arthur jumped as they clattered on the concrete floor; his knuckles went white gripping the handlebars. Ruled entirely by what went on inside his head, he looked behind him, then side to side. He started moving again, slamming into things left and right. His sour breath hung in the air around her, making Ava think Arthur was dying from the inside out.

"Come on, leave the bike," she said. "Let's go up to the house. To find Nan. She's there, right?"

Acting all confident, Ava pretended she was Mallory, telling herself Arthur was just a lonely, screwed-up kid. She tried to push aside frightening thoughts that he was dangerous.

"There's nothing to be afraid of, Ava. They say to go down there. Water heals."

Every time he said *they*, his eyes darted around the boathouse like he saw other people standing there. Jesus, Benno had said he did the best job ever of faking that he heard voices. There was nothing pretend about the way Arthur's face contorted, or how often his eyes blinked, or how loudly he moaned. Ava wasn't faking the beginnings of a panic attack either.

It didn't matter how shaky or dizzy she was, or how much her vision narrowed, Ava needed to get her act together. "You're going to be fine," she told Arthur. "I only met Nan once, but I like her a lot. I can't believe she really can fly."

Arthur stopped at the mention of his aunt and her plane. With one hand, Ava took hold of his elbow, and with the other she peeled his fingers one by one off the handlebars of Bobby's bike. Ava helped him walk through the open boathouse door to start across the lawn toward Herrick House. Two steps forward, one pause, she stopped long enough to leave James's inspiration right there on the grass where he might see it. Sweat traveled down her neck as the ocean came into full view.

They were on their way to the house when Nan came rushing toward them.

"Arthur, you scared me," she said. "I fell asleep on the couch, and when I went up to check on you, you were gone."

Nan pulled her nephew into a hug.

"I'm going to ride the waves." Arthur sounded like someone Ava had never met before, a little boy. "Don't make me go back there. To Mount Hope."

Ava's head was pounding. The word *waves* rang out, B-flat; *back there*, F-sharp and G.

Nan leaned into Arthur, putting an arm around his shoulder. "Oh, honey. Never again. I promise."

"Remember that ropes challenge we did together?" Ava asked Arthur. "You told me not to look back. To pay attention to where I was going. Nan's here. You don't need to be scared."

"You were real nice to me that day," Arthur said.

"I should've been nicer to you every day. I'm sorry I wasn't."

"Come on, you two, enough talk of that place," Nan said. "Let's go inside." After taking a few steps, she stopped and looked over her shoulder. "Coming?"

"No, you guys go ahead. Don't worry about me. I'll be fine," Ava said. "I've got something I need to do."

So concerned about her nephew, Nan didn't give Ava a second thought, leaving her alone on the path. Ava decided to ignore the advice she'd given Arthur, at least the part about not looking back.

Skidding down the hill, her stupid shoes offered no resistance. The closer she got to the dock, the louder the waves crashed, the sharper the seaweed smelled, the faster her heart beat. It was a rhythm she'd memorized the notes to; one so familiar she'd come to despise it.

It took forever to make it to the shoreline. Bypassing the dock, she forced her feet straight into the water. When the ocean was up to her ankles, Ava stumbled. She fell forward, pebbles and stone stabbing at her hands. Frigid water swallowed her up to her waist.

Ava refused to end up like Arthur. She could not wait for her dad to tell her his version of what happened on Patong Beach. She knew water—this thing she feared beyond all else—would trigger her memories and bring the final pieces of the story back to her. Ava stood to move deeper into the surf.

When she started to lose all feeling in her legs, Ava spread her arms wide and let herself fall face first into the salty sea. Water on her chest, her lips, her forehead. Jagged shells pierced her skin. Ava didn't scramble to get her footing. She didn't bother to anchor her feet in the sand. The enemy rushed in around her nose and cheeks, into her ears, drowning out her music. With lips closed tight, she refused to open her mouth to it. Ava had made that mistake before.

Willing the memories to come, she wondered how much longer she could last. She should have taken in more air before the plunge. Why not take a breath right now—

My mother has my hand and Poppy's, her two girls, one on either side. We are marching toward a shoreline that draws away from us. I look over my shoulder and see my father standing where we left him, mesmerized by something beyond us, hypnotized by the sea.

A gust of wind riffles the pages of my mother's journal. "Daddy," I shout, "My poems."

My father grabs the journal and breaks into a run. "Rain, no!"

When I look forward again, I see the ocean has become a blue-black wall of water. It's then that my mother realizes something is terribly wrong. With a jerk and a tug, she turns from it, dragging Poppy and me with her. We're a blur, running from the wave. We are flying. It is faster. My feet leave the ground as we're swept up in a wild rush. With only one hand frantically paddling, I struggle to keep myself above water. It's no use. All I can do is tighten my grip on my mother. Before the three of us go under, I grab the deepest breath I can. The punishing water surrounds us, spinning us, violently returning us to shore.

The last time I see my mother's pretty face, it's anything but. Creased and wrinkled, a silent scream is pasted there. My mother wrenches her hand from mine; it neither slips nor is it stolen by the wave. She turns her back on me and I watch as she pulls Poppy close. It's as if they are hugging under water.

I am airless and weighed down all at once. My arms and legs don't know what to do without her touch. My mother and sister disappear before my eyes. Without my anchor, knowing she didn't choose me, I let the ocean claim me.

Moving so fast from where we once were, there is nothing I can do but surrender. My body is battered by errant things. A beach chair, a table. Pieces of wood, metal. Glass. I hear a girl screeching. I realize then, it's me. When my bathing suit is ripped from my body, I think, fine, there is nothing left it can take from me.

Then I hear my father's voice above the roar. "Hold on." Hearing him triggers something fierce in me. There's a tree branch dangerously close to my face, and like a reflex, I reach for it. My grasp is weak and the water strong. As I cling to it, I picture my mother's face. I consider letting go of it. Like she let go of me. I open my mouth—to breathe or swallow, I'm not sure which. That's when from behind, someone yanks me up. His grip is tight, a crushing hold. Inside my chest is a flame, burning, burning. I gasp and wheeze, barely able to hear, but there he is again. "Hold on."

My father has one arm around my waist, and with the other he pulls us both, branch by branch over to a palm tree. The water is thick and brown now, muddy as it slaps us, urgent as it tries to tow us back to sea. Suddenly we are climbing. In between urging me to hold on to its trunk, telling me to go higher, my father cries out. "Rain. Poppy."

As swiftly as the wave overtook us, the sea releases its grip. No longer is it spiteful. When it recedes in swirling pools, my father coaxes me down. First he swims toward land hauling me, then he picks me up and runs. He never stops sobbing into my hair. I say nothing. All my energy goes to holding on.

My arms are locked behind his neck, my legs around his waist. When we are almost to the hotel, he shouts to a man standing on a balcony, staring wide eyed at our nakedness. I hear my dad yell to him, "Wing. Wing."

The tone and echo of the word "run" in any language is the same.

Inside my head, I beg my father not to do this. Do not leave me. Do not put me in the arms of this stranger. But my father peels me from his body. As I cry and cry, he says, "I know, I know."

And then the connection between us is broken, final.

I hear a splash as he heads back through the water. At first he is screaming, "Rain. Poppy." Their names are loud, clear. As the man with a camera that digs into my ragged flesh takes me from the hotel, away from my family, my father's voice gets softer, softer still, and then it's gone.

The man wraps me in his shirt and carries me like a baby. He covers my eyes and we are moving through town. I tell myself Mom and Dad and Poppy are right behind me. Soon we will all be going home.

One step inside a building, a whiff, and I know it's a hospital. A woman takes me from the man. They speak, but I can't understand what they are saying. She brings me to a room filled with people, so many people. Some of them are bleeding. Some of them are staring. All of them crying.

But I do not cry or scream or speak. I curl up on my cot and pull the cool white sheet over my head. I am alive and I am dying.

THIRTY-SEVEN

The sunroom was empty and Herrick House quiet by the time Toby made it back from Biddie's. He'd driven faster than he should have over twisting, turning roads, in an effort to beat Ava home before she gathered her things and took off. Though once he explained the unexplainable, there would be no stopping her.

To say he regretted arguing with Lorraine that morning was an understatement, a paltry way to account for the guilt he would always carry. He'd wasted precious seconds reaching for the poetry journal, placing him too far away to save his entire family but close enough to watch his wife choose between their daughters.

Despite the surety that words would prove inadequate, Toby planned to beg for Ava's forgiveness. For handing her over to a stranger. For leaving her alone in a hospital for a single second, never mind an endless day. Without revealing the horror of his task, Toby needed Ava to know, he did everything he could to find them.

Toby ran his hand over the indentation on the old sofa in the sunroom, a place he'd spent countless evenings with Lorraine after their girls had gone to sleep. He thought it remarkable, amidst everything happening now, that the ghost of his wife had begun to fade from that space. In the last few days, he imagined confessing his wrongdoings not just to Ava but to Nan. Yet Toby was prepared to sacrifice all that might be with Nan for a shred of forgiveness from Ava, the hint of a chance that they could put the horror of that day behind them.

He looked out the window. No sign of Ava. Drawing on Nan's confident example, he readied himself. When Ava hauled up from the woods and opened that sunroom door, he would sit her down and they would talk it out.

Back at the swing, Toby had every intention of telling Ava that Nan and Arthur, worn out and exhausted from their ordeal at Mount Hope, needed a place to stay before they went back to Boston for the boy's evaluation at McLean. He just couldn't come up with the words fast enough.

Now as he willed his daughter to walk through the back door, he rehearsed what he would say.

"Ava, this is where you live. We're going to counseling—together—you and me. I'll talk to you about everything. What I did and didn't do. The devastating choice your mother felt she had to make. I was wrong to send you to Mount Hope, but I won't let you go now."

Toby glanced at the lighthouse-shaped wall clock, a silly, inexpensive thing Poppy had insisted he buy at a souvenir shop on a day trip to Bar Harbor. The sweet memory was interrupted when he registered the time. Even if Ava had strolled home, wasting time on the path, it was taking too long for her to get from Biddie's to Herrick House.

Toby took the side door out, making his way toward the boathouse. It jarred him to see Nan and Arthur walking arm-in-arm up the walkway. If Ava saw them sashaying around the grounds, it might well push her over the edge.

"Have you seen Ava?" he asked. "She's coming for her things. She wants to move to Biddie's."

"Ava's sorry," Arthur said, looking over his shoulder. The boy was rattled. Not the calmer, stronger kid he'd been at breakfast. Twenty-four hours out of that hellhole and Arthur had seemed a little bit better. Now something was off about him.

"I hope we didn't have anything to do with that," Nan said.

"Things got so heated I didn't even have a chance to tell her you're here with Arthur."

"She knows. We met her coming out of the boathouse. Arthur went for a walk and got lost. She brought him to me. I asked her to come inside with us, but she said not to worry. There was something she needed to do. Last I saw her, she was headed to the dock."

As if Toby had guzzled a pot of Biddie's bitter blend, his heart began skipping beats. Ava would never willingly go close to the shoreline. And hadn't Mallory said the same thing right before she'd hurt herself?

Toby wanted to fly down the embankment, but his feet were glued to the walkway. *Move,* he told himself. Why couldn't his mind and body ever get this fight or flight thing right? So what if he showed up down there and everything was fine. Embarrassment Toby could handle. Ava ticked at him he could live with.

"Get Arthur to the house. See if you can track James down. One of you meet me back at the dock. Please, hurry."

Taking the trail that led to Biddie's, Toby nearly slid down the hill. His lack of agility wasn't suited to the rugged terrain or the steep drop to the shore. A banging in his head matched the beat of his heart. His blood pressure had to be through the roof. His out-of-shape body slowed him down. Minutes in, his legs began to cramp. The heaviness that traveled down both elbows to the tips of his fingers was nothing compared to the knife that got him right between his shoulder blades.

Then he saw her.

Ava was moving toward the thin line where water meets sky. Toby needed to go faster, much faster.

Looking on, he watched her fall to her knees. Not letting one stumble slow her resolve, she popped right back up. She swayed to and fro like she had at the airport.

He tried to call to her, but the words wouldn't come. His throat was closing tighter by the second, as if someone's hands were wrapped around his neck.

The scent of lavender perfume overcame him. Every sound became sharper: his feet pounding ground, a mix of voices in his head, his and Ava's. He could swear he heard Lorraine.

"Hurry, Toby. Hurry."

Disoriented yet determined, Toby wouldn't take his eyes off his daughter. It was like looking at Ava through a keyhole; the girl on one side of a door and him on the other.

Ava thrashed and beat the water as she moved further from him. When the ocean was up to her waist, she stretched her arms out by her sides and fell forward. Then her body went still, her arms limp, her hair a fan on the surface of the sea.

No matter how fierce Toby's will to get to her was—to drag Ava from the surf, up the incline by the dock—his legs wouldn't move. Before he made it anywhere near her, Toby collapsed under the crushing weight of everything he had ever failed to do for her.

The agony of wanting his family back filled his chest. It became unbearable, a vise around his heart.

As his field of vision narrowed, Toby struggled to speak. "Come back," he whispered. But there was no one there to hear him. With his daughter lying face down in the Atlantic, Toby was drawn back to the Andaman Sea.

I'm looking out to the horizon. Ahead of me, Poppy is there, skipping across the beach with Ava, one of my daughters nearer the water than the other. Lorraine and I trail our girls, side by side, hand in hand.

"We'll move to Maine for good," I say.

"Everything will be better there," Rain says.

Then it all goes black. I am cold and wet, and all I can hear is crying, my sobs mixed with Ava's.

A woman shouts. "Ava needs you. Go."

I cannot tell who's speaking.

"Open your eyes. Hold on to our girl."

Slumped on the ground, Toby could barely lift his head, but lift his head he did. Dizzy shapes and shifting patterns distracted him, and still Ava came into focus. Watching her swim toward a boulder lodged in the ocean floor, near the dock, Toby experienced a faraway sense of gratitude. With her arms wrapped tightly around her chest, she rocked against the boulder. Toby could almost feel the stone against his own back, the waves lapping his face. Ava was safe.

Toby had never been so tired. Like smoke swirling around his head, the smell of the sea became so intense, so overwhelming, he no longer cared to breathe. In that brief moment, split off from himself, it occurred to him that there was one more place he might look for Rain and sweet little Poppy. What a fortuitous way to learn what he'd longed to know.

THIRTY-EIGHT

Four weeks after her father had a heart attack because she went searching for what the sea held in wait for her, Ava knelt on the side lawn next to James, putting the final touches on her tribute to the people she loved. Honoring them with blue flowers and found art.

The memorial garden outside Herrick House had been her idea. She'd planned every inch of it, plotting exactly where each perennial would go. James helped her dig the earth and turn the soil. Biddie drove her all over town to find the right seedlings.

"Where do you want the sign to go?" James asked.

He'd been keeping the last piece of the garden art a surprise for her. Ava loved the one James had made for Amelia and Liam, to accompany the mother and baby sculpture she had helped him deliver. That sign, with its silver and gold metallic splashes of paint, their names etched in black, was haunting. And though it fit the piece he'd designed to commemorate them, it wasn't right for Ava's cheery, full-of-color garden patch. Secretly she hoped James knew what she'd envisioned, the pretty thing Ava forced her mind to rest on these days.

"You decide," she said. "But let's do that last, okay?"

"The whole thing is perfect," James said wrapping his arms

around her.

Like she had in countless dreams, Ava stroked his cheek, letting her fingers rest on his lips, on the scar left by surgeries he'd had as a baby. Another touch of the cruelty of nature.

"You want us to come back when you're done?" Toby asked.

Ava hopped up, brushing bits of dirt and grass from her jeans. When she saw her father coming down the hill with Nan, she didn't react quickly because the pair had scared her. Though Ava still had panic attacks, they were shorter and more controllable since she'd been meeting with Sarah a couple times a week. Ava didn't leave her boyfriend's side in a rush because she had anything to hide either. Ava hurried to her dad and Nan, guiding them to her creation, because it was as much for her father as it was for her. And it was all about the presentation. With Nan on one side and Ava on the other, they linked arms.

"It's not that I don't love the attention, but you both know I can walk by myself, right?"

Her dad had been forceful and brave since he'd been home from the hospital. Whenever he felt the urge, he talked about the surgery, about being in ICU. Ava understood how almost dying could flood a person with so much fear it was hard to find the words to describe it.

Maybe he was stronger because she was.

"Ready?" Ava asked.

James stood up and backed away from the garden so Ava could explain things. She pointed to the clusters of salvia, the purple flowers Poppy's someday husband might have been named for. Ava was the only one who knew that little story, and right then she decided to keep it for herself.

"That's Mom," Ava said, though there was no real need to explain the sculpture next to the salvia patch either.

Ava watched her dad take in the likeness of woman holding a book, a circle of zinnias planted about her feet. Of course it was Mom.

"Absolutely gorgeous," Nan said, taking Ava's hand and squeezing it. "You guys are so talented."

Ava didn't let go of Nan's hand for what seemed like a long time. She wanted her to know how much she loved her being there, how grateful she was for what she'd done for them, rushing to the dock, saving her dad's life. Nan had given them their chance to start over, to set things right.

"James, your work is stunning," Nan said. Bending down, she touched the sculpture of the little girl lying on her back, pointing toward the sky.

"It's Poppy playing the cloud game," her dad said, rubbing his eyes, croaking out the words.

"Actually Ava did most of it," James said.

"You were the one who taught me how to sketch my vision," Ava said, lacing her fingers in his. "He helped me find all the objects I wanted to weld together. It was hard, but I think it turned out fine."

She liked saying the same words James would use whenever he stepped back to admire his art. These pieces—the ones they stared at now—would be the only ones Ava would ever make. Found art belonged to James like writing music belonged to her.

Her father came to her then, and without a word, he pulled her close. He hugged her so hard Ava worried she would hurt the wound that ran like a zipper down his chest. "I love it," he whispered. "So much."

With his arm around her shoulders, she leaned into the weight of him, letting him love her and the garden. Ava couldn't remember a time when she felt happier.

"It really captures her," he said. "Only I don't remember Poppy ever playing that game without you."

"I almost added a sculpture of me, but I decided to take Arthur's advice. Pay attention to where I am, not where I've been." As soon as Ava said his name, she wished to take it back.

Nan got a sad look on her face every time someone mentioned Arthur.

"It's a commemorative garden anyway. It's for them," she said.

Her dad motioned for Nan to come to him. "You're right. We all have a lot more living to do. Together."

Nan smiled, laying her head on Dad's other shoulder. Ava didn't know if her father was officially asking permission to include Nan in their family, but if he was, if he ever did, Ava's answer would be yes.

"Speaking of together, Dad told me you're leaving tomorrow."

"For a few days," Nan said. "Arthur's doctor thinks we should try a new medication. I want to be around for that."

Selfishly Ava was glad when Nan used basic words like doctor and medication when it came to talking about Arthur. She didn't think she could take it if Nan dropped the words psychotic break and schizophrenia into every conversation.

"I wish I felt up to going with you," Dad said. "You shouldn't have to do this alone."

"I could go," Ava said.

Bending down to pull a lonely weed, her back to everyone, Ava could feel all eyes on her. Even the birds stopped singing.

"We could stay at the house in Wellesley," she said. "You could be with Arthur at the hospital all you want. I'd bring my guitar to work on the song I'm writing for Mallory's boy. I could cook at night when you get home."

"That's more than generous of you," Nan said. "Why don't we talk about it after dinner? Tonight, I'm cooking for you."

Nan's pretty face lit up. It was as if the offer to go with her was gift enough. She didn't know Ava still felt like she owed Arthur. Not just because she'd probably made him worse by blaming him for things at Mount Hope. But because seeing him that day in the boathouse, a victim of the crazy thoughts dancing inside his head, gave her the courage to go after the rest of what haunted her. Like it or not, standing above the Reach that afternoon, Ava knew the water could trigger the rest of the story, but only if she was brave enough to disappear inside it. If it weren't for Arthur, Ava didn't know if she would have gone back to get the final pieces. To accept what really happened.

After Ava remembered everything clearly, she no longer blamed her father. In the end, he did choose them. All of them. It was partly Ava's fault he'd stopped on that beach for those brief seconds. She was the reason he wasn't closer to them when the wave hit. Every time Ava thought about it, she ended up telling herself it wouldn't have mattered. Her dad would never have been able to save them all. Plus James was right. People do crazy things in bizarre circumstances. A little girl might ask her father to protect her poems. And he might actually do it.

It was easy enough to forgive him for handing her off to a stranger, asking the man to take her to a hospital. It had to be awful going back to search for her mother and sister.

The thing that hurt the most was thinking about her mother—of her choosing Poppy over her.

Last week, in the first counseling session she'd had with her dad, Ava had asked him why he thought Mom picked Poppy. Doing his best to control his sadness, he said he didn't know. Surprisingly, it didn't frustrate Ava—him saying so little—that he wouldn't venture a guess. Actually, she respected him for it.

For whatever reason—if there were any reasons all—they would never know why her mother picked her sister, the brave and fearless one. And not the girl who'd only days before had finally learned to swim. Ava didn't hate her for holding on to Poppy. She just didn't know how to feel about being the one her mother let go.

Her father stroked her hair to bring Ava back to the place where real live people stood. People who went out of their way every day to make sure she knew they loved her. It was as if he could read her mind.

"I've been thinking a lot about what you asked me the other day," he said. "I think I know why Mom let you go. It was because Rain knew I had you."

They hugged again. "I'll always have you," he whispered.

In her father's arms, Ava realized how much she had missed letting him take care of her.

"So is anyone hungry?" Nan asked, wiping her tears with her sleeve.

Dad made a face, sticking his tongue out like Poppy used to. "Lobster without butter? I hardly see the point."

"Be quiet," Nan said. "You'll love it. I made a lemon dipping sauce. And if you don't complain all through dinner, I might let you have a sliver of Biddie's peace offering. She dropped off a blueberry buckle."

"Peace offering? Are you sure the woman isn't trying to kill me?"

James and Ava exchanged a look, stifling their laughter as Dad and Nan turned back toward Herrick House. When they'd made it onto the path, James ran behind the tree that shaded part of the garden. Out he came with the squirming brown paper bag they'd stolen from the fridge. It was now or never.

James held it away from his body as Ava took his hand and they ran to the dock. Before the planned release, they looked over their shoulders and stood on their toes to make sure Dad and Nan were out of view. Though they would figure out soon enough where dinner had gone.

Two of the lobsters practically leapt out of the bag in a one, two splash. The other two with their claws tangled, remained trapped. When James let go of the lobsters, bag and all, Ava shrieked. And for a second she had a flash.

Click, a picture of the ocean floor, dark and frightening.

Then James laughed, C-sharp then B, and the image floated away on the air. He slid his arm around her. "Wonder what's for dinner now," he said.

"Let's go find out."

Walking up from the dock, they paused at the garden they had made together.

"Oh, no. The sign," Ava said.

James bent down and pulled a work of art from an ordinary plastic shopping bag. The piece of wood had scalloped edges painted white, with turquoise flowers and blazing orange letters. It read: BLUE POPPY GARDEN.

James staked it right in front, facing Ava so she could get the whole picture. The memorial was nothing like she'd imagined. It was brighter and more beautiful than any marker, any ghost art, she had ever seen. Her mother and her sister would have loved it.

AUTHOR'S NOTE

Every year thousands of distraught parents place their trust in residential, emotional-growth boarding, and/or wilderness schools and programs aimed at modifying the behavior of hard to reach, troubled teens. With little to no government oversight and regulation, the billion-dollar-a-year industry capitalizes on parental distress and dwindling local resources for adolescent psychiatric care, basing their segregated intervention on a philosophy of tough love or shock incarceration techniques to coerce adolescents into submission. Most programs of this nature do not require the consent of the teen sent away. The National Institutes of Health (NIH) and the Community Alliance for the Ethical Treatment of Youth (CAFETY) have position statements cautioning parents about fear-based programs like the one depicted in this novel, claiming that positive outcomes are exaggerated and that there is strong evidence that such treatment makes behavioral as well as underlying mental health issues in teens worse.

If you or someone you know is considering private residential treatment for a troubled teen, please reach out to your health care professional or school counselor for advice and support.

ACKNOWLEDGMENTS

I am deeply grateful to the following champions of this novel:

Katrin Schumann—for her generous feedback and unending encouragement.

Julie Basque—for her honest critique and enduring friendship.

Kimberly Witherspoon—for her responsive, insightful counsel.

Michelle Toth and Andrew Goldstein—for their astute editorial guidance and commitment to my work.

Grub Street Writers—especially Eve Bridburg and Chris Castellani—for reminding me that a career is so much more meaningful in the context of community.

Maia Szalavitz—for her tireless efforts to bring issues related to the ethical treatment of teens into our public discourse and for sharing with me authentic details about wilderness behavioral camps. Her book, *Help at Any Cost: How the Troubled-Teen Industry Cons Parents and Hurts Kids,* is an invaluable resource.

Julie Wang—for sharing her love of resilient wildflowers with me and for letting me tour the original Blue Poppy Garden in Maine.

Ann Hood—for believing in the power of this story even in its earliest draft form.

And to my family—my husband Tom; my daughter Caitlin and her husband Matt; and my son Stephen—for their unwavering faith in me and my mission. The four of you mean everything to me.

LYNNE GRIFFIN

photo © Elena Seibert

Lynne Griffin is the author of the novels *Life Without Summer* (St. Martin's Press, 2009) and *Sea Escape* (Simon & Schuster, 2010). In partnership with GrubStreet Writers in Boston, she facilitates the strategic writer program, Launch Lab. Lynne is also the author of the nonfiction parenting guide, *Negotiation Generation* (Penguin, 2007). She teaches family studies at the graduate level at Wheelock College and is the Social-Emotional Learning Specialist for an independent school in Boston. As a companion to the novel, *Girl Sent Away*, Lynne has written, *Talk About It: An Adolescent Mental Health Prevention Guide for Parents and Teachers*. To learn more about Lynne's work visit www.LynneGriffin.com or follow her on Twitter @Lynne_Griffin.

To invite Lynne to speak at your school, organization, or agency, email PR@LynneGriffin.com.

CPSIA information can be obtained at www.ICGtesting.com
Printed in the USA
LVOW10s0003130116

470313LV00008B/398/P